mostly good girls

mostly good girls

LEILA SALES

Simon Pulse
New York London Toronto Sydney

SIMON PULSE

An imprint of Simon & Schuster Children's Publishing Division

1230 Avenue of the Americas, New York, NY 10020

First Simon Pulse hardcover edition October 2010

Copyright © 2010 by Leila Sales

SIMON PULSE and colophon are registered trademarks of Simon & Schuster, Inc.

For information about special discounts for bulk purchases, please contact Simon & Schuster Special Sales at 1-866-506-1949 or business@simonandschuster.com.

The Simon & Schuster Speakers Bureau can bring authors to your live event. For more information or to book an event contact the Simon & Schuster Speakers Bureau at 1-866-248-3049 or visit our website at www.simonspeakers.com.

Designed by Mike Rosamilia

The text of this book was set in ITC Baskerville.

Manufactured in the United States of America

2 4 6 8 10 9 7 5 3 1

Library of Congress Cataloging-in-Publication Data

Sales, Leila.

Mostly good girls / by Leila Sales. — 1st Simon Pulse hardcover ed.

p. cm.

Summary: Sixteen-year-olds Violet and Katie, best friends since seventh grade despite differences in their family backgrounds and abilities, are pulled apart during their junior year at Massachusetts' exclusive Westfield School.

ISBN 978-1-4424-0679-7

[1. Best friends—Fiction. 2. Friendship—Fiction. 3. Preparatory schools—Fiction. 4. Schools—Fiction. 5. Ability—Fiction. 6. Creative writing—Fiction. 7. Massachusetts—Fiction.] I. Title.

PZ7.S15215Mos 2010

[Fic]—dc22

2010007190

ISBN 978-1-4424-0681-0 (eBook)

"Us Two" by A.A. Milne, from NOW WE ARE SIX by A.A. Milne, © 1927 by E.P. Dutton, renewed © 1955 by A.A. Milne. Used by permission of Dutton Children's Books, A Division of Penguin Young Readers Group, A Member of Penguin Group (USA) Inc. All rights reserved.

This book is dedicated to Terry Hayes Sales,
who made my education possible.

And to Allison Smith, who has always been
the Katie to my Violet,
and the Violet to my Katie.

mostly good girls

So wherever I am, there's always Pooh,

There's always Pooh and Me.

"What would I do?" I said to Pooh,

"If it wasn't for you," and Pooh said: "True,

It isn't much fun for One, but Two

Can stick together," says Pooh, says he.

"That's how it is," says Pooh.

—from "Us Two," in *Now We Are Six*, by A. A. Milne

My Junior Year To-Do List,
by Violet Tunis

1. Get a perfect score on my PSATs.

2. Get A-minuses or better in all my classes.

3. Do many awesome projects with Katie.
   (Note: Projects must be awesomer than
   anything we did last year.)

4. Improve this school's literary magazine.
   At least to the point where I don't have
   to pretend like I am not really the
   editor, like the editor is someone else
   who happens to share my name
   (huge coincidence).

5. Pass my driving test.

6. Maybe become famous for something,
   so that people everywhere will know and
   respect me?

7. Make Scott Walsh fall in love with me.

Mr. Thompson's sordid past

Poor Mr. Thompson. Mr. Thompson is my precalc
teacher, and he is also the only male at the Westfield
School. Unless you count Mr. Roebeck, the bio teacher, which
I don't, because he is approximately two million years old and
the only manlike thing about him is that he wears neckties.

Oh, and also there are the maintenance men, but nobody
counts them, because they are manual labor. We generally don't notice them at all, except on Maintenance Man
Appreciation Day. This is a holiday in March, but they don't
get the day off or anything. All that happens then is, whenever
we see one of the maintenance men around school, we have

to say to him, "Thank you for all your hard work!" Inevitably, the maintenance men will respond by looking like they want to kill us, or themselves, or everyone, and then they'll sort of grunt, "You're welcome," and go back to emptying the trash receptacles in the bathroom stalls.

But Maintenance Man Appreciation Day is only one day out of the year. The rest of the time we lead an entirely man-deprived existence, with the exception of poor Mr. Thompson, who is our Brad Pitt, Elvis Presley, and James Dean all rolled into one.

Mr. Thompson is, at the absolute least, twice my age. He has an awkward, scrappy beard and high-top sneakers that are persistently too white, as though he polishes them on a regular basis. When he gets excited about a mathematical theorem, his voice squeaks. On his upper arm is an unarguably stupid tattoo of a smiley face, the result, my best friend Katie believes, of drunken misjudgment. Katie tells the tattoo story like this:

When Mr. Thompson was a young and impressionable math undergrad, he got it into his head to pledge a fraternity. All the new pledges had to drink a lot of alcohol—like *one keg each*, Katie says. (She doesn't care that this isn't physically possible.) In a drunken stupor Mr. Thompson wandered away from the frat house, fell in with a gang of thugs, made out with a sexy homeless leather-clad hippie transvestite, and got a smiley-face tattoo at the local drug dealer's house.

Unfortunately, he never made it into the frat—due to some technicality, Katie explains, vaguely. And the sexy homeless hippie transvestite turned out also to be a gypsy, so she disappeared into the cloudy night, leaving Mr. Thompson with nothing but a broken heart and a goddamn stupid tattoo.

Now, I hope I've been clear here: Katie *made this story up*. It is a *total lie*. However, this doesn't stop all the lowerclassmen from believing it. I mean, the tattoo is right there! Clearly visible! So obviously the rest of the story must be true, too, right?

So, in short, Mr. Thompson is all around a little bit lame. Plus he is married and has a three-year-old son. But! He is undeniably male, and so every girl at Westfield flirts with him. Constantly.

In class today, for example, Tasha sashayed up to his desk while the rest of us were silently trying to integrate an expression. Tasha cooed, "Mr. Thompson? I'm having a lot of trouble with this problem."

Mr. Thompson said, "Just give it your best try. We'll go over it in a few minutes."

Tasha said, "Yeah, but it's really hard. I think I need extra help."

Mr. Thompson said, "Do you want to come back to the math office during lunch?"

Tasha said, "I was thinking more like Saturday. At ten p.m. At your house."

By this point in his career Mr. Thompson doesn't even have the decency to look scandalized by this sort of sexual harassment. He just looked tired and told Tasha to sit down.

Everyone else in the room was in hysterics. Mostly because there was no way Tasha needed extra help from Mr. Thompson. Because she is not technically in his class.

I'll grant you it's only four weeks into the school year, so maybe he hasn't memorized all his class rosters yet, but *still*. Mr. Thompson does not notice much. The Tasha Incident was, Katie wrote to me in a note, *further proof that he is in a DRUNKEN STUPOR.*

I responded to Katie's note by scrawling, *Oooh, hopefully that means he'll get another tattoo this afternoon!*

When Mr. Thompson confiscated this note, he just read it, sighed, and said to us, "Katie? Violet? Please try not to write notes in class." Katie and I nodded solemnly. Then he dismissed us all ten minutes early to lunch, which meant that everyone in my math class got *two* helpings of bread pudding!

I think Mr. Thompson may quit soon. It's just this hunch I have.

Dots, dashes, stars, and exclamation points

In English class this morning, Katie and I made a list of how far every girl in our grade has gone. The hardest part was remembering everyone. For the longest time our list had only fifty-two names. Turned out we were forgetting Rachel Weiss.

Once we had written down all the names, we marked them with cryptic symbols to indicate their sexual experience. The symbols had to be cryptic in case someone else was reading our list over our shoulders, which probably someone was, because the other option was to listen to Lily Vern explain, for the twentieth time, why Wordsworth is the only poet who has ever mattered. So we used a dot for kissing, a dash for second base, a star for third, and an exclamation point for going all the way. If you hadn't even kissed anyone, you got nothing.

The list looked like this:

Pearl *

Hilary •

Mischa !

Katie –

Violet

And so on.

Katie and I had a whispered argument over her dash. "You have not been to second base," I hissed as Ms. Malone put up a Williams Carlos Williams poem on the overhead projector.

"Yes I have," Katie insisted. "The summer after freshman year, with that guy I met on the Vineyard. Brad."

"I remember Brad," I said, "and I remember that he tried to feel you up. But you specifically said, *right after it happened*, that he failed to feel you up enough for it to count as second base. It was over the shirt, wasn't it?"

"It was over the bra," Katie said, like that made all the difference, "and I'm counting it now, *retroactively*, because sixteen is too old to have never been to second base."

I refrained from pointing out that, by her logic, sixteen is also too old to have never been French-kissed, so what does that make me? There must be something deeply flawed about me that no boy has ever wanted to kiss me. Not that I have even spoken to that many boys who I actually wanted to kiss. Pretty much just Scott Walsh.

Maybe I should just start lying, like Katie was doing, or counting things that obviously don't count, like, "Remember the time my cousin David kissed my cheek? I get a dot for that."

Wait. No. Ew.

Exclamation points only

Mischa and Zoe are the only girls in the junior class who have had sex, so they got the only two exclamation points on our list. For the rest of the morning, whenever Katie and I saw them, we exclaimed, "Mischa!" or "Zoe!" This cracked us up, but Mischa and Zoe were less amused, since they weren't in on the joke. Not to mention that Mischa is never amused by anything. That is just her way.

Katie and I got lunch from the cafeteria and carried it outside. The breeze had a bit of a bite to it, the first hint that it really was autumn. The midday sun shone down brightly, filtering through leafy branches of elm and maple trees and onto the bench swing in the courtyard where Katie and I sat. Katie rocked us lightly back and forth as I picked apart my ostensibly chicken sandwich, looking for a single piece of actual chicken. Westfield is pretty expensive, and I'm not sure where all the tuition money goes, but definitely *not* into the cafeteria's budget.

Around us the courtyard was filled with girls sitting on benches or lying on the uniformly green grass, propped up against backpacks and doing their reading. A few girls had taken off their shirts, trying to eke out that last bit of summer tan, even though technically we're not allowed to do this. Westfield doesn't have a strict dress code, but "Keep your shirt on" is a standard rule, and one that I like to follow. It was a little too chilly to be parading around the schoolyard in a bra or bikini top, and anyway, I don't tan—unlike Katie, or Pearl, or Genevieve, or my other perfect-skinned classmates. I freckle.

The school building, resplendent in aged brick and ivy, encircles the courtyard. To our left extended the playing fields, and then, far beyond them, I could see the tips of the Boston skyline rising into the clear blue sky. I felt like I was in one of those photographs that the school sends to prospective students. Except for the shirtless girls. They generally get cropped out of Westfield's promotional materials.

"I want a bra like that," Katie commented.

I followed Katie's gaze to see a well-endowed senior

sunbathing in an electric-blue bra. "Right, and you would know," I said. "Since you've apparently been to second base and all. So you're like the bra *expert* now."

Katie rolled her eyes at me. "Whatever, Miss Moody. Anyway, more important than my sexual experience—"

"Your *awe-inspiring* sexual experience," I put in.

"Right, more important than that, guess what Mischa! did in physics today?"

"What?"

"Made fun of Emily for using a drugstore-brand hairbrush instead of a *designer* hairbrush."

"Did she really?" I shook my head. "That is so bitchy. Why is Mischa so bitchy? Why does Emily's hairbrush even have *anything* to do with her?"

Katie nodded her agreement. "But you know what made me feel a little better about it?"

"The knowledge that Mischa will die someday?"

"No. The fact that I can put an exclamation point at the end of her name."

I cracked up, and we both shouted "Mischa!" across the courtyard with hearty enthusiasm.

Getting comfortable with our . . . never mind, I can't say it

Sex ed has got to be the most embarrassing subject a high school could possibly teach. It's also useless, since the only thing Ms. Wheeler lectures about is various forms of birth control: the pill, condoms, sponges, etc., all of which may be *academically* interesting but is still *practically* meaningless, since I don't know any boys. Well, okay, I know Scott Walsh and a few other Harper Woodbane guys—but I can't imagine ever being in a position where exchanging sexually transmitted diseases with any of them would be an option. Learning how to protect myself from chlamydia is nice, but if Ms. Wheeler really wants to sexually educate me, she could start by teaching me how to talk to a boy without choking on my own saliva.

Today in sex ed Ms. Wheeler talked about what our "options" would be if we got pregnant, which is ridiculous, since everyone knows that if you get pregnant, you get kicked out of school. The Westfield School offers a few key perks that our local public schools do not, including

a) no one ever brings a gun to school.

b) every student goes on to a four-year college.

c) none of the students are ever pregnant.

Those are the rules.

Still, Ms. Wheeler told us that if we got pregnant—presumably through immaculate conception, since 96 percent of us aren't sleeping with anyone—then we could get an abortion, or we could carry the baby to term before giving it up for adoption.

Rachel was taking copious notes, I assume because she thought there was going to be a test on this material, not because she was truly worried about getting impregnated. Rachel, like me, doesn't have even a dot next to her name. I also couldn't help glancing at Mischa(!) to see how she was taking all this. She sat in the back of the room, painting her nails, looking bored and virginal. Playing it cool, Mischa.

Pearl raised her hand and asked, "But if you get pregnant, can't you keep it?" We laughed at her because, like, *no*, you can't keep it. We've all met Pearl's mom. She's the dean of admissions at Harvard Business School, and she's just counting down the days until Pearl is old enough to be CEO of a multinational corporation. If Pearl thinks she can just give all that up to become some *child raiser*, she is even more of a moron than I thought.

Ms. Wheeler, though, is the sort of teacher who doesn't believe in telling students that they're wrong—which may be why she teaches sex ed as opposed to math. So she just hinted to Pearl that it's hard to be a full-time college student while mothering a toddler. Duh, Pearl. Then Ms. Wheeler had us all say "vagina" a bunch of times in unison, so that we will become comfortable with our vaginas.

Do you see what I mean about sex ed?

The precious Jewells

Pearl is not the first from her family to attend Westfield. Her oldest sister, Ruby Jewell, graduated from here seven years ago. She went on to Harvard, finished in only three years, and is now getting her medical degree and just got married to a Harper Woodbane alum who works for a corporate law firm.

Opal Jewell, Pearl's next-oldest sister, graduated from Westfield four years ago. She's not the genius that Ruby was, but she's still smarter than most. After Westfield she spent a year abroad in Paris, and now she's at Hampshire College.

Sapphire Jewell, next in line, graduated from Westfield two

years ago. She was lovely but, let's face it, not quite the shini-est jewel in the necklace. She had trouble getting into any college, even with her parents' connections and money, but at last they pulled the right strings and she started at UMass.

Pearl Jewell is in my class, and she is dumb as a pile of kindling. If it weren't for her sisters, Pearl never would have gotten into Westfield. She couldn't even have gotten into Miss Newbury's, Boston's other (and worse) all-girls school. Sometimes she can't walk without crashing into walls.

All the Jewell sisters look freakishly similar, with straight blond hair, big blue eyes, tiny waists, and perennially tanned skin. Sometimes I see photos of them in our alumni magazine, posed in age order, and I feel dizzy.

There is a fifth child in the Jewell family. His name is Bob. He's a chubby brunette kid in glasses. It's obvious to me that Mrs. Jewell once had an affair with the pool boy at her country club. There can be no other way to explain Bob Jewell's existence.

Like an amusement park, except with wild animals

We had to choose the theme for our junior yearbook during this week's class meeting. We didn't even get extra time to accomplish this task—Ms. Freck, the Westfield headmistress and junior-class advisor, was just like, "Girls, you have forty-five minutes to choose your theme. Go to it."

She put Hilary in charge of leading the brainstorming, since we'd elected Hilary yearbook editor at the end of last year. Hilary is Katie's and my next-best friend, which means she falls a distant second. She has a kind-of commanding presence, but that wasn't going to get her far with our class. You need to have the commanding presence of Mussolini to make anything happen in our class meeting.

"Okay," Hilary said, standing at the front of the classroom and squaring her shoulders for battle. "Remember, we're looking for themes that will inspire design ideas. So think about concrete themes with obvious illustrations. And for now we're just brainstorming, guys, so don't worry about an idea being perfect. We just want to get a bunch of thoughts out there, all right? So, who wants to start?"

Everyone wanted to start. "Outer space," suggested Tori, the aspiring social activist with dyed-blue hair.

"Boston," suggested Melanie, whose father works for the United Nations.

"Sports," suggested Sydney, the tall girl with chronic back pain.

Hilary wrote all these ideas on the whiteboard.

"I don't think sports should be our theme," piped up Rachel, the one who Katie and I forgot about when listing all the names of our classmates. "A lot of us don't do sports, so that idea would focus too much attention on certain members of the class."

"Here we go," Katie muttered to me. And, as if on cue—

"But a lot of good illustrations would come from sports," Sydney shot back. "And I think personal fitness is a value we all share, regardless of whether we actually participate in any sports teams."

"I'm not opposed to personal fitness," Rachel said. "But sports teams come with a number of negative connotations—cliquishness, groupthink, hazing. I don't want those values represented in my yearbook."

"Excuse me," Hannah spoke up. "As captain of the swim team, I want to say that we would never condone hazing."

"And as editor of the yearbook," Hilary said through gritted teeth, "I want to say that we're *just brainstorming*. Can we get more ideas on the board, please?"

"Picture books," suggested Mandy, the moody computer genius.

"Candy," suggested Lily, whose favorite movie of all time is *Homeward Bound*.

"I think candy would be too limiting," said Mischa, also known as Mischa! and the biggest bitch in the junior class. "What if we broadened that out to food?"

"Can we have candy and food be two separate suggestions?" Lily pleaded to Hilary.

"What about food," Mischa proposed, "but with the word 'candy' in parentheses next to it, so we'd know we're going to focus on candy?"

"Because we'd forget to focus on candy," Lily answered. "And I don't want pictures of, like, steak in my yearbook."

"I think that would be hilarious, actually." Emily, the narcoleptic, jumped in. "Can we definitely add food to the list?"

Hilary looked ready to murder someone.

The junior class yearbook, I should note, is completely not worth this level of hassle. It is sixteen pages of inside jokes and photographs, stapled together and bound as a paperback. It's mostly intended to be practice for when we're in charge of the *real* school yearbook next year. Primarily it just gives my class something to bicker about.

"Is there something we can do?" I whispered to Katie. I felt that Katie and I, as Hilary's friends, had a special obligation to make this process less appalling.

"I think by staying out of it," Katie said, "we set an excellent example."

"Except no one is following our example," I whispered back as the rest of our class moved on to deliberating music as a potential theme, and whether or not deaf people would feel left out (even though there are no deaf girls in the junior class).

"I would suggest something myself," Katie said to me, "but this is such a sham of a democracy, I just can't debase myself by participating."

I raised my hand.

"Oh my God." Katie rolled her eyes. "Don't tell me you're stooping to their level."

"Only by speaking up will our voices be heard," I replied.

"Your voice will be ignored whether you speak up or not," Katie predicted.

Hilary called on me. "Thank you for raising your hand,

Violet," she said pointedly, as though her approval would inspire our classmates to follow my example.

"You're welcome, Hilary," I said, equally pointedly. "I'd like to suggest the theme of safari. We could draw pictures of jungle animals and people wearing pith helmets and stuff like that. And we could each say where we'd want to go on a safari, or what we'd want to bring with us."

I held my breath, ready for the inevitable backlash, but weirdly it didn't really come. A bunch of girls were nodding. "I went on a safari once," announced potentially anorexic Genevieve (not raising her hand). "I bet it would make a really pretty yearbook theme."

The only vocal dissenter was Mischa, who was still wedded to her food idea. "Safari is too much like last year's theme," she snapped.

Katie swiveled her head to glare at Mischa. "Last year's theme was *amusement parks*," she said. (Katie may hate participating in classroom conversations, but she's good about taking my side.)

"I'm just saying . . . ," Mischa began, trailing off when she realized that she had no idea what she was saying.

"Let's put it to a vote," Hilary said, using a yardstick to rap the whiteboard, which now listed twelve suggestions. "All in favor of outer space . . ."

Tasha's hand shot up. "I think we should close our eyes when we vote," she said. "So that we're not biased by other people's opinions."

Hilary took a deep breath—in through her nose, out through her mouth. "I don't think that will be necessary," she said.

"Really?" Tasha countered. "Then why do we vote for the president of the United States by secret ballot?"

"Because president of the United States matters a lot more than yearbook theme?" Katie muttered.

"Maybe we should first vote on whether or not to close our eyes when we vote," said Pearl.

"Yeah," said Sydney, "except would we close our eyes as we voted on that, or not?"

Pearl looked stymied. I wanted to laugh at the whole situation, but it would have been like making fun of a crippled kitten.

"Using the impossibly minimal power vested in me as your yearbook editor," Hilary said, "I declare that we are going to vote with our eyes *open*. All in favor of outer space, please raise your goddamn hands."

Surprisingly, my suggestion of safari turned out to be the class's favorite. "Congratulations!" Hilary beamed at all of us. "Your yearbook theme is safari! And just in time for fifth period, too. Great work today, guys!"

"Hilary deserves to be martyred for her work here today," I commented to Katie as everyone bolted to her feet.

Katie raised an eyebrow. "You mean we should kill her?"

"Oh. No. I guess not. I just meant we should worship her. But without killing her first."

"Personally, I would rather be dead than be yearbook edi-tor," Katie said as we shouldered our bags. "But I guess that's just me." And we headed to our next class.

My family has *never* taken a tropical vacation

My parents love academia. I mean, *love* it. They first met in graduate school at Boston University. My dad was studying English literature, and my mom was studying sociology. You may think this would be such a huge cultural divide that they would never be able to find any common ground whatsoever, but somehow they did.

My mom went straight from college to grad school to being a professor, so she has never existed in the real world. My father spent three years postcollege teaching English as a second language to schoolchildren in a remote village in Japan. But that's not actually the real world either.

My parents insist on eating dinner together as a family every weeknight, which would be fine, except that we discuss exclusively topics like the new book my dad's working on (*Ernest Hemingway: Hero? Or Antihero?*) and the data my mom has collected about urban housing patterns. In other words, stuff that's vitally important to them, and vitally unimportant to everyone else in the world.

They're proud of me for going to Westfield, and they often speak rhapsodically about how amazing it is that I get to read Tolstoy at such a young age, and what wouldn't they have given to attend such a great school, etc. But they also think Westfield makes me too stressed out, which is blatant hypocrisy, since *they* are too stressed out. If you think it's easy to figure out if Hemingway was a hero or an antihero, you are dead wrong.

At dinner that night I shared my triumph with my parents. "The class chose *my* idea for the junior yearbook theme," I told them. "Possibly because it was the only theme that didn't promote hazing or offend deaf people. But still."

"That's great!" my parents chirped, both beaming with pride. My parents are proud of me no matter what I do, be it suggesting a yearbook theme or getting a B on a math test. They have incredibly low standards.

"So do you get anything for that?" my dad asked.

I stuck some mashed potatoes in my mouth and stared at him blankly. "Like what? A trophy?"

"No, what I mean is, do you get credited in some way for suggesting the theme. Is your name listed in the yearbook?"

"My name is going to be listed in the yearbook anyway," I explained. "Due to how it is a yearbook, which is a book that lists people's names. But, no, I don't think I'll be called out specially as the girl who said 'safari.'"

My parents are big into getting credit for things. They act like every time I get a good grade on a vocab quiz, Ms. Freck should personally commend me in an all-school assembly. What my parents don't understand is that nothing I do is all that impressive. Coming up with a yearbook theme is nothing compared to my classmates, who regularly play concertos at Symphony Hall or feed starving youths in Africa or invent periodic elements or whatever the hell it is they do all the time. Really, my parents just have no point of comparison.

Shortly thereafter I excused myself from the table to start my history reading. "You work too hard!" my father called after me, as he headed into his study to spend the rest of the night pondering Hemingway.

"We should all take a tropical vacation sometime soon!" my mother called as she disappeared into *her* study to stare at bar graphs.

Like I said: The hypocrisy in this family. It is *out* of control.

Katie's family talks only to God

It's debutante season. I am aware of this only because I overheard Mischa and Pearl, in the homeroom during my free period, discussing their dresses for cotillion. Cotillion is a big party where girls make their *debut* into Boston society. Not everyone gets to be a debutante. Not everyone even gets invited to be a guest at the debutante ball. You have to come from a certain sort of family. *Not* my sort of family.

I had been trying to do my homework, but now I turned to Katie and said, quietly enough that Mischa and Pearl couldn't hear, "I think it's preposterous that there still exists this classist, sexist ceremony in our otherwise enlightened city. Think about it! They round up a bunch of rich white girls and show them off as now eligible for *marriage*. A debutante ball is no better than a livestock show. I wouldn't come out even if they asked me."

"They asked me," Katie said, "but I still won't come out."

That brought me up short. Katie and I are similar in so many ways that I sometimes forget we come from different backgrounds. My parents save every penny of their professorial salaries to send me to Westfield because they believe there is nothing as valuable as a good education. Katie's dad is an investment banker and her mother doesn't work, and they send her to Westfield because girls in her family have *always* gone to Westfield, like since the 1800s. But Katie wants nothing to do with that whole preppy Boston scene, so she usually doesn't talk about it.

Katie's full name is Katharine Cabot Putnam, which no one ever calls her, though she does own some jewelry with her monogram on it, which she never wears. The Putnam is from her father. The Cabot is from her mother. Both are a pretty big deal. For example: One of the classrooms at Westfield is named the Putnam Room. And there's a famous poem about the Cabots. It goes like this:

And this is good old Boston,
The home of the bean and the cod,

Where the Lowells talk to the Cabots
And the Cabots talk only to God.

Of course, Katie doesn't talk only to God. She talks mostly to me.

Still, blood is thicker than water, as they say, which I guess means Katie gets invited to cotillion no matter *who* she talks to.

"Mummy doesn't understand why I don't want to come out," Katie said, thumbing through her physics textbook. "Not like she's angry about it, just like she honestly doesn't get how a living girl could *not* want to be a debutante."

I wasn't sure I got it either. As I mentioned, debutante balls are no better than livestock shows; however, if I had Katie's pedigree and someone was *begging* me to make my debut, then, you know, I might secretly consider it. "Maybe you should do it," I suggested. "I bet there are awesome desserts at cotillion." Personally, I will do many undesirable things, like babysit for total demon children and eat dinner at my Uncle Rick's house, if I believe that a good dessert will come at the end of it.

But Katie shook her head. "First of all, it's classist and patriarchal and anachronistic, as you yourself just pointed out. So no. And second of all, I would need to bring along an escort. So *definitely* no."

"I could be your escort," I offered. "Just to help you eat the desserts and all."

"It has to be a boy escort."

"A boy?" I feigned shock. "Where on earth do you find one of those?"

"Do I look as if I know?"

"Hey, make Scott Walsh escort you!"

"Oh, yeah," Katie said. "Absolutely. I'll be like, 'Hey, Scott, I know we only see each other like three times a year, so you may not even remember my last name, but how do you feel about being my date to a really lame socialites' party that I don't even want to go to?'"

"Yeah! Call him up and say that!"

"Sure. But just on the off chance this Scott Walsh plan doesn't pan out for me, maybe we should come up with an alternative."

Katie and I both wracked our brains.

"Oh, here's an idea," I said at length. "Maybe you should crash a car into some guy, knocking him unconscious, and then slowly nurse him back to health. He'll be so grateful to you for saving his life that he'll definitely agree to escort you to cotillion."

"But I can't drive. I can't even take driver's ed until the winter."

"Which makes it all the more believable that you'd crash!" I said.

"But won't he hate me for crashing into him in the first place?"

31

"He'll have amnesia," I explained. "So he'll just remember that you were the one to heal him, not that you were the one to run him over."

Katie drummed her fingers along the cover of her textbook, considering. "How long does it take to nurse someone back to health?"

"A month?" I guessed. "Two months."

"Wouldn't work, then." Katie shrugged. "Cotillion would already be over."

"Damn," I said. "Guess you shouldn't go, then."

"Guess not."

Before we were friends

I t's weird to think about now, but before Katie and I became best friends, we were sworn enemies. For three days.

Our hatred began in Lower School, when we were Littles. It was two months into seventh grade, and our history teacher assigned us to work together on a report about the events leading up to the Revolutionary War. Because this was my first year at the Westfield School, I barely knew Katie, and I was dubious about working with her. I was dubious about working with anyone, as I had been ever since one time in elementary school when I was supposed to do a project with a girl in my class who spelled "the" as "tha" and did not seem to notice that was a mistake. Since then I had steered clear of group projects.

But Mrs. Boyle's group project was not an optional one, so Katie and I arranged for me to go over to her house one Sunday afternoon so we could discuss the Stamp Act and the Sugar Act and all those other thrilling acts. My mother drove me from our house in Arlington to Katie's house in Chestnut Hill.

We pulled up in front of the Putnams' crisp white mansion, with its grand front stairway, Greek columns, floor-to-ceiling windows draped in voluptuous curtains. Eventually, I would grow to think of Katie's house as my second home. But at the age of twelve, it struck me as the biggest building I had ever seen that wasn't actually a museum.

"Enjoy it," my mother said as we opened our car doors, though I couldn't tell if she was being sarcastic or not. "From now on, this is what it's going to be like."

My mom and I climbed what seemed like a thousand stairs to the Putnams' front porch, and I swung the ornate brass knocker. A long moment passed before Katie opened the door.

"Hi!" Katie grinned at me. She looked then more or less the same as she looks now: honey-colored hair, rosy cheeks, tiny button nose. The main difference is that Katie was tall for seventh grade, but she stopped growing right around when the rest of us started, so a few years later she would wind up one of the smallest girls in our class. "You should have just come inside," Katie said to me. "The door's not locked. We never lock it. I guess we should, but . . ." She shrugged her shoulders in a *What can you do?* sort of way.

Katie's mother showed up behind her. Mrs. Putnam was wearing a green polo shirt and crisp slacks embroidered with colorful palm trees. She looked younger than my mother, and tan, even though it was November.

"So good to meet you!" she enthused, extending her hand to my mom. "I'm Bunny Putnam."

She looked like a bunny too: Petite. Cute. My mom shook Mrs. Putnam's manicured hand with her own nonmanicured one. "Thank you for having Violet over," she said. Katie and I slid into the living room, leaving them to their mom-talk.

"May I take your coat?" Katie offered, which seemed very adult to me—until she took my parka and tossed it on top of an antique-looking desk.

"Is that from Harvard?" I asked, pointing to the desk chair. I could see the university crest on the chair's back.

"I guess," Katie said. "My dad went there."

This impressed me, since in those days I was having a recurring nightmare about not getting into Harvard. I used to wake up panting, my heart racing in terror. I laugh about it in retrospect. When you're twelve years old, you just don't know how many colleges are out there. Now that I'm sixteen,

I know that there are at least four schools I could go to and still be happy. If I don't get into Harvard next year, I'll just go to Yale, or Columbia, or the University of Chicago. No big deal.

A large dog bounded into the living room, a rawhide clamped in its jowls. "Buster!" Katie cooed. "Hello! Hello, darling!" She hugged him around the neck and said to me, "This is Buster."

I gave Buster a little salute. He wriggled out of Katie's embrace and lumbered up onto the leather couch, sprawling to take up the entire thing.

"You can pet him if you want," Katie offered.

I shook my head. "I'm not really a dog person."

"That's cool." Katie shouted in the general direction of the ceiling, "Matthew! Come downstairs and put your dog outside!"

"You do it!" a muffled voice replied from upstairs.

"I have a guest!" Katie shouted back. She rolled her eyes at me. "Brothers. Anyway, want to do a project?"

I answered yes, thinking she meant our history project.

She did not.

"Perfect!" she exclaimed. "I have a good one: Let's set up all the furniture in the TV room like a maze, and then we can train Buster to go through it. We'll put treats at the end to incentivize him. And we can time, like, how long it takes him to learn his way through the maze, if he gets faster the more he does it, stuff like that. I know you said you're not a dog person, but it's okay; you won't have to touch him. You just have to help come up with a good maze. Oh, and you can record data about his times and whatever."

I furrowed my brow and opened my mouth to say, "No, let's not. Instead, let's make a collage about five causes of the American Revolution." But I didn't say that. Because Katie's idea sounded a lot more fun. And because she was already running off toward the TV room.

So we spent the next three hours forcing Buster to run through a maze of furniture, and rearranging the maze to make it more and more complicated, and giving Buster so many doggie treats that eventually he threw up all over the rug. I was just thinking that maybe Katie would become my first real friend at Westfield, when I looked out the window and saw my mother climbing the Putnams' front steps, there to pick me up. "Oh, *no*," I gasped. "We never did our history project!"

Katie shrugged. "It's okay."

"No, it's not! It's due Wednesday."

"Wednesday is *days* from now," Katie said, unruffled.

"Wednesday is less than *three* days from now."

"Less than three days is still days."

I glared at Katie. So it was going to be exactly the same at Westfield as it had been at my old school. Nobody worked hard; nobody cared. Once again I was going to have to do the whole assignment by myself because I was the only one who cared about doing things right.

"Fine," I said. "I'll just do it."

"No. I'll do half and you can do half," Katie said.

"But how do I even know that you'll do it?"

Katie set her jaw, and her expression grew steely. In the years to follow I would see her give this look often—to her mother, to Mischa, to Mrs. Freck, even sometimes to Hilary. But this was the one and only time Katie looked at me with such disgust.

"I mean, we're getting *graded* on this," I said. "I don't want to get a bad grade just because you didn't do your half."

The doorbell rang. My mother. Katie and I stared each other down, both refusing to look away.

At last Katie said, "I *will* do my half." She shoved an upside-down piano bench (part of Buster's maze) out of the way and marched to open the front door.

For the next two and a half days I toiled away, alone, at my part of the history project. I raged to my parents about how awful Katie was, how awful Westfield was, that it was filled with slackers, just like everywhere else. Every time I saw Katie at school, I pointedly looked away.

But when I showed up to school on Wednesday, there was Katie, and there was Katie's half of the project. Finished, as promised, and finished, I had to admit, better than my own half. Much better.

"Oh," I said when I saw it.

Katie lifted her chin, arched her eyebrows, and had the good grace not to say "I told you so." Instead she said, frostily, "I did it last night." Even at the age of twelve Katie was effortlessly successful.

I swallowed my pride. "I'm sorry I said I didn't think you'd . . . well, you know." Because apologizing is hard, particularly when you're twelve, although I'm not much better at it now.

Katie shrugged and replied, "After you left on Sunday, Buster did the whole maze in less than one minute." Because that was way more important to her than some silly school project.

That is how I became best friends with Katharine Cabot Putnam. And we've never looked back.

Strive for success

That was seventh grade. Nowadays we are juniors, and we know we're juniors because today was PSAT Day, the day we get back the results from our practice SATs. According to the official College Board, the letters *PSAT* don't stand for anything. But for us at Westfield, they stand for "Perfect Scores Are Triumphant." Or sometimes they stand for "Please Skip; Avoid Teachers," because so many juniors skip class on PSAT Day to have nervous breakdowns.

The results from our PSATs first go to Ms. Freck. The day they arrive, our headmistress meets with each member of the junior class, one by one, in alphabetical order by last name, to discuss her individual results and what sort of prep work she needs to do before the real SATs. These meetings go on all morning. Other than a few choice orthodontist appointments, this was probably the longest morning of my life.

Since my last name's near the end of the alphabet, my meeting with Ms. Freck came just before lunch. I wasn't able to focus beforehand. No one was. We were all too busy trying to figure out what scores our classmates got.

It's totally out of line for someone to just announce how she did on a test, so you have to listen carefully to what your classmates say and try to interpret their vague comments. "Not as good as I'd hoped" coming from Hilary would mean anything less than a perfect score of 240, whereas an "I did awesome" from Pearl would probably mean like 80, which is the score you get for filling out your name correctly.

Westfield girls are viciously competitive, so knowing that so-and-so failed a math test or that someone else achieved an elusive A on a paper for Ms. Malone is an incredibly intriguing piece of news. The school tries to minimize this competition for grades by keeping our GPAs secret even from us. It's rumored that no girl has graduated with a perfect GPA in all of Westfield history, but of course there's no way to prove that claim, since no one ever knows what her GPA is. We spend a lot of time trying to weight and average our course grades, but that's all just guesswork. So PSAT scores are the one official ranking we have of who is actually better than whom.

Katie got out of her meeting with Ms. Freck just in time for physics class. She slid into her desk, smiling slightly, like she knew a secret.

"How was it?" I asked.

"Good." Katie exhaled quickly and stared down at her desk, still smiling, just the littlest bit.

"So you'll probably get into college, then?" I asked, watching her closely.

"It's starting to seem like it," she answered, super casual.

I narrowed my eyes. She wasn't helping. Though maybe that was because everyone else in our physics class was listening in, wanting to know how Katie Putnam did on her PSATs. I wanted her to just write down a number on a piece of paper, tell me the answer—but even between best friends you don't do that. "How do you feel?" I asked her. "Happy?"

Katie shook her head no, still smiling that creepy little unexcited smile, and stared me straight in the eye. "Relieved," she said. "I feel relieved."

I was still puzzling over Katie's response when I left midway through the class period for my own meeting with Ms. Freck. Nadine Thomas was just on her way out of our headmistress's office, and she shoved past me without speaking, looking like she'd been crying. Ms. Freck ushered me into her office, with its stained glass windows and antique standing lamps, though the first thing that I noticed was the box of Kleenex on her desk. As headmistress she is always prepared for student freak-outs.

"Thank you for coming," Ms. Freck said—like I'd had a choice—as I sat down in a wooden chair with the Westfield crest carved into it. The crest includes our motto, *Fortiter ascende.* This translates roughly to "Strive for success." I felt, as I sat in that chair, like the words were digging into my shoulder blades, branding themselves across my upper back, like a tattoo I would never be rid of.

"Violet, you did very well," Ms. Freck told me as she opened my file. "You should be proud of yourself."

I smiled at her weakly, since this must be the line she feeds every girl. *You should be proud of yourself.* Well, sure, there are lots of things I *should* be, but that doesn't mean I *will* be, now does it?

Without any more fanfare Ms. Freck handed me the sheet of paper containing my test results. I took them in instantaneously. Math: 63. Verbal: 70. Writing: 78.

So that was it, then. That was the answer. Just numbers on a page.

Just numbers on a page, but I saw them and they crushed me. I had wanted so much more than this.

"Obviously, your scores are strong." Ms. Freck's voice sounded like it came from very far away. "But since you have six months before you take the real SATs, there's certainly time for you to get tutoring in math and verbal. And writing, too, if you want it, though I think you're all set with that section. No surprise that the editor of our literary magazine is a good writer! I'm going to give you a list of some of the test-prep companies and private tutors we recommend. . . ."

I sat through a few more minutes of that sort of talk before Ms. Freck dismissed me. I saw Lily Vern on my way out, waiting for her meeting with Ms. Freck, looking petrified. I tried to smile at her, even the sort of unexcited smile that Katie had given me, but I had nothing inside.

I didn't go back to physics. Instead I went to the homeroom, where no one was bothering anyone. I curled up in a corner of the room, put on sunglasses, and read *Winnie-the-Pooh* until lunchtime.

As soon as lunch period started, Katie showed up in the homeroom and beelined to my corner. "Are you okay?" she asked, crouching next to me. "You didn't come back to physics, so I didn't know if . . ."

"I'm fine." I put on a fake smile. I had been practicing fake smiling, readying myself for this moment. "Really, it's fine. I did totally fine."

"Okay," Katie said, sounding like she didn't believe me. "So why are you hiding in the homeroom?"

I shrugged and leafed through my book.

"You know the PSATs mean nothing for your future, right? Colleges don't see them. Jobs don't see them. They're just

SAT practice. No one cares about your PSAT scores, in the long run."

"Totally," I said. "I know." *The only one who cares about my PSAT scores, in the long run, is me.*

"And it's not like your standardized test scores are any indication of how creative you are, or how good a leader, or speaker, or athlete, or logical thinker. They don't even really test how smart you are." Katie pressed on in her reassurance, and I realized that she must have given herself this exact same pep talk after seeing her own scores. That must have been why she didn't want to talk about her PSAT results during physics—because she was upset, just like I was.

I felt guilty, then, for sitting around and moping and making Katie bend over backward to cheer me up, like I was the only one allowed to be unhappy. From the way I was acting, Katie probably thought I had *failed*. Whereas, in fact, I only *felt* like I failed.

"You're right," I said, standing up. I couldn't let Katie go on pandering to me, when, honestly I had gotten a higher PSAT score than like 85 percent of the country—even if I currently felt worse about myself than probably 85 percent of the country. I guess 85 percent of the country didn't expect very much from themselves. "I was just feeling a little down, but it's no big deal. Let's go to the cafeteria."

We ate lunch, and Katie was careful to talk only about cheerful things: television, silly stories from crew practice,

criticism of Tori's new hair-dye color. During her afternoon
free period Katie ran down the road to the convenience store
and bought me a king-size Snickers, my favorite candy bar.
I didn't deserve her sympathy, but I appreciated it anyway. I
have the best, best friend in the world.

Perfect Scores Are Trouble

Hilary's the one who told me. I don't think she was trying to cause trouble or gossip. She just assumed I knew. Even if she hadn't told me, I was bound to have found out sooner or later. That's just how Westfield works.

"Crazy about Katie, isn't it?" is what Hilary said as she sat down at the desk next to me in history class.

"Hmm?" I replied. I was making a list of all the pieces we had so far for the fall issue of the Westfield literary magazine. Conclusion: Not enough that I could insist on cutting any of the ones I hated.

"It's crazy about Katie," Hilary repeated. "I mean, if anyone was going to get a perfect score on her PSATs, my money would have been on Katie, but still. I bet Lily is pissed off. Even she got only a two-thirty, I heard. . . ."

I stared at Hilary, not saying anything. I felt this pressure building up behind my nose, like I was going to cry, but I wasn't. I wouldn't. I'm not one of those girls who cries in school.

"Violet?" Hilary had noticed my silence. "You okay? Hey, you knew already, right?"

"Oh, yeah," I choked out. "Of course."

"I figured. I mean, you and Katie are best friends."

Which was, of course, precisely why Katie hadn't told me that she had aced the PSATs. Because we're best friends. And she hadn't wanted to hurt my feelings.

What *had* she told me, though? Oh, right—that nobody looks at your PSAT scores, not colleges, not jobs. That the PSATs don't test anything worth testing. Easy for you to say, Katharine Cabot Putnam. It's easy to say the PSATs don't matter when you have the luxury of having perfect PSAT scores.

"Strive for success," the motto tells us. Wow, thanks a lot for that awesome advice, Westfield. Look, I strive all the time, okay? It doesn't get me anywhere. And Katie? Katie barely strives at all.

"How do you even *know* all this?" I asked Hilary. "Do you have like a chart for recording all of our test scores?"

Hilary shrugged. The answer was that Hilary knew all this

48

because Hilary knows everything. It's her gift. Like how Katie's gift is winning, and Mischa's gift is being a prissy brat, and my gift is being subpar.

"Today we're going to resume our discussion of why various American factions did or did not want to commit forces during World War Two," our history teacher said. I hadn't even noticed her come into the room.

I opened my notebook and held my pen above it, like I was a diligent student about to take notes. But really all I could think about was Katie. Perfect, perfect Katie.

I know it's not okay to be jealous of your friends' clothing or money or hair or whatever. But sometimes I am jealous of Katie's entire life.

I am so low maintenance

The weekend after PSAT Day all I wanted to do was stay home and study, as if studying really hard now could somehow reverse my mediocre test scores. As much as Katie was my best friend in the entire world and I never grew tired of her, I did feel too tired to hang out with her success.

But then Hilary made the only plans that could possibly entice me out of hibernation: She somehow arranged for herself, Katie, and me to get ice cream on Saturday night with Scott Walsh and a couple of his Harper Woodbane friends.

I have no idea how Hilary pulled this one off. Knowing Hilary, she probably just said to him, "So, want to hang out?"

Hilary can manage to say that sort of thing without coming off like she has a disorder. Plus, unlike Katie and me, Hilary doesn't have a debilitating crush on Scott, so that helps.

Katie and I developed our crushes on Scott Walsh the very first time we ever saw him, at the seventh grade Westfield–Harper Woodbane dance. Harper Woodbane is Westfield's brother school. We do dances and school plays and stuff with them so we won't feel like we live in a nunnery, only actually I feel like I live in a nunnery anyway. In the four years since first discovering Scott Walsh, we have never stopped loving him, because we have never met any guy better than him. Though, to be fair, we don't meet that many guys.

Obviously, Katie and I had to meet at the Putnams' an hour before ice cream time so we could try on outfits together. Katie is smaller than I am, but I leave half my wardrobe at her place, and she leaves half her wardrobe at mine, so regardless of which house we're at, we can both find something to wear. Seriously, though—"What do we wear?" I asked Katie, pawing through a pile of shirts.

She surveyed the mess of clothing covering her bedroom floor. "I read in a magazine that guys like low-maintenance chicks," she said.

"Okay, great. Let's go for the 'low maintenance' look, then." I put on Katie's mom's old Radcliffe sweatshirt. "I am so low maintenance!" I tried saying to the mirror. "Man, I just throw on any old sweatshirt, and I am ready to go!"

"We could just show up naked," Katie suggested.

"Right, good, naked *is* low maintenance."

"We'll be like, look, I didn't think this evening was important enough to get dressed up for. Hell, I didn't even think it was worth getting *dressed* for."

"What magazine did you read this in, again?" I asked.

Katie shrugged. "*Cosmo? Seventeen? National Geographic?*"

"I'm not sure about this. How do we know this whole 'low maintenance' thing isn't just a lie, designed to make clueless girls like us go out with their crushes looking like slobs? Or naked."

"Maybe." Katie collapsed face-first onto her bed, a tank top dangling from her fingers. "But it seems likely, doesn't it? That guys would like low-maintenance girls?"

"Katie," I said, sitting down on her legs, "I have *no idea* what guys like. Maybe low-maintenance girls. Maybe blind girls, or boneless girls, or mermaids."

"I like mermaids," Katie said.

"Shut up," I said.

Like a triple date.
Kind of.

We were late to our ice cream date with Scott. This was Katie's fault. She lives only a few blocks from Coolidge Corner, but she insisted that we leave her house nearly fifteen minutes late, because we didn't want to seem "overeager."

"If we're there right at eight o'clock, then Scott will be able to tell that we never hang out with boys," she reasoned.

"And that's a problem?" I asked. I was standing by the Putnams' front door, holding my purse and cardigan, while Katie lolled on the living room couch with Buster, rolling his ears around her fingers.

"Yeah," she said, "because then we seem like losers."

"But we *are* losers," I said.

"But we can't let him *know* that. You're supposed to lie to boys."

"Did you read that in *National Geographic* too?"

Katie wrinkled her forehead and stared up at the ceiling, like she couldn't quite recall. "Nooo," she said. "I think I just made that up."

I grabbed her arm and hauled her out the door.

"Bye, Mom!" she shouted upstairs as I pulled her away. "I'll be home in a couple hours!"

I shouted, "Unless Scott wants us to stay later, in which case we'll stay out!"

"Dumb." Katie shook her head as we headed down her block. "If Scott wants us to stay later, then we'll *definitely* have to leave. You're always supposed to keep men wanting more."

"Wow," I said. "You're just a fount of wisdom about the male psyche tonight, aren't you?" And then, "Just because you aced the PSATs doesn't actually mean you know everything about everything."

Katie slid me a sidelong glance, and I thought maybe she was going to apologize for keeping her score a secret from me, but instead all she said was, "I know."

"Were you ever planning on telling me?" I tried not to sound hurt.

Katie threw her head back, looking up at the stars. "It's just the PSATs."

Because I guess when you already have as much going for you as Katie has, the PSATs really don't matter to you. Just another astonishing feat in her string of astonishing feats. Getting a perfect score on the PSATs is only about the hundredth-most interesting thing about her. You know. Yawn.

I still felt like it mattered. But I didn't say anything else about it as we walked down the road. If I was upset about this, that was my problem. What was Katie supposed to do— apologize for being who she is? It's not her fault she's perfect and I'm not.

By the time we reached Coolidge Corner, it was already twenty minutes past eight. Because we're not overeager, see. Hilary was sitting with two boys on the hood of a parked car while Scott stood talking to them. Hilary threw us a dirty look—the sort of look you'd give your friends when they're twenty minutes late to meeting you, so you've had to make pleasant conversation with three guys all on your own.

"Hey, Katie," Scott said. "Hi, Violet."

With that one greeting from Scott, all thoughts of Katie's PSAT scores vanished from my consciousness. "Hi," I replied in a totally natural, mature way, while inside my head I was like, *Oh my God, Scott said my name. My name was said by Scott. Hmm, did anyone say my name? Oh, wait, Scott did!* Etc. I tried to archive this moment in my mind so that I could replay it for the rest of my life, like the next time Spanish class got particularly boring.

"This is Raymond," Hilary said, gesturing to the guy on her left, "and this one"—guy on right—"is Dale."

I smiled at them in a cursory way. They both looked like typical Harper Woodbane boys in their loafers, expensive jeans, polo shirts (but no ties; it's the weekend), and slightly gelled hair. Raymond's hair was shaved a little too much, so his head looked square, while Dale had some acne. I'm not claiming they were ugly or anything—I mean, they go to Harper Woodbane; you're practically not *allowed* to be ugly there. Every student at Harper Woodbane has to look clean-cut and wholesome and athletic all the time, which Raymond and Dale did. All I'm saying about them is, they were no Scott Walsh.

Scott is a solid six inches taller than me and trim without ever looking too gangly. He has dark brown hair that I have to restrain myself from tousling and a smile that could sell toothpaste by the bushel. He always stands and moves like he's perfectly at ease in his body, and also I am obsessed with the casual-preppy way he dresses. And that's just what he's like on the *outside.*

I couldn't understand why someone who looked like Scott would hang out with two normal-looking guys. For that matter, I couldn't understand why Scott would hang out with me. I'm not very skinny, and my hair is never quite curly and never quite straight, and most of the time I am wearing uncool shoes. Scott should be hanging out exclusively with supermodels. They are probably the only people he can relate to, in terms of attractiveness.

"I was just telling Hilary about drama class on Thursday," Scott said to Katie and me as we leaned against the car. "We're doing *The Tempest*, but we theorize that Mr. Moritz has never actually read it. So on Thursday we made up this word—'dink'—and then we inserted it into our lines as many times as we could. Just to see if he would notice. Like, 'We are such stuff as dreams are made on, and our little dink is rounded with a sleep.' It got to the point where everyone was saying it at least once per line, and Mr. Moritz *never noticed*, at least until Chris started laughing. And then he asked what was going on, but all Chris could say was 'dink.'"

Everyone laughed appreciatively, except for me, because I was busy searching my brain for some intelligent and witty response. I think this is how conversation usually goes—someone tells a story, and then you reply to it, and, just like that, you have a conversation. But I couldn't think of a single reply to Scott's story. I was too worried I'd say something boring. I noticed that Katie didn't say anything either, so she must have been having the same problem as me, because Katie *always* has something to say.

Fortunately, the boys didn't have this difficulty. Raymond

said, "Dink!" and Dale said, "Mr. Moritz is an idiot," and Hilary said, "Let's get ice cream," and suddenly we were all headed into the ice cream parlor, while I was still brainstorming potential clever responses to Scott's story. ("How did you come up with the word 'dink?'" Who cares. "I like *The Tempest.*" *Double* who cares. "To be or not to dink?" No, don't say that; that's not even from *The Tempest.*)

We got our ice cream and sat down at a table in the corner. Girls on one bench, boys opposite us. Katie pulled out her cell phone, typed something into it, and put it back in her purse. An instant later, my phone buzzed in my pocket. I pulled it out, and there was a text from Katie. It read, If this is a date, aren't they supposed to pay for our ice cream? I rolled my eyes at her.

"Wait a second," said Scott. "Did you"—he pointed to Katie—"just text her?"—a point to me. (*Oh my God, Scott just pointed at me! See that finger? It pointed AT ME!*)

"Uh," Katie said. "Maybe?"

"Would you care to share with the rest of the table?" Scott asked me and Katie. I shut my phone and shook my head. "Secrets, secrets are no fun," he admonished us, wagging his finger, and I giggled. "All right." Here Scott pulled his own phone out of his pocket. "Give me your number," he said to me.

"What?" I shrieked. I stared at him across my cup of mint chocolate chip. I was aware that boys sometimes ask girls for their phone numbers—I had seen this happen in television shows—but I didn't know this was the sort of thing that could actually happen to me.

"Your number," Scott repeated in a soothing tone, like I was an easily frightened feral animal. "I want to text you too."

"Oh." Right. I told him my number. He typed rapidly on his keypad. A moment later my phone vibrated again. It said, tell me what katie texted you.

I laughed. "What?" Hilary asked, trying to read over my shoulder. "What did he say?"

"Nothing." I hid my phone under the table and smiled at Scott. He smiled back at me. (*Scott Walsh smiled at me! Scott Walsh LOVES me! He obviously wants to be my BOYFRIEND!* Etc.)

I texted him back, Never. Secrets, secrets are so fun.

Scott's phone buzzed, then a minute later Hilary's phone went off, then Raymond's, then mine again, and all of a sudden we were all texting one another.

After a few minutes of texting back and forth, we turned it into a game. The goal was to send a text that would make another person at the table laugh, without laughing yourself. You got a point every time your text made someone else laugh, and lost a point every time you were the one laughing. We all sat there, staring fixedly at our cell phones, our lips pursed as we tried to hold back giggles.

Katie kept getting me because she knows exactly what I find funny. At one point she texted, Aren't you glad we didn't show up naked? and I laughed so hard Hilary suggested that I lose *two* points.

Scott was best at not laughing. It must have been all his theater experience. He looked no more amused by our texts than he would have been by reading stock reports. Somehow, this made me want to make him laugh even more, so I bombarded him with text messages.

What, you don't laugh? I texted.

Then, You have ice cream on your nose.

Still nothing. Have you ever noticed that Dale looks kind of like an elf?

Dink.

That last one made Scott crack, finally.

"Who sent it?" Hilary demanded. "Who gets the point?"

Scott pointed at me again (obviously, our relationship was progressing by leaps and bounds). "Violet," he said, still chuckling. "Funny girl."

I kicked my legs a little bit under the table, but not so hard that anyone could tell. Probably. And I sent one last text from my cell, this one to Katie: Who just called me funny? Oh, wait, Scott did! OMG. Etc.

Killing my game

It was getting late. We had finished our ice cream and were all hanging out on the hood of Scott's car again. Eventually he said, "I need to get going."

"Me too," we all chorused, like every one of us had suddenly remembered a pressing engagement at eleven o'clock on a Saturday.

"Can your mom still drive me home?" I asked Katie.

She checked the time on her phone and winced. "You might have to spend the night, Vi."

I made a face. "Really? I have to be up early tomorrow. I'm babysitting for Ronnie."

"Sounds like a way fun Sunday," Katie said, who knows that the only thing I like less than babysitting for annoying kids is waking up early to do it.

"Where are you trying to get back to?" Scott asked me.

"Arlington," I replied.

"I live in Arlington too," Scott said. "I can drive you home."

"*Really*?" I squealed. "Oh my God, that would be *amazing*!"

He laughed. "You *really* don't want to spend the night at Katie's, do you?"

Right, Vi. Maybe try for a little subtlety? "Oh, no, I do—I would—but getting a ride home—like, that's great!"

Um, that may have been subtle, but it wasn't *English*.

"I do have to stop for gas on the way home," Scott told me. "And pick up some stuff from the store."

I bobbed my head furiously. "No problem. Gas. Store. If you're giving me a ride, you know, whatever." And then we could spend even *longer* together! Time getting gas! Time at the store! Time together, just me and Scott!

"Or, if you want, I can drive you," Raymond piped up. "I live in Lexington, so your house is on my way. And I don't need to stop for gas or anything."

Before I had a chance to speak, Scott replied, "That'd be perfect. Thanks, man."

"Where in Arlington do you live?" Raymond asked me, pulling car keys out of his jeans pocket.

I stared at Raymond blankly. It had taken my brain approximately one eighth of a second to construct a fantasy about Scott driving me home and gradually, over the course of the fifteen-minute trip between Brookline and Arlington, realizing that I was the only one for him. We would have stopped for gas, and he would have treated me to candy from the convenience store. He would have walked me to my front door and then kissed me under the front-porch light. Now this fantasy was suddenly not coming true, and I couldn't process it.

But there was no way out now. I couldn't say, "No, thanks, Raymond, I'll sleep over at Katie's," because I had just been going on at Scott about how *great* it was to get a ride home. And I couldn't say, "No, thanks, Raymond, I'd rather Scott drove me," because, um, then everyone would know I had a giant crush on him. And that's supposed to be a secret.

I glanced at Katie, who shrugged helplessly, and then I put on my "good sport" smile—the sort of smile I use when I get a B on a paper I worked really hard on and I want everyone to know that *it's no problem, I think a B is JUST GREAT, honestly*—and I said to Raymond, "Thank you. That is very kind of you to offer."

So everyone said good night, and Katie and Dale walked off in opposite directions toward their respective homes, and Scott and Hilary took off in their cars, and I buckled myself into the passenger seat of Raymond's Jeep.

Turns out Raymond is not a great driver. I wouldn't even describe him as a *good* driver. Every time there was a red light, he slammed on the brakes just before reaching it, so we came skidding to a halt, slamming me against my seat belt. I couldn't think of a tactful way to explain to him, "Look, the light turns *yellow* before it turns red, so if you see a *yellow* light, you might want to consider *slowing the hell down.*"

It did make me more hopeful for my own driving test in January, though. If Raymond could pass his, then it can't be that hard.

"How long have you had your license?" I asked, like I was making polite conversation and not just trying to figure out how likely we were to get into a car crash.

"Nearly four months," he said.

"And how long have you had your car?" I asked.

"Yeah, same. Four months. What good's a license without a car, right?"

"Totally," I said, like all our parents give us cars just because we pass the driving test.

I didn't have much to say to Raymond after that (other than "*Be careful that's a stop sign!*"). But it didn't matter, since he kept up a steady chatter about sports, including Harper Woodbane's upcoming game against Exeter, and how well he had done at fantasy baseball this year. I hadn't attended a coed school since I was twelve years old, but as I recalled, this was exactly the sort of discussion that boys used to have back in sixth grade. I was relieved to see I hadn't missed much over the years.

When we finally jerked to a stop in front of my house, I unbuckled my seat belt, stopped gripping the car door, and said, "Thanks again for the ride, Raymond."

"No problem," he said. "Hey, do you want to go out sometime?"

"Um." I was already halfway out of the vehicle. "What?"

"Go out," he said. "Sometime."

"Like on a date?"

"Sure," Raymond said. "Yeah. I guess. Like on a date."

"No," I answered quickly, because, like, *why* would I want to go on a date with Raymond? Not that there's anything obviously wrong with him, but he is just *some guy*, and merely being a) male and b) my age is not reason enough for me to date someone. What I wanted to say to him was, "Are you honestly so delusional as to believe that we have *anything* in common? Did you consider your fifteen-minute-long soliloquy about sports to be a *successful conversation?*"

But I couldn't say that aloud. Because that is mean. So instead what I said, to soften the blow of my rejection, was, "Thanks for asking, but I'm actually not allowed to date."

Total lie.

"Really?" he asked.

Absolutely not. "Absolutely." I nodded. "My parents are

strict about that sort of thing. They say if they're investing this much in my education, they want me to get the most out of it. And not waste precious studying time on boys."

That sounded impressively genuine.

"Man, I'm sorry," Raymond said emotionally.

"Yeah. But if that ever changes, well, I'll give you a call. Okay, thanks again, bye!" I flung myself out of Raymond's car like I was rescuing myself from quicksand. He drove off. He wasn't even halfway down the road before I pulled out my phone and called Katie.

"Hey, lady," she answered.

"Oh my God," I said. "Raymond just asked me out."

"Damn," Katie said. *"Why?"*

"I have no idea." I explained to her the whole conversation, ending with my turning my parents into celibacy-obsessed, overcontrolling nutcases.

"Great job," Katie said. "Great escape, really, massive style there. But did it occur to you, Violet, that now every guy at Harper Woodbane will think you're not allowed to date until college?"

"Oh," I said. "Not really."

"Every guy," she repeated. "Including Scott Walsh."

I sank down onto my front stoop, frowning into the nighttime. "All the more Scott Walsh for you, then, right?"

"Oh, right, I'm sure that his first move once he hears you're off the market will be to ask me out. But this was pretty poorly played on your part," Katie said. "I might even call it a game killer."

"Would you?"

"Totally. Total game killer."

"Because my game was just so spot-on beforehand?"

"Oh, yeah," Katie said. "Your game was smokin'."

I groaned. "I hate everything."

The Wisdom

As editor of Westfield's literary magazine—ambitiously entitled *The Wisdom*—I am constantly shocked by how poorly written our submissions about anorexia are. Actually, I may be more shocked by the way the rest of the LitMag panel always stands up for them.

During our Tuesday lunchtime meeting I read aloud the newest attempt, an anonymous submission. These sorts of pieces are usually anonymous, I guess because the writers don't want their classmates to know they're anorexic, but perhaps also because they don't want their classmates to know they write such god-awful poetry. I tried to keep my voice neutral, like I was giving the piece fair consideration.

I want to be thin
Because that means I win
I must be thinner than my kin
Thinner than my sister, Lynn
As thin as my skin
(Which is yang to my yin).
Hunger is a sin
As bad for you as a shark's fin.
I would laugh and grin
If only I were thin.

I cleared my throat, to indicate that the poem ended there, and looked around the table at my panel of eight literary-minded classmates. "What did we all think?" I asked.

"I liked it," offered Lolly, a sophomore.

I nodded at her, as though this were a valid opinion. "What did you like about it?" I asked, hoping she would be like, "Oh, wait, now that you mention it . . . nothing."

Instead Lolly fiddled with her pen, lowered her lashes dramatically, and murmured, "The poet just seems to do a great job of capturing what it's like to have an eating disorder, that's all."

She said nothing more, and I knew she was waiting for the

rest of us in the room to wonder if she, Lolly, might possibly have an eating disorder too. Personally, I wasn't all that curious. Lolly had spent the first half of our lunch meeting chowing down on turkey meat loaf, so if this was her version of anorexia, she wasn't doing a good job of it.

"Do we agree or disagree?" I asked the rest of the girls. "Does the poet convince you that this is what it really feels like to have an eating disorder?"

They all nodded. Either everyone else in this room was crazy, or I was. Actually, they probably just wanted to be nice to the author, whoever she was, who was pouring out her heart and soul and body-image issues into this poem. What was wrong with me, that I didn't want to be nice to some poor anonymous girl?

"So we like the content," I reiterated, and again everyone nodded, refusing to back down. I tried another tack. "What about the form?"

"I like the way she rhymed every line," said Dolores, a freshman. "Very Shakespearean."

"Shakespeare didn't rhyme every line like that," shot back Nina. It figures. Our classmates' poetry we can't critique. But Shakespeare, *that* we can argue about for hours.

"'Parting is such sweet sorrow / That I shall say good night till it be morrow,'" Dolores smugly rejoined. Dolores is a theater chick. "*Romeo and Juliet.* That's two rhyming lines in a row right there."

70

"Let us," I said, "stick to the work at hand, and maybe not bring Shakespeare into it. This untitled anorexia poem—as awesome as it probably is—is not quite Shakespeare, I think we can all agree." I hoped we could all agree. "So," I went on, "some of us liked the way every line rhymed. What about word choice? Word choice is very important in poems."

"I liked the 'yang to my yin' bit," Tasha said.

"Really?" I blurted out, then bit my lip before saying, "'Cause I thought that part sucked." My job as editor was not to tell everyone when something sucked. That was considered an abuse of power. My main job, in these meetings, was to be an unbiased mediator. So instead of offering my own opinion, I said, "If we *had* to give this poet edits, what would we suggest?"

Everyone pondered this question in uncomfortable silence. No one wanted to come off as the bitch who was hating on an anorexic.

"Maybe she shouldn't use the bit about shark fins?" Emily said at last. "I mean, I think it's great . . . but I'm not exactly sure what it means for something to be as bad for you as a shark's fin."

"But you're not supposed to be sure," argued Lolly. "It's creative language. It's a metaphor."

Lolly could define a metaphor in her sleep, but goddamn it she wouldn't recognize one if it galloped up and punched her in the stomach.

I wish Katie did LitMag with me. She maintains that she's too busy with crew practice to have time, and that she's not a "joiner" anyway, which may be true, but at least if Katie had been there, someone would have been on my side.

In a last-ditch attempt I appealed to the LitMag advisor, Mr. Thompson. He had been obliviously grading math tests in the back of the room. Much as I hated to put him on the spot, I needed backup.

"What did you think, Mr. Thompson?" I asked innocently. "Given the *Wisdom*'s very high literary standards, is this poem strong enough to do justice to such a sensitive topic?"

"Um." Mr. Thompson had not been paying attention. That's what we got for choosing a math teacher to advise our literary magazine. Actually, that had been the intention: We had all agreed that an advisor from the English department would interfere too much, would look at our LitMag meetings as an opportunity to rehash her graduate thesis with us helpless teenagers. Mr. Thompson's graduate thesis was on fractals, so there was no danger there. Plus, he was a guy, so we wanted him there for eye candy. Well, given his smiley-face tattoo and bright white high-tops, maybe not candy. Maybe something less delicious than candy, but still edible. Eye banana.

He scanned the poem in question and concluded, "I'm pleased that the author feels comfortable enough in the Westfield community to share her difficult experiences with us."

Mr. Thompson may be eye banana, but he's still a math teacher, and math teachers don't know shit about poetry.

"What would your response be," I asked my panel, "if someone's opinion was that having an eating disorder is very troubling and sad, and that writing poetry is a great way to work through those issues, but that being anorexic does not automatically make you a poet? What if someone suggested that even though a poem is about an important topic, it may still be a bad poem?"

Everyone gaped at me, as though I had just said, "What if someone told you that I eat dead babies?"

"Never mind," I said. "Let's vote."

The poem passed with eight yes votes and one abstention (mine).

I don't know how this can be true, since every year we win some kind of award for it, but seriously, the *Wisdom* must be the worst literary magazine ever published.

Moneymaking schemes

Katie and I need a new source of income. We are practically paupers. Katie will get a trust fund when she graduates from college, but that's approximately twelve million years from now. Until then she has to use her parents' credit cards for everything, which, she keeps moaning, is *not* the same as being independently wealthy. Meanwhile my parents give me a paltry allowance, which I have to subsidize by babysitting. And I have just decided that I hate babysitting.

"From now on," I declared over lunch in the cafeteria with Katie and Hilary, "I will babysit in houses only where the parents can *guarantee* me that they will have better food than my own parents."

"Hear, hear." Katie raised her plastic cup of lemonade.

"The next time some desperate parents beg me to take care of their children," I raged, sawing at my slice of chicken breast, "I will ask them for a full accounting of all the boxes of cereal in their pantry. And if they don't have at least three types of sugar cereal, then I will say no. No, I will not babysit for your whiny children in your cereal-deprived sham of a household."

Hilary, who was nibbling on baby carrots that she had wisely brought from home, asked me, "What brought on this sudden empowerment, exactly?"

So I explained: On Sunday, I babysat for a four-year-old boy, Ronnie, who accidentally on purpose let his dachshund out of the house. Ronnie and I had to run all over the neighborhood chasing after it. It took us forever to catch the dog, because Ronnie kept complaining that he couldn't run that fast. Also he kept stopping as he got distracted by motorcycles, ambulances, the sidewalk, etc.

Once we finally captured the dog and towed it back into the house, Ronnie claimed I had made him run so fast that now he was nauseous. He refused to go down for his nap without ginger ale to soothe his stomach. Sadly, there was no ginger ale in his house. But that's not the sort of explanation that satisfies a four-year-old. So he just kept shrieking, "I want ginger ale! My tummy hurts! I need it!" until he tired himself out and fell asleep in his clothes.

At this point I figured the only thing that would make my day at all worthwhile would be a heaping bowl of CocoKrispies, or possibly Lucky Charms.

"But do you think," I asked my lunch table, "that this god-forsaken family had Lucky Charms?"

"No," guessed Hilary.

"Given the arc of this story so far, I'd say it's doubtful," Katie agreed.

"They did not!" I slammed my fist down on the table, knocking one of Hilary's carrots to the floor. "They had something called *Fiber Flakes*. And not even milk to eat it with. Only *soy milk*."

"That sucks," Hilary said.

"That's why," I said. "No more babysitting."

"Shouldn't the rule just be 'no more babysitting for brats'?" Hilary asked.

"No, Violet's right," Katie said. "No more babysitting."

"But what'll you do for money?" Hilary said.

That was when Katie and I decided to become pool sharks. It was the only logical plan of action.

The way to be a pool shark is, you go to some bar or billiards club. You have to look really hot; that's key. Ideally, you should be blond and wear a lot of mascara. Then you sidle up to some men playing pool, and you watch them for a while with your big, excited eyes. Periodically, when they do something impressive, like hit a ball, you should squeal.

Eventually, you say to these men (while batting your mascara-drenched eyelashes), "Oh my goodness, you're so good at this game! Will you teach me how to play?"

And they say yes, of course, because you are so beautiful. They will teach you, while you act giggly and awestruck. Once you have been suitably taught, you have to say, "Let's have a little fun. Let's *gamble.*"

So then you bet the random men, say, two hundred dollars that you'll beat them at pool. They accept your bet, and then—stunningly—you turn out to be awesome at pool! And you beat them! And make two hundred dollars! And spend it all on sugar cereal!

(The sugar cereal bit is optional.)

Anyway, that's how to be a pool shark. It's pretty straightforward. And, not only is it a solid source of income, but also it's a great way to meet boys. I could really use a new way to meet boys, since so far the only males I've interacted with in the month of October have been Scott and his friends, Katie's little brother, and the cashier at the convenience store.

After school I went over to Katie's to practice pool sharkery. Her dad has a pool table in the basement. I don't like going out on school nights—I feel guilty when I'm not home studying—but Katie talked me into it.

We discovered that we're pretty good pool sharks. We put

on our tiniest tube tops and loads of makeup, so we had that part down pat. And Katie is blond, which, as I mentioned before, is ideal, if you can manage it. When I become a full-time pool shark, I will probably bleach my hair, but on this afternoon I was making do with my normal brunette style.

So we looked the part, and with a little practice we became excellent at shimmying around the pool table, waving about pool cues seductively, throwing back our heads and laughing. Really, the only thing we couldn't do well was: actually play pool.

After we had perfected our feminine wiles, we spent a while trying to hit pool balls. I missed the balls entirely, pretty much every time. Katie was a little better than me because she is by definition better than me at everything. So she usually hit a ball . . . but it never technically went into a pocket. After half an hour neither of us had yet scored a goal, or a basket, or whatever you call it in pool.

"Here's the thing," Katie said, as she chased the number five ball around the table. "It's all well and good to pretend to be bad at pool. But it doesn't help you any if you're *actually* bad at pool."

"Oh, yeah." I rubbed my eyes with the heel of my hand, smearing mascara across my face. "So do you think we could be blackjack champs, then? And take Vegas for all it's worth?"

"We could definitely do that." Katie directed a few more failed shots at the five ball. "But until then, you might need to go back to babysitting. And I might need to go back to spending Daddy's money."

"Do I *have* to?" I whined, setting down my pool cue. "Honestly, the horrors out there . . . You can't even imagine what it's like on the frontlines of child care."

"I'm sorry, Vi." Katie picked up the disobedient five ball and flung it against the wall. It sounded with a loud *thunk.* "Life is cruel."

Dinner with the Putnams

By the time Katie and I had finished being pool sharks and washed off most of our makeup, it was late enough that I just stayed for dinner. This meant I wouldn't get home and start my homework until after nine o'clock, which meant I would get only a few hours of sleep, which sucked, but that was just my punishment for going over to Katie's on a school night. I live on the edge.

The Putnams have an enormous dining room that I've never seen used. Whenever I'm over for dinner, we eat in the kitchen. Mrs. Putnam serves premade dishes from the organic grocer in Newton, and Buster hangs out under the table, slobbering and waiting for scraps. When Katie's dad isn't home for dinner—which is most of the time, since he works roughly one hundred hours a week—Buster will try to climb on to Mr. Putnam's empty chair to be eye level with the rest of the family. For some reason the Putnams think this is adorable, even when Buster drools into the water pitcher.

Tonight, for a change, Mr. Putnam joined us for dinner, though I barely noticed his presence, as he mostly sat silently, still in his business suit, drinking bottle after bottle of Sam Adams. The dinnertime conversation raged on around him.

"Honey, it's not too late to sign up for the deb ball," Mrs. Putnam said to Katie, a smile on her face. I have never seen Bunny Putnam not smiling.

"I already told you, I'm not going," Katie snapped, picking apart a chicken wing with her fingers.

"I know you said that, honey, but what I'm saying is, it's not too late, if you've changed your mind."

"I could be your escort," Matthew piped up. "I took cotillion class last year."

Cotillion class is this after-school course that a lot of seventh graders go to where they're taught to waltz and fox-trot and do other things that will be useful at a debutante ball and pretty much nowhere else for the rest of their lives. Any Westfield girl who knows any boys usually knows them from seventh-grade cotillion class. I never went, because my parents said it sounded "expensive and pointless." Which may be exactly why Matthew did it.

"Great, thanks, Matthew," Katie said. "I'll bring my little brother to my deb ball with me. That's what all the cool kids do."

"I still remember my deb ball," Mrs. Putnam said, getting a faraway look in her eyes. "I felt like a princess in my long white dress. Don't you want that, sweetie?"

"Not really," Katie said. "Because guess what? I'm not actually a princess."

Mr. Putnam stood up to get another beer from the fridge.

"I just want you to have every opportunity," Mrs. Putnam pressed on, sticking a green bean in her mouth. Katie's mom eats only about three different types of food, one of them being green beans. "You only get to be a teenager once, and I want you to live it to its fullest."

Katie exhaled through her nose. "Trust me, Mummy, I have *every* opportunity."

Mrs. Putnam flinched. She hates it when her daughter calls her Mummy, which only makes Katie do it more. Perhaps sensing a losing battle, Mrs. Putnam turned her attention to Matthew. Still smiling, she asked, "Did you get your science quiz back today, sweetie?"

"Um . . ." Matthew rolled his eyes toward the ceiling and answered, "Noooo."

"Really?" Mrs. Putnam asked.

"Okay, fine, yes, I did."

"And?"

"And I got a seventy-nine percent."

"A *seventy-nine* percent?" Mrs. Putnam set down her fork. "Seventy-nine?"

"That's nearly an eighty!" Matthew pointed out. Matthew is an eighth grader at Harper Woodbane, which grades at least as tough as Westfield does.

"But, sweetie, you shouldn't even be getting eighties. Look at your sister. She's never gotten an eighty in her life."

Katie held up her hand. "Whoa there, don't bring me into this."

"I'm just saying, getting a two-forty on your PSATs doesn't come out of nowhere."

"Jesus Christ, can we please just *shut the hell up* about my PSAT score?" Katie looked murderous. "For one meal, please? It's *just a standardized test*. It doesn't *matter*."

"Okay, well, Violet, then." Mrs. Putnam turned her smile on me, and I shrank back in my chair, because this was the first indication anyone had given of actually seeing that I was at the table. "Violet, honey, *you've* never gotten a seventy-nine percent on a test before, have you?"

"Um, well—"

"It's not a *test*, Mom; it's a *quiz*!" The veins on Matthew's skinny neck stood out as he tensed in frustration.

"Do you need me to talk to your teacher? Maybe he's not presenting the material appropriately."

"No, he's fine," Matthew said.

"Chip, did you hear your son got a C-plus on a science test?" Mrs. Putnam asked her husband, even though he had been at the table with us this whole time.

Mr. Putnam nodded thoughtfully and took a swig of beer. Apparently deciding that he had drunk enough that he could finally speak to his family, he said, apropos nothing, "Big crew race on Saturday, right, Kate? Head of the Charles?"

"Yes, Daddy," Katie answered, resigned.

"And what is your strategy going to be?"

I think Mr. Putnam is probably a nice, gentle man, and he parents as best he knows how, but it seems like the only thing he can ever think of to discuss with his kids is crew. And Matthew doesn't even row.

As Katie described how she was going to lead the Westfield boat to victory at Head of the Charles, Mrs. Putnam cleared the table, emptying her still-full plate into Buster's bowl. He trotted after her, wagging his tail lovingly.

I guess I shouldn't go to Katie's for dinner, because for some reason I always wind up finding it really depressing. But Bunny Putnam serves excellent desserts. So it's hard to stay away.

Aspiring toward contentment and Scott Walsh

Head of the Charles is one of the largest rowing regattas in the world, and it takes place every October on the Charles River. Hundreds of professional, college, and high-school teams compete—including Westfield, of course.

Even though Katie's been on our crew team for years, I still don't know much about the sport. Fortunately, Head of the Charles isn't really about watching the rowers. It's mostly about lounging around the boathouse Westfield shares with Harper Woodbane and keeping an eye out for Scott Walsh.

Or maybe that's just me.

Katie spent the morning of the race running around in a

Lycra suit, having harried conversations with Coach Nelson, and "warming up." I don't know why Katie warms up, since she is the team coxswain, which means all she has to do is sit in the boat and yell at the eight rowers. From shore I can never hear what she's shouting at them, but I assume it's something along the lines of, "Row, bitches! Faster! Pearl—are you rowing faster, like I told you to? No? Why not, huh? Do you want to *lose*? Hey, everybody, Pearl wants to *lose*! We have a *loser* on our team! What about the rest of you? Any of you want to lose too? Then, by all means! Row slower! What do I care if I'm associated with a team of *losers*?"

Whatever it is Katie shouts, she is apparently exceptional at being a coxswain. I don't know what it means to be an exceptional cox, since, as best I can tell, the only requirements are 1) having a loud voice and 2) being tiny. Maybe Katie's voice is superlatively loud? Maybe her body is superlatively tiny? All I know is that the other girls on the crew team agree that Katie is really something, and that she could probably cox in college, like even for a school with a Division I crew team. I'm not at all surprised by this. Katie has a knack for being excellent at things that I didn't even know it was possible to excel at.

Our boathouse is on the Cambridge side of the Charles River, a little west of Harvard Square. I sat on the wood ramp that leads down to the river, hugging my knees and watching the boats speed by. Reflections of the sun sparkled on the water. Across the river I could see the bright reds and yellows of the maple trees, and Boston's grand skyline. I thought about apple cider and my upcoming physics test, about jack-o'-lantern carving and whether I would ever be able to save the *Wisdom* from itself. Scott Walsh was nowhere to be seen, but, otherwise, this was the perfect New England autumn afternoon.

Mischa Amory and her Harper Woodbane boyfriend skittered past me, nearly tripping over my feet. Mischa was giggling and gripping his arm as they collapsed to sitting a few feet from me. He kissed her on the temple and threw his North Face fleece over her shoulders. It really *must* have been a perfect New England autumn afternoon, if even Mischa could feel it. Usually Mischa doesn't giggle. Usually Mischa just marches around school, her mouth pressed into a thin line, like she knows something you do not. Mischa has a very clear sense of right and wrong, which usually comes down to: She is right; other people are wrong.

When I saw Mischa's boyfriend pull a silver flask out of the pocket of his khakis and press it to Mischa's lips, I realized that she wasn't giggling in rapture over this lovely fall afternoon after all. She was giggling because she was drunk. Never mind that Ms. Freck stood ten yards away and could have caught them at any moment. Of course Mischa was drunk—I should have know better than to think Mischa could ever just *enjoy* herself like a normal human being.

I felt a sense of longing as I watched them on the boat ramp, Mischa nestled into the crook of her boyfriend's arm, his hand playing with her hair as they watched the race. I wasn't longing for her boyfriend, one of those burly athletes who lets his football throws do the talking. So un–Scott Walsh. Nor did I long to be drunk right now. I never had been drunk, but it seemed kind of risky—what if they fell in the river?

Really, I guess I just wanted Mischa's . . . contentment. I just wanted to sit on a boat dock, with or without the boyfriend, and with or without the flask, and feel content. I feel like I'm always working so hard to be content with what I have. It's the great paradox of my life. I'm pretty sure Katie is content with what she has. But then, I thought as I watched Katie command the Westfield boat down the river, Katie has everything. Who wouldn't be content with everything?

Genevieve is anorexic

Genevieve has been absent for two days now. The first day everyone just assumed she was taking a mental health day, which is normal, but today rumors began circulating that she has been hospitalized for anorexia. There are a number of signs pointing toward an eating disorder for Genevieve.

1. She drinks only Diet Coke.
2. Every couple of weeks she will make some gooey, creamy concoction, like tiramisu, and she will bring it into homeroom, and she

will demand in a crazed tone that the rest of us eat it. "All of it!" she will shrill. "As much as you want! Help yourselves! Yum!" So we do. And she doesn't have a single bite.

3. When she has a free period, she'll drive her Audi all the way to the mall to buy some zero-calorie, zero-fat, frozen-chemical pseudo ice cream, even though there's a perfectly decent Baskin-Robbins just around the corner from school.

4. I never see her eat in the cafeteria during lunch, not even on pizza day. And *nobody* misses pizza day.

5. No one in our class has gone anorexic yet this year, and odds are that *someone* will, so it may as well be Genevieve.

All her friends are huddled in the far corner of the home-room, crying together. They refused to go to fourth period because they were too distraught. When Ms. Freck came into our homeroom to try to make them go to class, Sydney shrieked at her, "You think discussing *The Scarlet Letter* is more important than *our friend's health?* How callous can you *be?*" So Ms. Freck let them skip.

Personally, I went to class because, while it sucks if Genevieve has anorexia, sitting around crying probably won't help her as much as, like, some food and an improved body image. Plus, Katie once calculated it out, and every one of our class periods costs our parents more than twenty dollars. I like to get my money's worth.

The moral of the story is, don't crash your car

Westfield doesn't offer driver's ed because it's too small, so instead I have to take evening classes at a driving school in my town. Week after week I have been reporting to this driving school in order to sit on a plastic chair in an overcrowded classroom with hormone-crazed teenagers trying to accumulate enough hours to take my driving test. I also have to do a few hours of practice driving, which is supposed to be the fun part. But most of my driver's ed experience is spent in this hellhole.

The teacher's name is Christine. Christine has frizzy hair, which she dyes bright red. I assume she is a cigarette addict, because every half hour or so she puts on an instructional video for us and goes outside for a while, then comes back in smelling like tobacco. Christine has a Boston accent. She often talks about her hometown, Dorchester, which she pronounces as "Dawchestah." She says she has been teaching driver's ed for fourteen years, which is, in my opinion, thirteen years and eleven months longer than any sane person would spend at this job.

On Wednesday, Christine began our lesson ten minutes late with a lecture about American Indians. Well, she just said "Indians," but I'm pretty sure that's politically incorrect. This lecture went as follows:

"Shut up," she started with, which is how she begins all her lessons. The room of thirty kids kept talking, except in slightly quieter tones. I took this "shut up" as the cue to hide my physics textbook in my lap.

"Shut up," Christine repeated. No one did, but she plowed on anyway. "Three hundred years ago America was filled with Indians. The Indians were kinda like us, but kinda different." Christine drew a feather on the chalkboard at the front of the classroom. I wasn't sure what this was supposed to represent. I get that if you're a teacher, having a chalkboard is a real perk of the job, so you want to draw on it as much as possible . . . but a feather, really? Was it supposed to be part of like a tribal headdress?

"One of the things that made Indians so different,"

Christine continued, "was that they did medicine different. Instead of doctors they had shamans." Christine wrote *Shammann* on the chalkboard. "Who can tell me what a shaman is?"

There was a long pause as all the kids in the class continued whispering to their neighbors, or fiddling with their cell phones, or applying their makeup.

"Who knows," Christine asked again, "what a shaman is?"

For heaven's sake. If Christine had posed this question at Westfield, she would have already gotten a dictionary definition and all relevant historical context. Unable to take the silence, I raised my hand and answered, "A shaman is like a medicine man."

"Good job!" Christine nodded. "So these medicine men used natural herbs and plants to treat their sick. Eventually they sold these herbs and plants to us Americans, and we used them as drugs." Christine drew a marijuana leaf on the chalkboard, next to the feather. There were some giggles, and two guys near me held their fingers up to their lips, pretending like they were smoking joints.

Christine looked pleased that she had gotten such a strong reaction, while I tried to figure out whether she actually *believed* this story was true, or whether she just thought we were all so stupid that this was the most complicated explanation of history that we could understand. I also wondered what all this had to do with driving a car.

No one else seemed quite so concerned, though. Instead my classmates said things like:

"That's not what a marijuana leaf looks like. I should know; I grow 'em in my bedroom."

"You do not."

"For twenty bucks I'll even give you some."

"Maybe we should get high before driver's ed next week."

"Tom's high right now."

"No, he's not."

"Bet you he is."

"Hey—Tom! You been doing a little what-what?"

"What?"

"Exactly!"

I considered excusing myself to the bathroom for the rest of the class period, but I was just too curious to discover the connection between shamans and operating a motor vehicle. Fortunately, Christine did not let me down.

"Now there are drugs in our society," she told us. "But don't do drugs while driving a car!"

Then she inserted a video into the television, dimmed the classroom lights, and went outside.

"Excuse me, *what*?" I asked aloud. No one replied.

So I went back to trying to study physics while the video played. But it was hard not to watch it. Based on the color quality and the characters' bell-bottom trousers, I'd guess that it was filmed around 1979. The plot was: There was some guy named Nick. One night he went to a party, where he got peer-pressured into smoking marijuana. Then he drove home and crashed into his neighbor's garage.

At the end of the film Christine returned to the classroom, reeking of nicotine, and asked us, "What did you all learn from this video?"

No one replied.

Christine rephrased the question. "When you watched this video, what did you learn from it?"

An unanswered question tears at my heart. I took pity. "Don't do drugs and drive at the same time," I said.

"Excellent!" Christine enthused.

The boys in the row behind me shot rubber bands at the back of my head. "Teacher's pet!" whispered one of them. "Narc!" whispered the other.

I stared down at my physics textbook and thought about how Katie, who still hasn't started driver's ed, constantly tries to convince me to date a boy from my class. "Driver's ed," she keeps telling me, "is a hotbed of dudes. Think about it: You're trapped in a classroom with them for two hours a week! Just introduce yourself! Then make out with them!"

And I have to keep telling her, "Katie. I can't make out with the boys from my driver's ed class. They are *all retarded.*"

Genevieve is not anorexic

G enevieve was back in school today. Turns out she just had the flu and was too delirious with fever to let any of her friends know where she was.

When she found out about the anorexia rumor, she got all indignant and went around complaining, "I can't *believe* you thought I'd been hospitalized!" Though she also sounded a little proud to be so skinny that her classmates had mistaken her for being in advanced stages of a life-threatening eating disorder.

Whatever, Genevieve. It was a totally rational assumption.

My R-rated life

Walking to Spanish class Katie asked me, "Do you want to go see *The Prep School Chronicles* at Coolidge this weekend? Maybe Saturday, before the dance?"

"That depends," I said. "Is it a horror movie?" I can't stand horror movies. Katie loves them, but that's because she has some kind of weird fascination with watching bad things happen. I hate when bad things happen, even in movies.

"No, it's a romantic comedy that takes place at a prep school. You love romantic comedies. Also, prep schools."

"Prep school sounds like a boring premise for a movie," I said. "Is it all about the students having too much homework and trying to decide on a theme for their yearbook?"

"According to the trailer," Katie said, "it's about the students partying and crashing sports cars and having affairs with their teachers. All of which, by the way, I think you and I should do a lot more often."

The idea of our doing anything like that made me snort with laughter. "That's supposed to take place at prep school?" I shook my head in disbelief as we walked past Señora Alvarez, checking her e-mail in the Spanish office, already four minutes late to teaching our class. "Can we even legally see that shit? How is it not rated like NC-17?"

"It's PG-13, I think. For teen drinking, drug use, and nudity."

"Fuck," I said. "For all the teen drinking, drug use, and nudity I do, my life is like G-rated."

"If it makes you feel any better," Katie said, opening the door to our classroom, "I'd definitely give you an R rating for language."

The unthemed dance

Westfield doesn't technically require us to attend school dances, but Ms. Freck encourages it as a way to show support for the class that planned the dance. Plus dances, unlike school itself, are not 100 percent female, so there is always the chance some boy might ask you to dance and then, at a later date, become your boyfriend.

This has never happened to me. But I'm pretty sure that's how the boyfriend thing is supposed to work.

A lot of Harper Woodbane guys come to Westfield dances, so it's also a great opportunity for Scott Walsh–watching expeditions. I don't see *nearly* enough of him, because I can

never think of a credible reason why I should be in his vicin-
ity. ("Heyyy, Scott! Fancy running into you here . . . on the
tennis courts . . . at Harper Woodbane . . . a school that I do
not attend.") In fact I hadn't seen him since our ice cream
date three weeks earlier—and by "our ice cream date" I mean
"that time he and I and four of our friends went to get ice
cream and Scott said my name approximately once." Now that
Scott had my number, I kept hoping he'd text me again. He
could even text me by accident, like if he was trying to reach
someone else whose first name starts with *V*. That would be
fine too. That's how unpicky I am. And then I could text back
something witty and charming and inside-joke-referencing,
like, *That didn't make me laugh. No points for you!* And then we
would strike up a texting repartee, until eventually he would
invite me to the dance. As his date.

However, the dance was tonight, and somehow none of
that had happened.

Instead a bunch of us went over to Katie's house and ordered
in pizza and spent like a million hours primping. Getting ready
was especially difficult, because we weren't sure what to wear.
Usually Westfield dances have a theme, like Studio 54 or Sock
Hop, and we dress accordingly. But this one didn't have a
theme, because the seniors couldn't get their act together to
agree on one. Probably all the proposed themes were deemed
offensive to deaf kids or nonathletes or dolphins or something. So the theme was School Dance, and that could have

meant anything from tube tops to cocktail dresses. Personally, I was wearing a short jean skirt, a bright-green off-the-shoulder blouse, and strappy sandals with a three-inch heel. I had no idea if this was appropriate attire or not.

"Unspecific dress codes are a major faux pas," Tasha commented as we crowded around Katie's dressing table, applying makeup in front of the mirror. "When my mother throws charity galas, she always says that it's the hostess's responsibility to inform guests what they're expected to wear. That helps them to feel at ease."

"This is yet another symptom of modernity's declining social standards," Katie mumbled dispassionately around her lipstick. I rolled my eyes at her and accidentally stabbed myself with eyeliner.

Mrs. Putnam drove us to school in her SUV, all the way telling us what knockouts we were, how the boys had better watch out, etc. Mothers live in a little fantasy world where that's true.

The dance was in the gym, which looked exactly the same as it always does, only less well lit, and with a DJ behind a table in the corner. Also there were random, incongruous decorations, like woven wall hangings and disco balls. I got the impression that every senior had tried to decorate the gym according to what she had wanted the theme of this dance to be.

My friends and I made a quick pass around the room, getting our bearings (no Scott Walsh yet), then settled into a spot where we could dance in a circle. The DJ played trashy pop songs and unremarkable hip-hop. I noticed Pearl and Mischa tottering around the gym, their Harper Woodbane boyfriends in tow. Dances are a fabulous opportunity to show off your boyfriend, if you happen to have one.

Hilary does not have a boyfriend, but she does have an ex-boyfriend. His name is Mike. Hilary and Mike broke up nearly three years ago, but he still shows up to school dances so that he and Hilary can have awkward, highly dramatic interactions. At our last school dance Hilary brought some other guy, which caused Mike—her ex from *eighth grade*, I would like to reiterate—to lock himself in the bathroom and refuse to come out until Hilary sent her new boy home alone.

My friends and I had been dancing for less then twenty minutes when Mike showed up and insisted on dragging Hilary away from us because they had "unresolved issues" to discuss "in private." What they still have not resolved by now, three years later, I cannot imagine.

My mother thinks Hilary and Mike will wind up married.

We danced for a while longer (still no Scott Walsh). Some guy approached our circle, grabbed Tasha around the waist, and tried grinding with her. Tasha sort of let him as she leaned in to mouth at the rest of the circle, *What does he look like?*

So we all stared at this guy, as he and Tasha rubbed their hips back and forth, and we made judgmental facial expressions. I shrugged and scrunched up my lips, trying to get across the message of *I'm not all that impressed, but go for it if you want to.* Katie gave a not-too-surreptitious thumbs-up. Tasha let the guy keep grinding with her.

Katie leaned over and shouted something at my ear.

"What?" I yelled back. School dances are loud. That's part of the reason why you have to look so pretty—because it's not like you can rely on conversation to get you anywhere.

"I said," Katie repeated, "why are no random dudes trying to hump *us* from behind?"

I snorted. "No sense of romance, obviously."

"What?" Katie shouted back.

It wasn't worth it. "Never mind!"

Two songs later Katie slammed a hand down on my bare shoulder.

"Ouch!" I shouted. "I am a fragile flower, Katie, for Lord's sake!"

She shook her head impatiently and pointed across the room. I followed her finger to see that Scott Walsh had at long last arrived, looking handsome as could be in a fitted blazer, dark-wash jeans, and red Converse. My heart swelled—and then sank so fast that I felt nauseous.

Scott Walsh had his arm around a girl.

"Isn't that . . . ," I started.

"Julia what's-her-face?" Katie finished. "The sophomore?"

"Yeah." Their backs were toward us. "You don't think they're . . . dating, right?"

"No way in hell," Katie said. "I'm sure they're just friends. Who like to go to dances together."

"And put their arms on each other's backs."

"Right. And make out."

Because right then, as though Katie and I weren't inspecting his every move from across the room, Scott leaned down and kissed Julia fully on the mouth. With obvious tongue. It looked like an amazing kiss. It looked like a kiss out of the final scene in a movie. I honestly thought I was going to throw up all over the gym floor.

I licked my lips, pressed my hand into my chest, and looked at Katie for help.

"Okay," she said, her brain visibly clicking away. "Either we go over there and slap her and cry and scream at him for betraying us . . ."

"Okay," I breathed.

"Or we leave. Your call."

I kept watching Scott and Julia. They had stopped making out now. He was doing some sort of funny dance, and she was giggling prettily. "Let's leave," I said.

Technically we're not allowed to exit and reenter our school dances, but obviously this was an extenuating circumstance. Katie and I snuck out the back staircase when the chaperones weren't looking and emerged into the cool night.

We trudged across the playing fields, my ears still ringing from the loud music. I scraped my sweaty hair into a ponytail, to keep it off my neck. The heels of my shoes kept getting stuck in the soil as we walked, so I took them off and dangled them from my fingers. My toes dug into the cool grass and earth.

"It probably doesn't mean anything," Katie reassured us.

"Oh, I know," I said.

"Lots of people kiss people, or date people, or whatever. It doesn't mean they're like *in love* or anything."

"Of course," I agreed, my stomach turning over at the word "love."

We wandered past the soccer goal, alongside the fence separating Westfield from the real world. School feels so different at night, when the fields are quiet and empty.

"When you come right down to it, Scott is just some guy," Katie concluded. "He seems pretty great, but if we got to know him, he'd probably turn out to be nothing special. We'll meet lots of pretty great guys someday."

"Oh, yeah?" I said thickly. "When's that?"

"College?"

"God, let's hope so."

We passed underneath the maples at the far end of the field. At length, I said, "I feel like I lost something that wasn't even mine." Katie nodded. I asked, "What does she have that we don't?" and Katie shrugged.

As far as I was concerned, Julia had to have *something*. She had to be smarter than me, or funnier than me, "or prettier than me, or skinnier than me, or richer than me . . . because if she weren't, then Scott would be with me.

"You can't beat yourself up over this," Katie said.

"I'm not."

"Oh, cool. Because you looked a lot like someone beating herself up over something that had nothing to do with her."

"Ha, ha." I stuck my tongue out at Katie. "I just really thought he and I hit it off that time we went to get ice cream, that's all."

"I know, I felt that way too. I guess he's just friendly."

I tore a handful of maple leaves off a tree. "That's not fair of him! It's breeding false hopes in innocent young girls like us."

"It's true," Katie agreed. "As a rule, I'm friendly only to people I want to kiss. That way no one gets the wrong idea."

"I blame Raymond," I said. "If he hadn't insisted on driving me home after ice cream, then Scott would have, and tonight he would be French-kissing *me*."

Katie laughed a little, sadly.

"It's easier for you," I snapped. "At least you've had a boyfriend before."

"Two years ago," Katie reminded me.

"And then there was that guy you went to second base with."

"It was over the bra, as you love to point out."

"Still. It's not like *you* live and die by Scott Walsh."

"Maybe not. I would really like a boyfriend, though," Katie said.

Suddenly the dark of the schoolyard was pierced by a beam of light flashing quickly across us.

"Christ." I held my arm up to my eyes. "What was that?"

"Security," Katie answered. "Get down!"

Katie knocked me to the ground, and we flattened ourselves on our stomachs. "This is really not good for my shirt," I muttered.

"Keep quiet," she hissed.

"Yeah, but it's dry-clean only."

"Do you want to pay eleven dollars, or do you want to explain to Ms. Freck why you're wandering around the school grounds at night?"

I lay there and kept quiet.

After a time, Katie giggled.

"What?"

"I was just thinking about what a colossal failure tonight has been."

As sad and betrayed as I felt, I couldn't help but smile a little into the grass. It smelled like autumn. "It's true."

"We're not really cut out for school dances, are we?"

"No," I said. "I think a more literary scene would suit us better. Like a Parisian salon."

"At least we have each other," Katie said, and I turned my head sideways to raise my eyebrows at her, since Katie is not usually big into displays of emotion.

She stared at me, and I think she was waiting for me to

say this back to her—"Yes, at least we have each other"—like how when someone says "I love you," you're supposed to say "I love you too." (Not that anyone other than my parents has ever told me they love me, but whatever.)

I opened my mouth to agree with Katie, but the words just didn't come out. Because ever since PSAT Day, I didn't quite feel like we had each other. Not like I used to. Because if Katie and I had each other, wouldn't she have just told me about her perfect PSAT scores? And if we had each other, wouldn't I have just been happy for her?

It's not that I was angry with Katie—you can't be angry with someone for being who she is—but, at the same time, I looked into her eyes and could say nothing.

At that instant, as we lay flat on our stomachs in the grass together, the lawn sprinklers turned on.

"Fuck!" Katie and I leaped to our feet, but we were already soaked. Bits of grass clung to our wet shirts.

"God*damn* it!" Katie screamed. "Why do I feel like I live in Dante's *Inferno*?"

I started to laugh then, really laugh. It was all so ridiculous. Katie and me, going to dances, dressing up, trying to meet boys. Ridiculous. After a moment of scowling at her soaked jeans, Katie gave up and laughed too. My hair was falling out of its ponytail in a damp, dirty, sweaty mess. I didn't care. Katie grabbed my hand and I grabbed my shoes, and together we ran through the sprinklers back to the school gym.

Westfield girls drink too much?

"Violet?" Mom tapped on my bedroom door on Tuesday evening as I was doing homework. "Have you been getting drunk at any school functions recently?"

"Um . . . ," I spun around in my desk chair. "No?"

"Okay, great, that's what I thought." Mom tossed a sheet of paper in the recycling bin. It was the Westfield stationery, instantly recognizable from its thick cream-colored paper and the engraved *Fortiter ascende* insignia at the top.

"Out of curiosity, what would you have done if I'd said yes?"

"Attended a workshop at your school about how to raise

a responsible daughter who doesn't drink alcohol," Mom replied.

I pulled out the paper. It was a letter from Ms. Freck, explaining that certain Westfield students had been drunk at Saturday's dance, and that this was not to continue, and that the school wanted to work with the parents to educate their daughters about alcohol abuse.

I quickly made a mental list of who this letter might have been referring to. Probably Mischa, Pearl, that whole crowd. I hadn't noticed their acting drunk at Saturday's dance, but, then, I had been too busy getting sprinklered to notice anyone getting sloshed.

"Won't the school be mad if you don't go to this thing?" I asked Mom.

She sighed. "Vi, I'm pretty busy. Of course nothing is as important to me as your health and happiness, and if I thought you had a drinking problem, I'd be the first mom there. But as it is, I don't have the time or desire to hear a lecture about how *other* teenage girls shouldn't drink so much. If there someday comes a time when I should stop trusting you, you just let me know, all right?"

"All right," I said, throwing the letter away again.

"Now go wash your hands so we can sit down to dinner. Do you want a glass of wine?"

"Nope," I said.

Mom smiled. "I figured."

Improving the world, starting with the Westfield gym

I was in the school computer lab, proofreading a senior's postmodern cautionary tale for the *Wisdom*, when Tori slammed a clipboard down next to me.

"Whoa," I said, startled.

Tori didn't bother with pleasantries like "Hello." "Will you sign my petition?" was what she said instead. She thrust the clipboard into my chest, so I could tell she wasn't really *asking*.

I glanced at the top of the petition. *We the undersigned,* it began in flowery cursive, before abruptly switching to printing. Presumably Tori's hand had gotten tired. *We the undersigned petition the Westfield School to remove the scales from the gymnasium, as they encourage students' obsession with their weight, which in turn leads to poor body image, eating disorders, and death.*

I looked up from the petition. "Death?" I asked.

"People can die from eating disorders, you know." Tori pushed her unruly brown and pink hair out of her face to fix me with a stern gaze.

"But has anyone at Westfield died from an eating disorder?"

"Not recently," Tori answered, which I interpreted to mean "never."

I looked back down at the petition. A lot of people had signed it already. I hadn't realized weight scales were such a big issue in the Westfield community. Or, potentially, they weren't an issue at all, but no one had the heart to stand up to Tori when she was off on one of her causes. Last year she had started another petition when she discovered that our cafeteria workers and maintenance men have to punch in and out on time cards to get paid for the exact hours they work. Tori was outraged, believing this to be worker exploitation. The cafeteria workers and maintenance men turned out actually to be cool with this arrangement, since it meant they got paid overtime, but Tori wouldn't hear their defenses. "They're brainwashed into believing they like what they get!" she insisted. Tori wears a button that says THINK GLOBALLY, ACT LOCALLY. Tori carries around a pocket-sized copy of *The Communist Manifesto* at all times. I wouldn't blame anyone for signing her petition against scales in the gym. She can be scary.

"Do you even use the Westfield gym, though?" I asked her.

Tori shrugged. She had a lot of other classmates to hit up for signatures, I could tell. She wasn't looking for an involved conversation about her fitness habits. "I don't," she admitted, "but I *would* if there weren't scales there. The scales make me *too uncomfortable* to use the gym."

Wow. I could not argue with that. Tori's desire to have me sign this petition obviously outweighed my apathy. I signed it, and she immediately marched away, an activist on a mission.

Sometimes I think I'm just really shallow and self-absorbed. I don't think globally *or* act locally. I didn't even know there were scales in the gym. I mostly just care about the *Wisdom* not totally sucking. And even that is a losing battle. I also want to get straight As in all my classes, but that's downright impossible. I don't know how Tori is able to do so much. I can't do anything.

It's a day party!
We're not invited.

I forgot about the parents' alcohol training workshop immediately after my mother mentioned it to me, but the day after it happened, it became the only topic of conversation at school.

"My father has gone and locked up all his wine," Tasha grumbled, as some of us sat around the homeroom during a free period. "Like he thinks I'm sneaking swigs of Chardonnay whenever he's not looking." Pearl and Mischa murmured their dismay.

"All right, what's going on?" I asked Katie. I had been trying all period to study for a precalc test, but these mutterings about liquor consumption were distracting me.

"That bullshit teen-drinking education program they made our parents go to last night," Katie reminded me.

"Oh, yeah. Did your mom actually go to that?"

"Of course. How did yours get out of it?"

"Uh, she just didn't go. She's not a student here, you know. The school can't have total control over her life."

"Really?" Katie raised an eyebrow. "I've never heard that point of view expressed before."

On the other side of the room Pearl was complaining, "I was going to throw a day party on Monday, but after this stupid alcohol program, my parents are making our house-keeper hang around all day to make sure I'm not drinking. Like a babysitter!"

"Uh, question." Rachel, sitting with her back against the wall, raised her hand as though we were in class. "What's a day party?"

Mischa and Pearl explained for those of us not cool enough to already know: A day party is when you don't have school, but your parents still have work. Like on a teacher-training day, which is what we have coming up on Monday. So your parents leave the house at eight a.m. or whatever, at which point you invite over all your friends for a raging kegger. You're wasted by ten a.m., and then sober by the time your parents come home at six. *Pure class.*

"Hey, Violet," Katie whispered to me, once Pearl and

Mischa were done describing this party that we were not invited to. "Want to have a day party at my house on Monday?"

"If by 'day party' you mean eating Oreos and watching *My So-Called Life* DVDs," I whispered back, "then totally. Party on."

What a safari really means

Ms. Freck vetoed our junior yearbook theme in class meeting today. Why she couldn't have vetoed it when we first chose it, why she had to wait until we had spent more than a month working on it, was unclear. She just told us that some unnamed student felt offended by the theme, so we had to change it.

"Who?" I asked from where I sat on the floor. "Who felt offended?" I felt particularly slighted here, since safari was my idea and all.

Ms. Freck shook her head and explained that it didn't matter *who*. So long as one of us felt uncomfortable with the theme, we should all feel uncomfortable. Class unity, supporting minority rights, etc.

"What's *wrong* with it, though?" demanded Hilary, standing beside Ms. Freck at the front of the room. Hilary had been diligently doing research ever since we chose safari as our theme. She'd even been to Harvard's library to find lesser-known academic safari books. The look on Hilary's face when Ms. Freck made this announcement was that of someone learning that her sole living relative has died in some tragic, unforeseeable factory accident.

"What's wrong is that a safari is not just about looking at animals in the jungle," explained Ms. Freck.

There was some confusion throughout the room. "I thought that's *exactly* what a safari's about," I whispered to Katie.

Katie nodded wisely and said, "Elephant tusks."

"You think someone's offended because safaris are actually about killing elephants and stealing their tusks?"

"That's my bet. So the provocateur must be some environmentalist. I nominate . . . Lily."

I glanced at Lily, who was leaning against a locker, calmly working on a friendship bracelet tied to her backpack. "You're way off," I told Katie. "This must have been politically motivated. How dare we support Africa in our yearbook when they allow genocide on a daily basis. Look at Darfur, et cetera. This is like an act of sanction. My bets are on Tori."

"You're so wrong."

"*You're* so wrong."

We were both so wrong.

"Safaris are extremely racist," Ms. Freck went on, "because they objectify black people. Tourists go to Africa to watch animals, and they watch native Africans as though they were animals too. That's not the sort of mind-set we want to encourage at the Westfield School. I congratulate for her sensitivity the girl who brought this matter to my attention."

That's when we all knew Mischa was the culprit, because she beamed like she had just won the lottery. This was not a lottery that I wanted to enter.

After class meeting ended, Katie and I walked together to Spanish class. Katie said to me, "Now, I'm no racist . . ."

"Right," I agreed, because I, too, am not a racist.

". . . but I still think that was total bullshit."

"It was," I said, "but that's not an argument that will change anyone's mind."

Katie got really angry all of a sudden. She hauled off and kicked one of the lockers lining the hallway. It made a loud crashing noise, and a few Littles jerked around to look at us.

"Relax!" I grabbed Katie's arm. "It's just a yearbook."

"It's just this *place* sometimes, you know?" Katie seethed, her body rigid. "This on top of that dumb alcohol meeting . . . Can't they ever let us just *live our lives?*"

I threw the Littles a fake smile, to reassure them that everything was fine here, and repeated through gritted teeth, "It is just a yearbook."

"It's *not* just a yearbook, Violet! It's about what the yearbook stands for. Why do we have to be *so* nice, and *so* behaved, every *goddamn* minute?"

I dragged her into class.

No matter what I told Katie, though, it was hard to relax when Ms. Freck announced she had taken the liberty of selecting a new yearbook theme for us. The theme was: animals. "This way you can still use all the drawings that you've done already!"

We should have just gone with "food" while we still had the chance. Hilary looked like she was going to faint from rage. Animals. Seriously, be more lame, will you, please?

Violet and Katie also drink too much

Katie and I were jogging around the field during gym class when she said to me, "I think we should get drunk."

"What, now?"

"No, Violet. Not *now*. I think Coach Nelson would notice. But soon. This weekend or something."

"Why?" I thought about how I had just reassured my mother that she didn't have to worry about my abusing alcohol.

"What do you mean, *why*? Getting drunk is an integral part of teenage development," she explained, slowing her pace so

I could keep up. "You're going to do it eventually, but you want the first time to be in a safe environment, like, say, your family room. That way you can learn your limitations and not end up passed out under a Mercedes with your cooch showing and strange men stealing your purse."

"That does sound bad," I agreed, panting as I jogged.

Katie nodded, her ponytail bobbing behind her. "But if we get drunk in a safe place—your family room, to again choose an example at random—the worst that will happen is we'll pass out on your sofa."

"With our cooches showing," I added.

"Ideally, we can avoid that part."

"You know when people get drunk they, like, lose control." Like Mischa at Head of the Charles, losing control of her constant commitment to being in a foul mood.

"I know."

"But doesn't that seem . . . not fun?" I managed.

"No, that seems like the *point*."

I didn't say anything. Not because I had nothing to say, but because we had been running for ten minutes and I was out of breath.

Katie didn't have this problem, though, and she continued, bouncing along, "Plus it'll be fun. Think how fun it always looks in movies. Teenagers getting drunk! Making out with boys in fits of unbridled passion! Don't you watch television?"

"There aren't any boys in my family room," I wheezed out.

"Whatever. It'll be a *project*."

I just sucked in air as I could, and Katie took my silence as a yes.

Cheers! *L'chaim! Salut!*

We couldn't get drunk that weekend. I was babysitting Friday night, and Katie couldn't go out on Saturday because she had an early crew practice the next day. She grew impatient. "In movies, teenagers don't have to plan to get drunk weeks in advance," she complained.

Fortunately, the following Friday fate was on our side, as neither of us had plans, and my mother was out of town for a conference at Stanford. This left only my father at home, who would be locked in his study all night, and who had zero interest in how my best friend and I amused ourselves.

Since I was supplying the family room, Katie supplied the alcohol. "Like my father will even notice that he's missing a bottle of vodka," she said, pulling it out of her duffel bag.

"Uh, how many bottles of vodka does he have?" I asked. Because my parents have *one*, so they would probably notice if it disappeared.

Katie shrugged. "Enough that he won't notice if one is gone."

I measured out one shot of vodka into each of our glasses, but before I could drink any, Katie said, "We need to change into our pajamas first."

"No we don't. It's so early," I protested.

"But what if we pass out? We'll want to be in our pajamas then. I don't want to pass out in this skirt. I like it too much."

I held up my glass doubtfully. "Are we planning on passing out?"

Katie sighed elaborately. "Well, *I* don't know, Vi. That's the thrill of it: *Who knows* what could happen? But put on your pajamas just in case."

So I changed into my flannel pants and a T-shirt that said I GOT MY FACE PAINTED AT RACHEL'S BAT MITZVAH. Then we raised our glasses of vodka once again.

"Cheers," Katie said.

"*L'chaim*," I said.

"*Salut*," Katie said.

"What does *salut* mean?"

"I don't know. I think it means 'cheers.'"

We tipped the vodka into our mouths. I drank maybe three drops, then spat it all out onto the sofa. "Katie!" I shrieked. "It's *revolting!*"

Katie's lips were puckered, and her tongue was darting in and out as she scraped at it with her teeth. "I think it's an acquired taste." She gagged.

"I think we need to mix the vodka with something. Like juice."

"Yeah, but that's not very hard-core," Katie objected as I went to the kitchen.

"*We* are not very hard-core," I reminded her.

I returned from the kitchen with a carton of orange juice, which we stirred into our vodka. I sipped the mixed drink apprehensively. It was still horrible, but less so. We turned on the television as I worked my way through my first drink.

"Well, that was fine," I said once I finished it. "What a pleasant evening's entertainment."

"Not so fast," Katie said. "We're not drunk yet."

"Right, but we *have drunk*, so doesn't that count?" I was already sick of the taste of vodka and orange juice. And I didn't like the idea of passing out. Where was the fun in that? Also, what if I threw up in the middle of the night, but was already passed out, and so choked on my own vomit? This really happens to people. We learned about it in driver's ed. Which, on second thought, might mean that it's false.

I started to explain this fear to Katie, but she was like, "Look, it's not a thing until we're actually drunk. Now that we have embarked upon this project, we must *follow through*."

"Fine." I mixed us each another drink. "How many drinks do you think we have to have before we're drunk?"

"Six?" Katie guessed. "Seven?"

The correct answer was three.

Here is what happened after three drinks:

Katie got very giggly and talkative, and she stumbled around my family room chattering about something that I now don't remember, but obviously it was very important to her at the time, because she kept repeating, "Are you listening, Vi? I just want to be really sure you're really listening, because I really want you to hear this." Approximately once every five minutes I reassured her that I was listening, and the rest of the time I lay in silence on my couch with my head pressed between my hands, and I stared at the television screen.

Here is what happened after four drinks:

Katie got very earnest and knelt beside me on the floor and kept repeating that I was her best friend in the entire world, and that she loved me, and that she would kill anyone who ever came between us. Meanwhile I lay on my back, staring at the ceiling and wishing I could fall asleep. But I couldn't, because every time I closed my eyes, the world seemed to spin and tip around me.

Here is what happened after five drinks:

Well, nothing different for me, because I had given up on vodka by then and started to drink water. But there was a fifth mixed drink for Katie, at which point she started to cry. This alarmed me enough that I even considered sitting upright. Katie's not a crier.

"Do you ever feel like you're not good enough?" Katie wept, and I didn't reply, because I had drunk too much for words at that point. But it didn't matter, because she wasn't looking for a response. She was just talking in this fuzzy, wandering way. "I just feel, every day, like I'm not good enough. And like I'm *never* going to be good enough. Like my life is just going to go on for sixty, seventy more years, and it will just be year after year of never being good enough. It's so much time, so long to be a failure, and I can't tell why it's worth it."

Tears ran down Katie's cheeks, and her voice was thick with snot. I would have gotten her a tissue, but I felt too dizzy to move and too confused to know what was going on, so I just patted her hair.

"Every time I do something right," Katie choked out, her words barely discernable, "it just feels like luck. And I know that one day my luck will run out, and then I'll do something wrong. And I don't . . . I don't want to wait for that to happen."

She fell asleep almost immediately after that, with snot

still drying on her upper lip and vodka left in her glass. But for me the world kept spinning, so I couldn't sleep for what seemed like ages. And when I finally drifted off, I dreamed only the most fitful dreams about *failure* and *mediocrity* and the space between them.

Katie and I contribute to the hole in the ozone layer

The morning after Katie's and my drinking binge, I woke up early. My stomach hurt too much for me to stay asleep. I cracked open one eye and saw Katie sprawled on the floor, a blanket beside her. Somehow the sight of her sleeping peacefully while I was awake and nauseous felt like an outrageous betrayal.

"Katie," I hissed. "Katie!"

"Hmm?" She rolled over.

I feigned innocence. "Oh, hey, look at that! You're awake!"

Katie licked her lips and smacked her mouth open and shut a few times. "My head hurts," she concluded.

"My stomach hurts," I countered.

"A headache is worse than a stomachache."

"Definitely no," I said. "A stomachache is way worse."

Katie groaned. "Want to trade?"

"I would kill to trade."

"Great," Katie yawned. "We'll do that." She flung her arm over her eyes and let it rest there.

I snuggled into the couch and considered saying something about Katie's drunken monologue last night. But I didn't. I didn't know if Katie remembered what she had said. And even if she did, now didn't seem the time for a heart-to-heart. Not with the sunlight streaming through the windows, not with my stomach feeling like it was at any moment going to stage its escape from my body.

Everything Katie had said about feeling like she was never good enough made total sense to me; that was how I felt most of the time at Westfield. But why Katie would feel that way too I couldn't imagine. Had she not *noticed* her PSAT scores, or any of her grades? Had she never looked in a *mirror*, for the love of God?

And then her saying that it just felt like good luck every time she did something right—that was funny. Because every time *I* did something right, it felt like winning an epic battle. No luck involved.

As for that last thing she said before falling asleep—about how she didn't want to sit around waiting for her luck to run out—well, I didn't know what she meant by that. But now wasn't the time to ask. Instead, I said, "We need to get rid of that vodka bottle."

Like idiots we had left the empty bottle sitting out on the coffee table. I didn't think my dad had looked in at us yet, but he could at any minute. And when he did, I didn't want him realizing that his daughter was a liquor drinker.

"Can't you throw it away here?" Katie asked.

"Oh, yeah, like my parents wouldn't notice that in their recycling bin. Hello, Katie, they drink *wine,* and usually not even that. Usually they drink sparkling water. Can you take it home and throw it away at your house?"

Without removing her arm from across her eyes, Katie replied, "Too risky. Can we just use your neighbors' recycling bin?"

"Uh . . . sure."

We pulled ourselves to our feet, stuffed the vodka bottle into Katie's duffel bag, and headed out my back door. It was a crisp fall morning in New England, perfect for apple picking, for hayrides, for long country drives.

"Ow, ow, ow," Katie muttered, pressing her hands to her temples. "Jesus Christ, does it have to be so sunny out here?"

In bare feet and pajamas, we crept to the driveway of my next-door neighbors, the Mahoneys. Their garage door was open, and we could see their trash cans inside.

"In there?" Katie asked.

I glanced at the motionless white curtains in the Mahoneys' kitchen windows and gulped. "Yeah. Let's do it."

Clutching the duffel bag between us, Katie and I slunk down the driveway, under the basketball hoop left over from when the Mahoneys' sons lived at home, and into the garage. I was so scared of getting caught that now I felt *doubly* like I was going to throw up.

"I'll open the trash can," Katie whispered, "and you put it in."

"No. Where's the recycling bin?" I whispered back, looking frantically around the garage.

"This is no time for environmentalism, Violet!" Katie hissed. "We need to get in and get out!"

"It's always the time for environmentalism! Come on, it's probably this bin here—"

"Hello?" I heard a voice from the driveway. Katie panicked and dropped her entire duffel bag into the trash can. And not an instant too soon. A second later, I saw Mrs. Mahoney framed in the garage door entry.

"Oh, Violet, Katie!" Her face broke into a smile. "It's just you."

"Hi, Mrs. Mahoney!" Katie chirped. I tried to echo that sentiment, but all I could do was make strangled little gasping noises as I tried to breathe normally.

"How are you doing, dears? I haven't seen either of you in a while."

"It's been too long," Katie agreed, clamping a firm hand down on my arm.

"How are things at your school?"

"Great, great," Katie said, and I squeaked out something that sounded like "great," sort of.

"Did you girls need help finding something in the garage?" Mrs. Mahoney asked. When I was little, and her sons were teenagers, theirs was always the garage that the neighborhood kids raided for extra soccer balls, Rollerblades, hula hoops, whatever. Ten years on, Mrs. Mahoney apparently still saw nothing odd about two girls skulking around her garage at eight a.m. on a Saturday. She probably assumed we needed to borrow goals for a game of street hockey or something.

"I think we're okay," Katie said. "We were just going. Thanks anyway!"

Gripping my arm, Katie led me out of the garage, waving brightly at Mrs. Mahoney. I waved, too—somewhat less brightly.

Katie didn't let go of my arm until we reached my backyard, at which point she fell down on the porch laughing. "Oh my God," she got out, between giggles. "That was *ridiculous.*"

I collapsed beside her. "That was so awful," I said.

"No, Vi. If we'd gotten caught, *that* would have been awful. Since we didn't, it's just funny."

"Are you kidding?" I inspected my bare feet, filthy from the driveway and the garage floor. "We failed in every regard!

We didn't recycle the vodka bottle, thus destroying the ozone layer. You threw away your *duffel bag.*"

Katie waved her hand, as if batting away a mosquito. "Whatever. I'll buy a new one. We succeeded in the most important regard: throwing away the bottle some place other than our own houses."

"And all it cost us was twenty years off our lives," I said, clutching my heart.

Katie laughed again. "Twenty years off *your* life, maybe."

I shook my head. "How do those girls do it? Like Claire, Pearl, Genevieve . . . When they throw parties and invite boys and drink thirty-packs of beer, what the hell do they do with all the empty bottles?"

Katie shrugged. "The ways of cool girls will always remain a mystery."

"However they do it, I seriously hope they recycle."

Katie nodded in mock concern. "Sure. I mean, under-age drinking, whatever. But underage littering is downright *criminal.*"

My potassium obsession

Two days after Katie and I got drunk, I was doing homework at my kitchen table when my mother, poking through the fridge, asked, "Violet, did you finish off the orange juice?"

I felt blood rush to my face. "Maybe?" I squeaked out. Mom gave me a quizzical look. "I love orange juice," I said shakily, which, while not strictly true, seemed an important lie to tell. It seemed like the only other option would be to say, "Orange juice makes a great mixer for vodka, *which I drink*." Instead I babbled on, "It is my favorite beverage. Orange juice, I mean. Did you know orange juice contains as much potassium as a banana? Not to mention vitamin C, vitamin A, vitamin . . . uh . . ."

"Okay," Mom said, not listening anymore. She wrote down *orange juice* on her grocery shopping list.

Over the next three days I guzzled a couple gallons of orange juice in order to prove that it really was my favorite beverage. I must have started getting way more potassium than usual, though honestly I didn't feel any healthier.

So, as far as I can tell, that's all that happens when you get drunk: You throw away a duffel bag, and you have to force-feed yourself orange juice. I guess it could be worse.

Scott Walsh in search of a handheld fan, and/or true love

Thursday was one of the best days of my life: Scott Walsh IMed me.

I was in my room, doing my history reading, but with my phone on the desk beside me and my chat program open on my computer. Obviously, I was hoping to be interrupted. But to be interrupted by Scott Walsh? That is *a dream come true*.

Here was our exact conversation, word for word:

SCOTT: hi vi
ME: who is this?
SCOTT: scott

SCOTT: scott walsh

ME: oh right yeah

ME: i remember you

SCOTT: haha yah

ME: whats up?

SCOTT: do u have a fan? like a hand held one

ME: . . . i dont think so . . .

SCOTT: i'm in this play next week and we're trying
to find fans

SCOTT: as props

ME: oh cool

SCOTT: i thought you said maybe you had one

SCOTT: when we got ice cream that time

ME: no, i don't, sorry

SCOTT: no prob

SCOTT: maybe katie was the one who said she had
a fan

SCOTT: ill ask her

ME: yeah, good plan

SCOTT: kthx

That was it. That was our whole conversation.

AMAZING, RIGHT? I vowed to save his screen name forever.

Katie called me after dinner. "Oh my God, Scott Walsh
IMed me today!" she squealed when I picked up the phone.

"I know!" I shrieked back. "Me too. I pretended like I only kind of remembered who he was."

"Did that work?" Katie asked.

"Who knows. Do you think this means he's in love with us, though? Since he IMed us?"

"Maybe. What about Julia, though? They seemed really happy together at the dance, and that was only two weeks ago."

"Maybe they broke up?" I suggested. "Let's do some recon at school tomorrow."

So we did recon, which mostly meant cornering Hilary before class the next morning and asking her if Scott and Julia were still together or not. Like I said, Hilary knows everything. She is truly a genius.

"Last I heard, yes, they are still happily together." Hilary slung her backpack over her shoulder and tried to leave the room.

"Yeah, only, when was the last you heard?" I demanded, blocking her path, still hopeful.

She gave me a scathing look. "Yesterday morning." Hilary tossed her hair and headed down the hall to class.

Katie pursed her lips at me. "So . . . does that mean Scott Walsh IMed us but he *doesn't* love us? *That* doesn't make any sense."

I felt irrationally deflated. "He's such a tease."

Sophistry in Spanish class

S ometimes our Spanish teacher forgets to come to class. That, or she hates teaching us so much that she knowingly doesn't show up. If that were the case, I wouldn't blame her: I imagine that when we try to speak Spanish, we sound like a personal affront to her native land (Venezuela).

Here are some things I can say in Spanish:

Dónde están las uvas? (Where are the grapes?)

Jugamos al fútbol. (We are playing soccer.)

Te quiero, Scott Walsh. (I love you, Scott Walsh.)

Plus some other sentences that would be equally useful if I found myself alone in a Spanish-speaking country. Katie can do slightly better than me (Surprise! Katie is better than me at something!). But that's only because she spent five weeks last summer on one of those teen programs in Madrid where supposedly you're there to visit museums and absorb the culture, but actually you just go out partying all the time, because in Spain they don't care if fifteen-year-olds overdose on Ecstasy and die. At least this is how Katie described it.

It's possible that I would get better at Spanish if Señora Alvarez actually showed up to class every day, but there's no way to test this theory, since she doesn't.

In the interest of fairness I should point out that the Spanish teachers' office is right next door to our classroom. And whenever Señora Alvarez doesn't come to our class, she's just in the office, checking her e-mail. So really, if we had any sort of desire to learn, we would walk next door and remind her that it's class time.

That's what we were considering doing on Friday, when Señora Alvarez once again did not make an appearance. Ten minutes into the class period Lily suggested, "Maybe we should go get her."

"Why?" asked Katie. She was drawing on the whiteboard. The only things Katie can draw are a star, a heart, and a scribble that resembles a frog. So she was drawing those, over and over.

Lily looked thoughtful. Why, indeed. "Because she'll feel bad if she realizes she's missed class again?"

"She will feel bad," Katie agreed, messing up her frog-scribble and trying to smudge it out with her sleeve.

Emily drooled a little onto the desk next to mine. Which is not as gross as it sounds, because she was asleep. Emily can sleep on command. She can sleep standing up. She can sleep during every free period, every bus ride, every class when a teacher doesn't show up. During the course of any given school day, she racks up a bonus two hours of sleep, easy.

As far as I'm concerned, Emily Ishikawa is the luckiest girl in my grade.

"On the other hand," said Sydney, "I haven't finished my physics homework. And it would be really nice to have this next hour free to do that."

I also had not finished my physics homework. Not that I planned to, necessarily, even if we got this next hour off.

"One could also argue," said Tasha, "that if Señora Alvarez doesn't show up for our class, then she just doesn't want to be here, and it would be cruel of us to make her come against her will."

Everyone nodded along with this, but I said, "Sophistry!"

"What's sophistry?" Tasha asked.

"It was a vocab word," I reminded her. "Sophistry: an argument apparently correct in form but actually invalid, especially such an argument used to deceive."

Sydney looked impressed. "That was a vocab word?" she said. "Shit."

144

"Are you sure it's a word? I can't find 'sophistry' in my English-Spanish dictionary," said Lily, thumbing through the pages.

"And do we really want to learn a language that does not even have a word for 'sophistry'?" demanded Katie.

"No!" a number of girls cheered.

So we staged our escape. Only we had to crawl on hands and knees out of the classroom, past the Spanish office, in case Señora Alvarez looked out and spotted us.

Unfortunately, just as the last of us was making her get-away, Señora Alvarez opened the office door, toothbrush in hand, and inadvertently knocked into a crawling Tasha. Tasha muttered, "Ow."

"*¿Muchachas?*" Señora Alvarez looked quizzically down at Tasha's prone form, and then up at the rest of us, huddled at the far end of the hall. "*¿A donde van?*" ("Where are you going?")

We all looked wide-eyed and innocent, mumbling, *"No sé."* ("I don't know.")

"Ah!" Her eyes lit up. "Is it class time?"

We looked vague and shrugged in a *Maybe it is, maybe it's not* manner. Señora Alvarez got that this meant yes, so she shepherded us back into the classroom. Emily was exactly where we had left her, head resting on her arms, drool congealing on her desk. She woke up as all of us sat back down.

"Mmm," she said, stretching and looking around blearily. "Is it time for class now?"

I checked the clock above the whiteboard, which showed that we were twenty minutes into the period. "Now?" I repeated. "Yeah. More or less."

Our youthful joie de vivre

There was a fire drill during English class today, so we had to postpone our vocabulary quiz for a second time. (The first time was last week: Ms. Malone got too excited about Emily Dickinson and forgot to take a break for the quiz.) I'm getting sick of remembering this list of fifteen words, and I'm ready to finish taking the quiz so I can finally forget them.

"Saved by the bell," Katie shouted over the fire alarm as we filed out of the building. "I couldn't remember the meaning of 'attenuate.'"

"To weaken," I shouted back. "You know that." *How* could

that girl get a perfect score on her PSATs and yet not know a word that has been on our vocab list for the past month? It was like she had decided, "Hey, since I already won the PSATs, I don't need to keep learning stuff!"

Katie said, "I thought 'enervate' meant to weaken."

"I think they both do."

"Trick question!" She looked scandalized.

Once we were outside and had escaped the loud ringing, we had to line up around the softball diamond by grade. The littlest Littles start at home plate, and the seniors line up behind third base. We also have to line up alphabetically within our grade. I am behind Nadine Thomas and in front of Lily Vern. I used to stand in front of Claire Woodrow. When Lily started at Westfield, in ninth grade, it really threw me off.

Ms. Malone counted our line approximately one million times before she satisfied herself that all fifty-three of us were there. The teachers kept yelling at us to be quiet, like they couldn't count heads if we were talking.

"Well, counting *is* pretty hard," Katie said on their behalf.

Finally, the alarm stopped, but before we could make a break for the school, Ms. Freck shouted into her bullhorn, "Wave to the elderly, girls!"

Right. Okay. Here's the deal with the waving: Our school is next to a nursing home. The residents there can look out their windows and watch us play field hockey or lacrosse or whatever it is we're playing. Assuming, of course, that they can still see, which I'm not sure all of them can, because they are real old. Anyway. Ms. Freck says that it brightens the elderly's days to watch our youthful joie de vivre. So we're supposed to wave to them basically as a civil service, like, *Hey, you can't walk unattended, but doesn't it give you hope for the future when you see our joie de vivre?*

"Has it ever occurred to you," Katie asked as we turned and waved youthfully at the unresponsive building, "that maybe that's not actually a nursing home?"

"Go on," I said, clenching my teeth in a fake smile at the nursing home (or not nursing home).

"Maybe it's just a building that, like, some people live in. Maybe we just *believe* that we go to school next to a nursing home. Just like they must *believe* that they live next to an insane asylum."

I dropped my arm, and we headed back toward the school building. "What if this *is* actually an insane asylum?" I mused. "And it's just that no one's told us?"

"Oh, good." Katie nodded approvingly. "Now you're thinking like a twentieth-century novelist, Violet. Keep it up."

Another attempt at fame and fortune

Katie and I developed a new moneymaking strategy. It was based on Harry Potter, which is my favorite book series ever. Katie dismisses Harry Potter as overhyped, though I happen to know that she cried solidly through the last eighty pages of book six. She claims there are "loads of better books out there that don't get the same attention as Harry Potter," but, when pressed, the only "better book" she can come up with is *Moby-Dick*, a book that a) Katie hasn't read and b) gets plenty of hype in its own right.

But Katie's misguided ambivalence toward Harry Potter was no barrier to our moneymaking scheme, which by the way was called: We Take the Littles on Harry Potter Tours of Westfield.

See, Westfield was built in the late 1800s—an architectural epoch best known for its secret passageways—and it has expanded since then, wantonly, randomly. With its boarded-up dumbwaiters, back staircases that lead to nowhere, and secret closets, Westfield is a *dead ringer* for a magical boarding school. I can't understand how Katie and I were the first people to capitalize on this.

We spent all our free periods for a week plotting the tour route. Some highlights: the staircase hidden in the back of the Spanish teachers' office that leads down to the admissions office, the boarded-up swimming pool underneath the English teachers' office, and the underground passageway that leads from the sophomores' homeroom to the maintenance shed.

In planning our route we even discovered a trapdoor to the roof that we had never known existed. Katie thought this was the coolest thing, but for some reason I hated it. The idea that there was anything about Westfield that I didn't already know made me feel off-kilter. "It's like going into your bedroom and finding all your books rearranged," I tried to explain to Katie. "Or biting into your mother's macaroni and cheese and it suddenly not tasting at all like the macaroni and cheese you've been eating your whole life."

But she rolled her eyes and said, "C'mon, Violet, it's just a trapdoor. Plus my mom doesn't make macaroni and cheese." So I guess she didn't know what I meant.

Our first tour was on Wednesday, during the Littles' lunch period. I wore my tour guide pin, which I used to have to wear when I was in Key Club and gave tours of Westfield to prospective students' families. I thought this was a clever touch.

Katie and I had advertised our tour with posters and fly-ers in the sixth- through eighth-grade homerooms, and I was pleased to see that six Littles showed up. This seemed like just the right number: Then they would all tell their friends about how fun it was, and next Wednesday we would have an all-new audience. Plus, six kids at five dollars apiece meant thirty dollars total . . . except I would have to split it with Katie, which meant I got fifteen dollars total . . . but still that was an excellent profit for a half hour of not very strenuous work.

"Welcome to the Harry Potter tour of Westfield!" Katie announced to our Littles. One of them looked so excited I thought she was going to faint. "I love Harry Potter!" she squawked. I glanced at this girl, in her falling-down socks and bowl-cut hairdo, and was reminded of a key fact: It's hard to be cool when you're eleven years old. I mean, it's hard to be cool at any age. But it's particularly hard when you're eleven.

"We are here to show you all the hidden aspects of

Westfield!" Katie went on. "The Westfield you never knew existed! The Westfield *behind* the Westfield!"

One of the Littles raised her hand. "Will you teach us to do spells?"

Katie and I glanced at each other. Calling our tours Harry Potter tours had originally seemed like a brilliant marketing campaign, but now that we were put on the spot, it occurred to me that our tours didn't actually have a huge amount to do with Harry Potter. Like, we had no magical animals. And presumably nothing evil would occur.

"No spells," I said. Before the Littles could get upset, I added, "Think of us as your own personal Marauder's Map to the school!"

That impressed them. Before anyone could ask any other tricky questions, Katie and I set off, letting the Littles scurry behind us. Stop one was a closet with a window in the back of it that directly faced Ms. Freck's office. We let each Little go in and peer through the window.

"She's at her computer," the first one reported.

"She's on the phone," said another one.

"I think she saw me," said the last one.

"All right!" Katie clapped her hands once. "Good time for us to leave, then, isn't it?"

We marched off to show them the hollow area behind one of the chem labs. We passed Mischa along the way.

"Hi, Mischa," I said innocently, as though I greeted Mischa

all the time, as though Mischa and I were like best friends.

"Hi, Mischa," Katie echoed, as if she, too, had any use for Mischa whatsoever.

Mischa narrowed her eyes at the train of me, Katie, and six Littles. "Dana!" she barked at one of them. One of our Littles stopped and said, "Yeah?"

"What are you doing?" asked Mischa.

Dana stuck up her chin. "A Harry Potter tour."

Mischa looked at me and Katie, and we sort of shrugged, as if to say, *Who knows where kids get these crazy ideas?*

"Does Genevieve know you're doing this?" Mischa asked Dana, who I now recognized as Genevieve's littler (non-anorexic) sister.

Dana shrugged. "She's not the boss of me."

We walked on. "Why is our Harry Potter tour any of Mischa's business?" Katie asked me quietly.

I answered with a snort, "Because *everything* is Mischa's business."

The Littles seemed impressed by the hollow area (with the exception of Falling-Down-Socks Girl, who sniffed, "I already knew about that"). And they were even more impressed by the next stop on the tour: the boarded-up dumbwaiter on the third floor.

Unfortunately, as they were all oohing and aahing over the contraption, Ms. Freck showed up.

"Good afternoon, girls," she said. All the Littles turned

around and fell silent. Ms. Freck did not look happy. "Who wants to tell me what is going on here?" she asked.

Please don't say, "Harry Potter tour," I silently begged the Littles. *Please don't say . . .*

"It's a Harry Potter tour!" chirped Falling-Down-Socks Girl, who I originally thought was just dorky, but who I now realized was downright satanic.

Ms. Freck's eyes glinted as she processed this information. "Girls, please head to the cafeteria," she said to the Littles. "That is where you're supposed to be during lunchtime."

Before they scurried off, Dana had the presence of mind to ask, "Do we get our money back?"

I thought Ms. Freck's eyebrows were going to jump off her face, but all she said to Dana was, "Go to lunch."

Then she took Katie and me into her office for a lecture. A few of her key points:

1. During lunchtime Lower School students need to be in the lunchroom, focusing on their eating. Otherwise they will miss lunch and will thus develop unhealthy eating habits.

(Katie's comment when we talked on the phone that evening: "Harry Potter tours are in *no way* the leading cause of unhealthy eating habits among Westfield girls.")

2. It was inappropriate of us to take money from Littles. Westfield is a "money-free zone," which means that yes, your parents do have to pay tens of thousands of dollars for you

to go there—but once you are there everything is included, and our tours were excluding the poorer students.

(My comment to Katie that night: "Look, if any of the Littles had said to us, 'I really want to go on this tour, but, I'm sorry, five dollars is just breaking the bank for me,' then I'm sure we would have given them some sort of 'tuition break' and just let them come anyway."

Katie's comment: "I was unaware that Westfield opened its doors to 'poorer students.' We need to look into this at once.")

3. Certain areas of the school are off-limits for a reason—namely, because they are dangerous—and we shouldn't have been poking around in old dumbwaiters, because someone could have gotten hurt, and, frankly, Ms. Freck cares only about our safety.

(Katie: "No one told me that the hollow wall behind the chem labs was *off-limits* or *dangerous*."

Me: "Though, to be fair, the next stop would have been the boiler room, and I'm pretty sure that *is* off-limits."

Katie: "Well, *I* don't recall reading that rule in the student handbook.")

4. The students have access to one of the school's photo-copiers in order to further their academic and extracurricular pursuits, and we abused that privilege when we photocopied the flyers that advertised our tours.

(Katie: "Harry Potter tours *are* my extracurricular pursuit!"

Me: "Plus, seriously, is Westfield so financially screwed that the budget can't support the cost of our copying a piece of paper a few times? What is my *tuition* for?"

Katie: "Basically, they are saying that all my extracurricular pursuits have to be *school sanctioned*. And if we create our own activities, well, those don't really count, and then we're *abusing privileges*.")

5. Junior year is an academically crucial time in our lives, and Katie and I do not have the time to stop studying and start gallivanting around the school's back corridors.

(Katie: "It was all of half an hour!"

Me: "Actually, Freck might have a point there.")

Needless to say, Katie and I expressed none of these thoughts to Ms. Freck. We just nodded as though we were processing her feedback, even though Katie got very red in the face and I could tell she was fighting the urge to scream at Ms. Freck.

Ultimately, Ms. Freck let us go, saying, "I know you're good girls and didn't mean to hurt anyone. In the future, just think more carefully about your actions." We had to give back the thirty dollars, so there goes one free trip to the movies, but otherwise it was all nothing more than a slap on the wrist.

Right after we left Freck's office, Katie and I had to rush off to our respective classes, so we didn't get to debrief until our phone conversation that night. At the end of rehashing it, Katie asked me, "Why do you think Ms. Freck was so upset about the whole thing?"

"I don't know." I had approximately eight hours of homework staring me in the face, and I didn't have the energy to psychoanalyze our headmistress. "Probably for all the reasons she said, right? Fostering bad eating habits. Discriminatory to poor people. Et cetera."

"But all those reasons are obviously bullshit," Katie pressed.

I sighed. "Because she wants to run a dictatorial regime and our underground, unsanctioned tours were thwarting the total control that she wields over the school?"

"Yeah." Katie sounded satisfied. "I think that's exactly why. And she may have won this round, but I think we should fight back."

Katie sounded like she was about to launch into some plan, but to be honest, the last thing I wanted today was another project to get us in trouble. All I wanted was to do my reading so I could go to sleep before two a.m. So I just groaned and said, "Go do your homework, anarchist."

Filled to the brim
with girlish glee

There are a few commonly accepted facts about Boston's other all-girls school, Miss Newbury's. One is that all the girls there are sluts. Two is that they are completely devoid of ambition, except for the ambition of marrying rich. Three is that if they, by some twist of fate, go on to a legitimately good college, it is only because their parents are huge donors there. To be fair, I've only ever met one Miss Newbury's girl, at a school dance a few years back, and she struck me as really normal and smart. But she was obviously a fluke.

Of course, if you asked any Miss Newbury's girl about

Westfield, she'd tell you that everyone here is a raging bitch
who will stop at nothing, no matter how unscrupulous, to get
ahead. She would probably also mention that Westfield girls
are pathetic prudes, or lesbians, or both.

The Miss Newbury's/Westfield feud goes back to approximately 1898—which is, by the way, when *they* were founded;
we are six years older.

Despite this centuries-old hatred, Katie and I went to see the
Miss Newbury's–Harper Woodbane production of *The Mikado*,
because, um, Scott Walsh was in it. And isn't that reason
enough?

The performance was at Harper Woodbane, because they,
unlike Miss Newbury's, have an honest-to-goodness theater.
And I don't just mean a big assembly hall—though they have
one of those, too, of course. But the theater is a separate
building, and the only thing they ever use it for is school plays.
It has special acoustics because the architect who designed
it (Michael Godfrey, Harper Woodbane class of '54) works
exclusively with theaters. Some of his other buildings are on
Broadway.

Harper Woodbane is the only all-boys' school in the Boston
area, which is why they do plays both with Westfield and with
Miss Newbury's. Although when they collaborate with Miss
Newbury's, I feel like they are cheating on us.

Katie and I bought our tickets and found seats near the
back of the theater, where we had an unobstructed view of

Scott's girlfriend, Julia. We spent the time before the first act criticizing her.

"I can't believe Scott's dating a sophomore," Katie said. "That's like dating a child."

"I concur," I said, even though Julia is like nine months younger than Katie. I added, "She looks like a child too. She's too skinny to be a real teenager."

"That's because she's a ballerina."

"Ballerinas have brittle bones. So Julia will probably die sooner than us."

Katie snorted. "You're almost making me feel bad for her."

"I feel worse for Scott. When she dies, he'll be all alone."

"He'll still have us," Katie pointed out.

"Indeed. And what a comfort I'm sure he will find that in his time of need."

The lights went down then, so we didn't have time to get into what we thought about Julia's clothes (too trendy) or her hair (too shiny) or her complexion (sometimes her cheeks flush and it's hideous).

The Mikado is a Gilbert and Sullivan comic opera set in Japan. I had to admit that the Miss Newbury's senior who played Yum-Yum, the leading female character, had a beautiful voice—even though she was probably still a dumb slut, being a Miss Newbury's girl and all. And Scott was *super hot* as Nanki-Poo, the earnest leading man.

During intermission we went out into the foyer to stretch

our legs and buy sodas. Katie commented, "I wish the characters didn't have to have such dumb names."

"They're not dumb," I said. "They're Japanese."

"I don't buy that." Katie shook her head. "I know plenty of Japanese people, and none of them are named *Yum-Yum*."

"All right," I allowed. "Maybe that was just what Gilbert and Sullivan thought Japanese names sounded like."

"Racists," Katie tossed out. "Imperialists."

"But exactly who are these 'plenty of Japanese people' you know?" I challenged her.

"Emily Ishikawa," Katie replied.

"Okay. But you know Emily's not actually her *given* name, right? It's just what she goes by at school because she doesn't trust us to correctly pronounce her real name."

"Fine, but I don't think her real name is *Yum-Yum*."

Katie had me there.

The second act passed uneventfully. It was followed by a reception in the foyer. We ate cookies, and Katie tried to teach me the lyrics to one of the songs from the play. It's called "Three Little Maids from School." Katie knows it because she sang in Lower School chorus.

> *Three little maids from school are we*
> *Pert as a schoolgirl well can be*
> *Filled to the brim with girlish glee*
> *Three little maids from school.*

"Sounds kind of like Westfield," I commented. "Only what's 'pert'? Are we pert?"

"Shh," Katie said, "we haven't gotten to my favorite part yet." She continued on with,

> *Three little maids who all unwary*
> *Come from a ladies' seminary*
> *Freed from its genius tutelary*
> *Three little maids from school!*

"That does remind me of us," I said. "Only none of us are named Yum-Yum, as we've already established. Also, there are only two of us."

"We could make Hilary be the third little maid from school with us," Katie suggested.

"I don't really think of Hilary as being 'filled to the brim with girlish glee.'"

"But you think of yourself that way?"

"Totally. I am totally gleeful."

"Hey, Scott's here!"

"Oh my God." I whirled around just in time to catch him casually placing a kiss on top of Julia's head. I felt a powerful surge of emotion—some combination of jealousy, loathing, and wanting to stab myself in the chest with a knife.

"Oh, yeah," Katie commented. "You look so filled to the brim with girlish glee right now, Violet."

"No one is ever going to kiss the top of my head!" I wailed, watching Scott from across the room. He was still in costume and had only half removed his stage makeup. He kept his arm slung around Julia's shoulders as he chatted with a circle of teachers and parents. They were all talking to him, and he kept nodding and smiling. They were probably telling him how great he was in the play. At one point he said something that made everyone in the circle laugh. Scott looked totally at ease—and why wouldn't he be? Who wouldn't be at ease with a starring role and a crowd of admirers and a ballerina girlfriend? Who wouldn't be at ease when life was so easy?

"Let's go say hi," Katie said, once the adults surrounding Scott had dispersed.

"No way," I said, staring at him. "He's with Julia."

"So?" Katie rolled her eyes. "I didn't say, 'Let's go kiss him.' Let's just go, you know, say what a great job he did. Smile a little. Then beat it. You think Julia's going to be like, 'Stay away from my boyfriend, you creepy stalkers'?"

"Actually," I said, "yes. That's exactly what I think she will say."

"You're severely troubled, you know that?" Katie grabbed my elbow and hauled me over to where Scott and his girlfriend were standing.

"Hi," Katie said.

Scott looked up from Julia. "Oh, hey! Katie, Violet. You guys know Julia right?"

I gave her a tight smile. "Hi, Julia."

Katie, meanwhile, ignored Julia entirely. "You were great in the play," she told Scott.

"Your singing voice is so beautiful," I added.

"Thanks," Scott said.

Then no one said much of anything. "Yeah, you were great," I reiterated under my breath, because I am an idiot who cannot handle silences.

"Well, Julia and I are headed to the cast party," Scott said at last. "Thanks for coming! See you later!" He and his girl-friend took off.

"Well," Katie said, after we had stood there for a moment. "I guess our work here is done."

"I should say. But it was ever so productive, wasn't it?"

"Oh, yeah," Katie agreed. "That bit where we spoke to Scott? Awesome."

"He obviously fell in love with us just on the basis of that conversation."

"Two little maids from school are we," Katie sang. "Dumb as a schoolgirl well can be. Filled to the brim with insanity. Two little maids from school!"

Thanksgiving is a tough row to hoe

Thanksgiving is always a golden opportunity for my parents and me to sit in a car for four hours, battling our way through holiday traffic, until we eventually arrive at my Uncle Rick's house on Cape Cod, where we are treated to overcooked turkey, limp carrots, and my aunt and uncle's unwarranted bragging about their two sons.

Noah and David are the sons. Noah is twelve years old and David is a year older than I am. Their parents think everything their sons do is brilliant, even though the only thing Noah does is watch TV, and the only thing David does is be an asshole.

Uncle Rick is my father's little brother. Katie theorizes that he has an inferiority complex from always being compared to my dad when they were growing up. "I've seen it all before," she says wisely.

Whatever the deep-set emotional causes, Uncle Rick never misses a chance to point out how he is better than my dad. Sometimes he likes to talk about how he makes more money (because my dad is a professor, whereas Uncle Rick is a sell-out). Sometimes he likes to point out how his wife is a better cook than my mom (which is false but has never been put to the test, since we always celebrate holidays at Uncle Rick's and never at our own house). Sometimes he likes to mention how he owns a purebred golden retriever, whereas my dad has no pets at all (the idea, I think, being that my dad is such an incompetent that he would be unable to keep a pet alive).

But mostly, Uncle Rick likes to mention how his sons are better than my father's children (i.e., me). This line of commentary can take on many forms. Like when David became quarterback for his high-school football team—"a first for this family," Uncle Rick commented archly, like I should have tried harder to become a football quarterback at Westfield. Or, a couple years before that, Uncle Rick just couldn't get over the fact that I had to have braces while David did not. "Tough row to hoe, eh?" he kept saying to me with evident delight. Coincidentally, Thanksgiving dinner that year consisted almost entirely of corn on the cob and saltwater taffy.

That's why this year I was thrilled when, after creeping along I-93 at approximately two miles an hour, we at last arrived at Uncle Rick's and the door was opened by none other than twelve-year-old Noah, sporting a brand-new pair of—yes, that's right—braces.

"Hey, Noah!" I greeted him enthusiastically since, in the grand scheme of Uncle Rick's household, Noah is a lesser evil. He grunted before darting back to the living room, so as not to miss any more precious seconds of television airtime. My parents and I hung up our own coats.

"Hello, hello!" Aunt Cynthia emerged from the kitchen, wiping her hands on her apron. "Rick!" she called into the living room. "They're here!"

"We-e-ell!" Uncle Rick came into the front vestibule too and gave us all big hugs. I tried not to squirm against his fleshy gut. "The prodigal son, at last!" he said to my dad.

"You all must have gotten trapped in that horrible traffic," Aunt Cynthia fluttered, which was just her passive-aggressive way of pointing out that we were late.

"You still driving that Toyota?" Uncle Rick asked Dad. When Dad nodded, Uncle Rick widened his eyes and exclaimed, "Really!" which was just *his* passive-aggressive way of pointing out that Dad hasn't bought a new car within the past five years.

I knew the grown-ups would continue in this vein for a while, so I went to watch TV with Noah and the dog. Like I mentioned, Uncle Rick and Aunt Cynthia brag way too much about their sons; however, it is true that Noah is a champion television watcher. He has an uncanny sense for how long commercial breaks are, so he can effortlessly switch between a favorite program and a second-favorite program without ever missing a frame. Of course he has a DVR, too, but he hardly needs it—he devotes maybe six hours a day to television watching, so it's not like he ever "misses" a show because he's out "doing something else."

Eventually, Aunt Cynthia called us all to the dinner table. Noah moaned like his limbs were being slowly detached from his body without the use of anesthesia, but heroically, he managed to turn off the TV, and we went into the dining room.

"I suppose I should ask David to come down here," Aunt Cynthia said, looking up the stairs. "He's been locked in his room all day, and I just hate to disturb him. Homework, you know. He gets *so* much homework." She widened her eyes at my parents and me, as if David were the only person in the history of the world to have homework. I almost snorted in her face. Like, *come on.* I had three textbooks waiting in my parents' car, not to mention an annotated *Macbeth.* I'd challenge David to a homework contest any day of the week. I had so much homework, I'd begged my parents to let me skip Thanksgiving this year to stay home and study. Then Mom asked if *she* could stay home too, but Dad was like, "Oh, no. If I have to go through this, we *all* have to go through this."

Once David came downstairs, Thanksgiving began in

earnest. We went around the table and said what we were grateful for. Noah's list included MTV, VH1, Fox, and SOAPNet. Uncle Rick mentioned both his enormous salary, for allowing him to provide for his wonderful family, and his still-thick crop of hair (cue jovial laughter and tousling Dad's bald patch). I said I was grateful for my family, but actually I am considerably more grateful for mint Milano cookies and highlighter markers.

After we all thanked God/ourselves/TV network execs, the conversation moved on to college admissions. "David has been working *so* hard on his applications," Aunt Cynthia informed us all. "Haven't you, sweetie?"

David shrugged.

"Where are you applying?" Mom asked politely. "Violet will be looking at colleges next year, of course, so I'm interested in hearing about your process."

"I'm applying early to Trinity," David said, sounding impossibly bored by the whole thing.

"Just like his old man!" Uncle Rick bellowed.

I glanced at Noah, hoping we could commiserate in hatred for his family, but no such luck. Noah had his iPod out under the table and was half watching an old *Simpsons* episode as he methodically shoved mashed potatoes into his mouth.

"Trinity should be no problem for David," Aunt Cynthia announced, "because he's top of his class. He's going to be valedictorian."

Now, this claim could not have been true, since it's my understanding that valedictorians are not selected in November of senior year but rather in, like, June. Even if it were true, I've seen David's school, and let's just say that being top of the class there would not require that much effort. I could probably do it even with massive brain damage. I decided not to share that with the family.

"What about you, Violet?" Uncle Rick asked. "Top of your class? Going to follow in your cousin David's footsteps to valedictorianism?"

"Uh," I said, looking at my dad for support. "Actually, we don't have class ranks at Westfield. And we definitely don't have a valedictorian."

There is an old rumor—possibly started by Katie—that Westfield once tried having a valedictorian. They announced her name one week before graduation. Mysteriously, the next day, she turned up dead. The school asked the salutatorian to take over delivering the valedictory speech. But the next day, just as mysteriously, the salutatorian also died. So the school asked the girl ranked third to take over as valedictorian. But then she wound up dead too. And on and on until, by the actual day of graduation, the reigning valedictorian was the girl who had originally been ranked eighth. Fortunately, she was going to Princeton in the fall, so it's not like she wasn't worthy of the honor.

Now, *is this story true?*

No. I think if there were a week in which seven out of fifty seventeen-year-old girls died, Westfield would not still have its good reputation. But this story is true *at heart*, and that is why we keep telling it.

I considered sharing this story with the Thanksgiving dinner table when my Uncle Rick said, "No class ranks? No valedictorians?"

"No," I confirmed, and Uncle Rick narrowed his eyes, trying to figure out whether this made my school better or worse than his sons'.

"Why do you have to go to that special school, anyway?" David demanded.

There is no good answer to this question. People have asked me before—in fact David asks me pretty much every Thanksgiving—and I still haven't settled on a true yet uncontentious response. "Because my parents love me enough to spend thirty thousand dollars a year on my education" is not a good answer. Neither is "Because I'm really smart." And neither is "Because in sixth grade the other kids teased me for being a nerd and I cried all the time, so my parents sent me to a school where everyone is a nerd so that I would be happy."

Just imagine what Uncle Rick would have to say about any of those statements.

Instead I said to David, "It's a great education," which is maybe a *little* snobby, but so what. I was annoyed.

"Don't see what you need such a great education for."

Uncle Rick chuckled. He is very self-amused. "Your father's got eight years more education than me, and what'd it get him? Nothing much!"

That did it. My parents lost it. It's one thing for my aunt and uncle to criticize their car or their cooking or even their daughter, but to criticize the world of academia? Unacceptable. Like, *step off*, Uncle Rick.

"What did it *get* me?" My father balled up his napkin in his fist. "It got me *knowledge*, Rick. Knowledge is the most valuable human commodity. Perhaps you can't understand: I am one of the foremost *experts* on Hemingway—"

"On who?" Uncle Rick said with a laugh, even though obviously he knows who Hemingway is. Everyone knows who Ernest Hemingway is; at least, everyone who's related to my dad knows. Rick was just egging my dad on. And of course it worked.

"That's it!" my father declared, throwing his napkin across the table, but not quite forcefully enough to hit anyone. It landed in the water pitcher. He stood. "We're leaving. Girls, get your things."

So Mom and I also stood up—we could not have been readier—but then Aunt Cynthia was all flapping hands and, "Oh! Oh! Rick!"

And Rick threw his arms out wide, like, *What'd I do?* and he shouted, "Relax! It was just a joke. I was just joking around. Wasn't I just joking, kids?"

Noah and David nodded like zombies, though Noah's eyes were still on *The Simpsons* and David had a turkey drumstick rammed so far into his mouth I expected him to choke.

"I know how seriously you take school," Uncle Rick said to my parents and me. "I was only having some fun. Heck, school's great! It's not the most important thing, of course, but, well, it's still great."

We remained standing, waiting for my father to make a decision. *Leave!* I begged him silently. *Let's burn all bridges, leave in a huff, and never return!*

My father sat down heavily. "Not a funny joke, Rick," he said. "Pass the potatoes."

Oh, Dad. You so *owe me.*

Since I was already standing, I took this as an excuse to escape briefly to the palatial marble bathroom. I pulled out my cell phone and texted Katie, Today I am thankful that thanksgiving comes only once a year.

A moment later she texted back, My dad is already on his 5th beer of the day.

Honestly, it is a wonder that Katie and I turned out so normal.

When I dragged myself out of the bathroom and back to the dining room, Aunt Cynthia was serving corn on the cob. Noah waved her away, his eyes still fixed on the iPod beneath the table.

"Man," I said to my little cousin, in what was far and away the best moment of the day. "Braces, huh? Tough row to hoe, isn't it?"

Katie's boyfriend (is probably not a serial killer)

Katie has gone and gotten herself a boyfriend. Just. Like. That.

She called me on Saturday afternoon to ask what the our physics homework was, and I said we had to read chapter six in our textbook, and she said ew and asked how I enjoyed the rest of my Thanksgiving, and I said ew and asked how going to the movies with Hilary had been, and she said it was good and then she said, "By the way, I have a boyfriend now."

I was like, "What? Who?" I had been sitting at my desk, trying to write my English response paper, but Katie's statement came out of nowhere and completely astonished me.

I jumped out of my chair and started pacing around my room.

"His name is Martin," she said, all casual.

I wracked my brain. "Martin? Martin what? I've never heard of him. Is he from Harper Woodbane?"

"Nope." Katie sounded pleased with herself. "He went to Lexington High, but he's graduated now."

"Wow," I said. "How old is he?"

"Not too old. Eighteen. Nearly nineteen."

"Oh my God, you're dating a college guy?" I paced even faster. College may be less than two years away, but it's like a different planet. People in college drink alcohol all the time because no one cares, and they nearly all have sex. At least this is what happens in movies.

"No, Martin's not in college," Katie said.

"Oh." I paced up to my window and frowned out it, watching tiny snowflakes melting on my roof. "I don't get it. If he's graduated high school, but he's not in college, what does he . . . do?"

"He works at Starbucks."

I breathed on my window, hoping to create condensation, and tried to imagine my best friend, Katharine Cabot Putnam, as the girlfriend of a Lexington High graduate whose career was working at Starbucks. Katie in her Tiffany bean necklace, and him in his . . . Starbucks apron? Nope. Couldn't do it.

"Why isn't he at college?" I asked.

Katie sighed. "I don't *know*, Violet. I met the guy only like eighteen hours ago, and I didn't immediately say to him, 'Excuse me, person I barely know, but why aren't you actively pursuing higher education?'"

"Okay, okay." I turned away from my window and resumed my pacing. "But if you've only known him for eighteen hours, how are you already dating?"

"Uh, because he asked me, 'Will you go out with me?'" Katie explained, like this was deeply obvious. "And I said, 'Sure.' Does that make sense?"

Not really, I mouthed. But aloud I said, "I'm really happy for you, Katie. A boyfriend! My God, my little girl all grown up."

Katie giggled. She seemed happy. Who was I to deny her happiness?

"Did you kiss him?" I asked.

"Of course! If you don't kiss someone, he's not your boyfriend. He's just your friend. Who's a boy."

Seriously? I go to Cape Cod for two days, and I miss *everything*.

"When can I meet him?"

Katie paused for a moment. "I don't know," she said at last.

I sat back down at my computer. "What do you mean, you don't know?"

"He's pretty busy," she said.

I love how Katie can't even tell me why the guy's not in college, but she apparently knows the nuances of his daily schedule. "Pretty busy doing *what*?" I asked. "Working at

Starbucks? Because we can just show up there and visit him. Hell, we can go right now. My English response paper can wait."

"Honestly?" I heard Katie take a deep breath. "I'm just not sure you'd like him."

This made me immediately suspicious. "Why? I like most people. Other than Mischa Amory. And serial killers. Is Martin a serial killer?"

"No," Katie said witheringly. "But he doesn't . . . I don't know."

"Seriously," I said, "if you like him, I'll like him. I mean it. I don't think we've ever disagreed on anyone. We're like basically the same person, right?"

"Right," Katie agreed, though she sounded a little reluctant.

"Right. The biggest danger of my meeting Martin is that he might accidentally make out with me, because you and I are so similar that he'll mistake me for you."

"If you make out with my boyfriend, I will kill you," Katie threatened.

"I would think less of you," I said. "I've already told you my position on serial killers."

"Okay, fine," she relented. "He works at the Starbucks in Kendall Square in the evenings. I'm going to visit him tonight. You can come too, if you want."

"I do want," I said. "Of course I want." I didn't understand why Katie was acting so weird. Didn't she want to show off her boyfriend to me? More to the point, didn't she want to get my approval of him?

"He has some cute friends, too," Katie said, sounding more cheerful. "I met two of them last night. Maybe you'll be into one of them."

"Oh my God," I said. "Can we double-date?"

Katie laughed. "No way."

"Can we have a double wedding?"

"Only if it's at Disney World."

"That's perfect, actually," I said. "I always dreamed of a Disney wedding. How would Martin feel if all our groomsmen were dressed as Goofy?"

"I don't know . . . ," Katie mused.

"You don't know why he's not in college *and* you don't know his feelings on Disney weddings? What *do* you know about this guy?"

"That he's hot," Katie answered promptly. "You'll see."

Common people like you

When I showed up at the Kendall Square Starbucks that night, Katie was already there, wearing a strappy purple tank top, sipping a latte, and leaning over the counter to talk to the tall, scruffy-looking guy at the cash register.

"Violet!" She waved me over. "Martin, this is my best friend. Violet, meet Martin."

"Hi," I said, shaking his hand across the counter, sizing him up. His black hair was a little too long and looked unkempt, like he hadn't combed it in a while. On his chin was a couple days' worth of stubble. He had thick plugs through his ears and an actual tattoo on his skinny wrist. I didn't really see the "hot" that Katie had talked about, but at least he didn't seem like a serial killer. He just seemed like someone who didn't bathe very often. So far, so okay.

"Hey," Martin said to me. He had a deep, gravelly voice. "I'm just about done here. Just gotta count down in back and then we can take off." He popped the cash drawer out of his register and headed into the back room, untying his green Starbucks apron as he walked.

"So what do you think?" Katie demanded the instant he was out of earshot—or probably before he was even out of earshot.

I shrugged. "I'm probably not going to steal him from you, if that's what you're asking." This was a joke: I wouldn't know how to steal a boy if I tried.

"Martin is like everything I ever wanted in a guy," Katie told me, taking the lid off her latte to blow on it.

"Uh, really?" This was news to me. "I thought Scott Walsh was everything you ever wanted in a guy."

Katie heaved a big sigh. "You might not have noticed this, Violet, but Scott Walsh is taken. Which is not actually what I was looking for in a guy."

She had a point, but I still didn't get why she would invite some non–Scott Walsh guy into her life just because he happened to be available.

Martin emerged from the back room. Now that his apron was off, I could see that his T-shirt said ROCKET FROM THE

CRYPT on it—whatever that meant—and had a tear down the side. He pulled Katie toward him and gave her a kiss, right there in the middle of Starbucks, with all the lights on and the MIT students working on their laptops and the homeless woman napping in an armchair. Katie kissed him back while I willed myself not to look. I've watched Katie cry and I've watched her sleep; I've watched her do one hundred sit-ups and I've watched her try on a Versace dress; I've watched her bite into a whole onion and I've watched her fight with her mother—but there was something just weird about watching her stick her tongue into some stranger's mouth. Like she was a stranger herself.

"The guys are back at my apartment," Martin said when they broke apart. "Want to go?"

"Yeah, sure," said Katie.

"Yeah," I echoed, like my opinion counted, like they weren't already headed out the door.

Martin led us down the street to his car, a Toyota that looked roughly eight million years old. He unlocked the driver's door first, climbed in, then leaned over to unlock the front passenger-side door. I had to wait in the cold, hopping from one foot to the other, for Katie to unlock the back door for me. I shoved aside some crumpled-up Coke cans and dirty clothes to make room to sit down. Martin turned the key in the ignition a few times before it finally caught. The car started with a tremendous grating noise.

"Sorry," Martin said when the noise didn't stop. "The muffler's broken."

"I gathered that." I shouted to be heard.

While Martin hooked up his MP3 player to the car radio and skipped through a bunch of songs, Katie twisted around in her seat to beam at me. "Isn't it great that he has a license?" she said.

Somehow I took offense at this. "I practically have my license too. I mean, I'm going to get my license in January."

"He has his own car, too! Isn't it authentic?" she went on. Like half the girls at Westfield didn't have *their* own cars. Like Katie's family didn't have a three-car garage attached to their house.

"What'd you say?" Martin asked, yelling a little to be heard over the clanging muffler and the blaring music.

"I said that you're *awesome!*" Katie squealed.

I almost gagged.

We drove through Cambridge and into Somerville, into a neighborhood that I'd never been to before. The streets were narrow and lined with parked cars; the houses sat closely packed together. This wasn't where Westfield girls lived.

Eventually, Martin stopped in front of a wood, four-story row house, and we climbed out of the car. "This is it," he said. "Home sweet home." He unlocked the front door, and we climbed a narrow staircase, emerging into a living room that featured a three-legged table piled high with empty beer bottles, a lumpy brownish-green couch, an enormous stereo system, an even more enormous television screen, and three guys.

This was probably the most boys I had ever seen at one time, so I immediately felt like I was going to throw up. Fortunately, none of them seemed interested in our presence. Their eyes were glued to the giant TV, which was showing some cheesy music video.

"Yo," said one of the guys on the couch. He had a shaved head and a lip piercing. Without glancing away from the television, he stuck his hand in the air, and Martin high-fived it.

"Yo," Martin said back. To me and Katie he said, "I'm getting a beer from the fridge. You want?"

Oh, and he's *hospitable*, natch. I shook my head. Katie gave a bright, "Sure!" and Martin disappeared into the kitchen.

Obviously, my best friend hadn't learned a hell of a lot from our "getting drunk" experiment. I could hope only that she wouldn't end this night by crying to Martin's friends about how she never felt good enough.

Martin returned from the kitchen with two bottles of Stella Artois and a cracked mug of water for me. There wasn't any room on the couch, so he plopped down on the linoleum floor. After a moment I did the same. Katie sat next to Martin, leaning her head on his shoulder.

"Um, I'm Violet," I said to the guys on the couch, not necessarily because I thought they cared, but more because it seemed polite.

"Oh, yeah." Martin said. "I forgot. This is Katie and Violet. These are my roommates: Tommy, Nat, and that fat one's Lee."

Lee looked to be approximately half Martin's size. I gathered that calling him fat was some attempt at sarcasm. It wasn't clear which of these guys were the cute friends Katie had promised. Martin was far and away the best-looking one of this pack, and that was not saying much. So much for our Disney double wedding.

"What're we watching?" Martin asked, then took a swig of beer.

"One Hundred Greatest Music Videos of the eighties, or some shit like that," Nat said.

"I think it's Fifty Greatest Music Videos of the eighties," Lee countered.

"Some shit like that," Nat repeated, unconcerned.

"Please excuse my friend," Lee said to me, putting on an affected, half-British accent. "I fear he has a potty mouth."

"Oh, uh . . ." I looked to Katie for support, but she was busy gazing soulfully into Martin's eyes. "It's okay. I don't mind."

"I could tell from looking at you that you're a girl with class," Lee went on. "Nat doesn't really do class."

"I *do* anything," Nat shot back, and Martin snickered.

"That's a reference to sex," Lee told me, still in his affected voice. I blushed and smiled weakly. I remembered the last time Katie and I had hung out with a group of boys: Scott

Walsh and his friends, back in September. It hadn't been like this. Maybe because Scott and his friends were still in high school, and these guys were older? Or maybe because these guys were *authentic*, while the Harper Woodbane boys were . . . what? Fake? If Katie was right about that, then I just didn't see the appeal of authenticity.

"How can you tell I'm a girl with class?" I asked Lee.

Dropping the accent, Lee said, "Dunno. But you are, aren't you?"

I thought about that. I'm a girl with nervous stomachaches, an unrequited crush, and a B-plus average in honors physics . . . but I don't know if I'm a girl with class or not.

Katie came to my rescue, sort of. "Sure, Violet's got class," she said. "That's why she's not drinking." Here Katie took a big gulp of beer, as if to prove that *she*, for one, was not a girl with class.

I narrowed my eyes at her. I felt suddenly like my best friend was selling me out, which, by the way, is a shitty feeling.

Lee picked up an oddly shaped container formed out of dirty brown glass. It had a round bottom with two tubes sticking out of it. He pressed one tube against his mouth for a moment, and sweet smoke poured out the other end. He didn't look away from the TV the whole time, while I watched him, fascinated.

When Lee removed the glass tube from his mouth, he coughed slightly, then turned to meet my gaze. "Hey," he said, holding the container out to me.

A couple seconds passed as I tried to figure out if he wanted me to hold on to this thing for him, or what, and then he said, "It's a bong."

Oh, right. Of course. I thought suddenly of Christine's abstract chalk drawings of Indian headdresses in driver's ed. It might have been a little more educational if she'd drawn an actual, modern marijuana-smoking device.

Katie glared at me, like I had somehow given away the secret that we were not very cool.

Lee was still holding the bong out to me, and it wasn't until he said, "Do you *want* some?" that I realized why.

I laughed, but not really. "Ha-ha" was what my laugh sounded like. "No. Thanks."

I expected to be "peer-pressured," because that is what always happens in the driver's ed videos. But what actually happened was Lee shrugged and said, "'Kay," and passed the bong to Martin. Martin took a long drag on it before passing it to Katie.

I opened my mouth to speak, but Katie met my eye and gave me a defiant look. She held the bong up to her lips, quickly breathed in, took it away, exhaled, coughed, and passed it on to Nat. God, she was a natural. Katie, quick to pick up everything, was a natural even at pot smoking. I said nothing, she said nothing, and we never broke eye contact until Martin kissed her, distracting her.

We all kept sitting there for a while. VH1 cycled through

all the 100 Greatest Music Videos of the '80s and started showing the 100 Greatest Music Videos of the '90s. Martin finished his beer and opened another one. The guys had a prolonged conversation about a comic book that I'd never heard of. Apparently Lee works at Newbury Comics, so he knows about these things. Tommy fell asleep eventually, and the other three joked about searching his room for drugs while he slept, but they didn't actually move anywhere. The room was unlit except for the glow from the television set, and the sweet stench of marijuana hung musty in the air.

Katie was uncharacteristically quiet, though she kept a hand on Martin at all times, as if somebody else in the room, not realizing he was taken, was going to put the moves on him. I was pretty quiet too, because what, exactly, was I supposed to say? "I don't read comic books; I read real books; in fact I should be at my desk reading one right now"? "I doubt that a cinema ticket seller like Tommy can afford drugs, and how did you guys afford the stuff in this bong, anyway?"? Mostly I just kept my mouth shut and stared at the television, but even VH1 was grating on me.

Just when I thought I might die from boredom, Lee turned to me and said, in a burst of energy, "Oh, hey, I totally forgot: Want to see our passed-out friend?"

I had no idea what he was talking about, but Nat and Martin both laughed. "Oh, *man*," Martin said. "Ryan's here?"

"Of course," Nat said. "Dude, he came over after work,

drank a six-pack, and just passed the fuck out. I put him in your room."

"We know how much you love getting Ryan in your bed," Lee added, which was good for a few more chuckles. Even Katie laughed.

"Come on," Lee said to me, standing up and holding out his hand. I scrambled to my feet but didn't take his hand. I followed him down the dark, cramped hallway. We stopped in front of a doorway. "That's our passed-out friend," Lee said in a low voice.

I peered inside the room and saw another guy, I guess Ryan, sitting on the edge of an unmade bed, doubled over, his head resting between his knees.

"Want to see the best part?" Lee asked. Without waiting for my answer, he went into the room, lifted Ryan's torso by the shoulders, and then let go. Ryan's body immediately collapsed in on itself, his head falling back down between his knees.

"Isn't that sick?" Lee asked. "He always just goes back to that position. Here, you can try."

Hesitantly, I stepped into the dimly lit room. Like Lee had done, I put my hands under Ryan's shoulders and lifted up his chest. He weighed more than I had expected, and his head hung limp, eyes slightly open, but rolled back in their sockets so only the whites showed.

I took my hands away, and Ryan slumped back in half like a rag doll. I turned to look at Lee and found that he was standing only a few inches away from me. "Ryan's so funny," Lee said, looking me straight in the eye, exhaling an odor of beer and smoke.

And I said, "I want to go home."

I turned and walked past Lee, out of the bedroom and back to the living room, where I found Katie lying on the floor with her head on Martin's knee.

"Hey, Katie, can we get going?" I asked.

Katie snuggled into Martin's lap and said, "Nope."

I gaped at her. The bright lights of the television picture flickered across her face as she stared straight at it.

"Can I talk to you outside, please?" I said.

Katie sighed and, with great effort, pulled herself to her feet. She kissed Martin on the top of his head like a dog marking its territory, then followed me out the door. I led the way downstairs and outside, being careful to leave the front door open a crack.

"Jesus, Vi," Katie said. "It's freezing out! We couldn't have conversed, like, in their kitchen?"

I didn't even bother to answer. "What is *wrong* with you tonight?" I demanded instead.

Katie knitted together her eyebrows in confusion. "Me?" she said. "Nothing's wrong with *me* tonight. I'm just enjoying an evening with my new boyfriend, getting to know him and his friends. I don't want to leave yet because I'm having fun. What's wrong with *you*, Violet? You've been sulking ever since we got here. Martin has been trying to be nice, and you've basically ignored him. His friends were being really friendly; Lee was even flirting with you—"

"Hold on." I held up a hand to stop her. "How do you know Lee was flirting with me?"

Katie shivered. "I don't know. You can just tell."

"*I* can't just tell!" I also couldn't tell if Katie actually knew more about boys than I did, or if she was just acting like it. Either way, it annoyed me.

"So does that mean you're interested in him?" Katie asked.

"In Lee?" I responded as immediately as I had the time Raymond asked me out. "No."

"You," Katie said to me, "are a snob."

My mouth fell open. Katie might be abrupt sometimes, and she'll call a bitch a bitch when that bitch is Mischa, just as she'll call an idiot an idiot when that idiot is Pearl—but I had never known Katie to talk to *me* that way. "I'm sorry, you think I'm a snob because I'm not interested in Lee? Some nineteen-year-old loser whose last name I don't even know?"

"I think you're a snob because *nothing* and *no one* is ever good enough for you," Katie replied. "Lee seems fine. He's fine. But since he's not the pinnacle of manhood—since he's not *Scott Walsh*—you don't even want to get to know him. You've just decided he's a loser. And why? Oh, right, because he works at a comic-book store and doesn't live in a suburban mansion. *That's* why you're a snob."

This was so unfair. I had been sitting on the floor in that godforsaken tenement for the past two hours, subjecting myself to marijuana smoke and probably asbestos, too, all for Katie, just so I could get to know a guy who was obviously important to her—and this was how she thanked me? "*I'm* a snob?" I said. "Me? Look who's talking, Miss Katharine Cabot Putnam! Miss Debutante Ball! Miss Perfect Score On Your PSATs!"

"I can't help the way I was born," Katie snapped, "but I can help the way I act. You're not interested in Martin and his friends just because they didn't go to *Harper Woodbane*. Because they're not at *Harvard*, they're not good enough for you? Is that it?"

I stared at my best friend. Did she honestly think I was that shallow? *Was* I honestly that shallow? Was that my problem with them?

"No," I answered slowly. "It's because they didn't interest me. They didn't make me laugh once—not *once*, and you know I love to laugh. It seemed like they weren't really passionate about anything, like they didn't really want to *do* anything. I felt like they were just killing time, all the time."

"You don't know them," Katie said. She was shivering pretty hard by this point. She had left her coat inside, and her tank top and lightweight cardigan didn't help much in this weather. I could see my breath in the air as I talked.

"I like you," I told her, "not because you go to Westfield

or because your family has money. I don't care about any of that. I like you because you make me think. And you make me laugh."

I didn't look at Katie as I said this, but she probably wasn't looking at me, either. Like I said, we're not into shows of affection.

"Does Martin make you think?" I asked, turning back to her now. "Does he make you laugh? Would he even do a project with you?"

Katie looked up at the sky, at Martin's parked car, at a group of girls stumbling in high heels up at the street corner, and she ducked the question. "I've only known him for like a day," she said. "And he's nice. He's normal."

Because apparently that's all we look for in a guy: that he be *nice* and *normal.* "Can we please go home?" I was shivering by now, too.

Katie sighed and rolled her head around like she was making an enormous sacrifice on my behalf. "Okay, fine. Call a cab. I need to run inside and get my jacket, and say good-bye to Martin, and break Lee's heart by telling him that you're not into him."

As Katie opened their front door, I said, "I just think you could do better. That's all. I think we can both do better."

She paused on the threshold and said, not to me, but sort of to the doorbell, "I don't *want* to do better." And she disappeared into Martin's house.

Genevieve's boyfriend advice

C an you come over after school today?" Katie asked as we sat in the Spanish classroom on Wednesday, waiting to see if Señora Alvarez would make an appearance. It was a few days after we had hung out at Martin's apartment, and Katie and I hadn't talked much since then. I was playing it cool, waiting for her to explain, or at least apologize, for Saturday night. But so far, nothing.

"Uh, not really," I said, focusing on a worksheet about usage of the word *por* versus the word *para*, just in case Señora Alvarez showed up, just in case she remembered that she had assigned us homework.

"Why not?"

"Well, for one, this thing called 'homework.' For two, I have a literary magazine to put out, in case you've forgotten. I need to edit and format the whole thing before winter vacation." *For three, you think I'm a snob and I think your boyfriend sucks,* I thought but did not say.

"Oh, right." Katie clapped a hand over her forehead in mock revelation. "*The Wisdom.* Violet Tunis's ticket to an Ivy League college."

"We can't all rely on our PSAT scores," I pointed out waspishly. Katie raised her eyebrows and backed off her *Wisdom* mockery.

"Can you take *one* afternoon off editing? Pretty please? I want to bake cookies for Martin and I need your help."

I finished writing *por* and *para* at random down all the blanks on the page and turned to look at Katie. "I don't understand a single word you just said. Why do you want to bake cookies for Martin?"

Also, why did she want to involve me in this? Katie knew I was unimpressed by her boyfriend. Our argument outside Martin's apartment kept niggling at me. It was like she realized Martin wasn't worth her time, yet she didn't care. What did she mean when she said she didn't *want* to do better than Martin? Doesn't everyone always *want* to do better? And she's Katie! She's smart and funny and talented and pretty—she's capable of doing better *effortlessly*!

But instead she wanted to bake cookies for this guy.

"I think baking is something girlfriends do," Katie said with a vague wave of her hand. "I heard Genevieve say something about it in the homeroom once. She knows all about boyfriends."

"Okay, but why do you need my help?"

"Because I don't know how to bake."

"And I do?"

"Probably not," Katie conceded as Señora Alvarez made her harried entrance, eleven minutes into the class period. Katie dropped her voice so the teacher wouldn't hear. "But we're usually better when we do something together than when I do it alone. Or at least we have more fun."

This was obviously Katie's way of apologizing to me for our Saturday-night fight. I wrinkled my nose at her, both of us knowing that I would be at her house that afternoon. I can never say no to Katie.

The way to a man's heart

When we got to Katie's house after school, I hadn't even taken off my backpack before Katie started pulling every conceivable ingredient out of her kitchen cabinets. Flour, sugar, rolled oats, lemon juice, honey, vinegar, cumin powder—the Putnams' counter was starting to look like a farmers' market. Buster followed her around the room, his tongue hanging out, like he was hoping for a treat. Maybe he likes cumin powder.

"Do you have a recipe?" I asked hesitantly. Katie appeared to be "in the zone" and I didn't want to disrupt her focus.

"Let's use the cookie recipe on the back of the chocolate

chip bag," she said. So while she started measuring out the flour, I returned to the cabinets all the ingredients that weren't listed on the recipe. That was about 70 percent of the stuff Katie had pulled out. Like basil leaves. Turns out you don't put basil in chocolate chip cookies. Go figure.

"The recipe calls for half a tsp of vanilla," Katie called, sounding panicky.

"Okay." I tried to be soothing. "Half a tsp. Do it."

"Is a tsp a teaspoon or a tablespoon?"

I shrugged. "Does it matter?"

Katie slammed the bag of flour down on the counter, making a loud noise and causing the white powder to fly everywhere. Buster gave a high-pitched whine and retreated to the corner of the kitchen. "Of course it matters!" Katie said. "These cookies are my gift to Martin. They are my attempt to show him that I can care for him. They say the way to a man's heart is through his stomach, so I can't get to Martin's heart if my cookies have too much vanilla, or too little vanilla!"

"Hold up," I said. "They say that? About the stomach and the heart and stuff? Who says that?"

Katie was holding measuring spoons up to the light, her forehead wrinkled. "I don't know who. Everyone."

"Is this another Genevieve line? Because, seriously, Genevieve is an anorexic, so you can't just trust everything she says about stomachs."

"*No.* Not Genevieve."

"Is this from another one of your misleading magazines? Like the one that told us that men like low-maintenance girls? Do they now like low-maintenance girls *who cook?*"

"I think tsp means teaspoon," Katie said, ignoring me. "Only now I can't figure out which of these measuring spoons is the half teaspoon. Goddamn it, why does Westfield not offer a home ec class?"

"Because home ec is demeaning to women," I told her as I cracked eggs into the mixing bowl (dropping only a little bit of the shell in). "Duh. You think all we're good for is sewing and baking? No! We're also good at physics and lacrosse. This isn't the 1950s. We don't need to debase ourselves that way."

"I wouldn't feel *debased* if I knew how to make cookies. I'd feel useful."

"But see?" I sloshed the eggs around with a butter knife. "You just want to bake cookies to impress your man. That's an antifeminist approach. That's why Westfield didn't teach us how to bake."

"Right, but I can't do *physics* or *lacrosse* to impress my man," Katie said, dropping one teaspoon (or possible tablespoon) of baking powder into the batter. Some of it snowed down on the floor, and Buster helpfully lapped it up.

"That's because your man doesn't understand physics. Or potentially lacrosse."

Katie reacted instantly, whipping the beaters at me, and splattering yellowish batter all over my shirt. I guess I couldn't blame her. I had basically called her boyfriend stupid. Of course, I suspect that he really might be.

"Do you think the Westfield parents would like it if we had home ec?" I continued, emptying a bag of chocolate chips into the mixing bowl. "No! They'd wonder why they were investing in a single-sex education, which is supposed to be empowering, if really it was just teaching us to be docile and domesticated."

"Still," Katie said, apparently deciding that we were done mixing, and sticking blobs of batter on to the cooking trays with her fingers. "It would have been nice if they had covered the difference between teaspoons and tablespoons in math class, maybe."

"I'm pretty sure they did," I said, piling the batter onto the tray. "Just not in precalculus."

We stuck the cooking trays into the oven, which was pre-heated to 375 degrees, just as the recipe required, and we set the alarm for nine minutes, just as the recipe required. Katie and I collapsed onto stools, dripping with batter, exhausted by our cooking adventure. Seven minutes passed.

"Violet," Katie said to me suddenly. "Do you think there's a difference between baking soda and baking powder?"

"Definitely." I nodded. "I put the baking soda away right from the beginning, but I left the baking powder out for us to use. They're in completely different containers. I am basically a cooking expert."

Katie frowned, pulled herself to her feet, and removed the now-empty chocolate chip bag from the trash. She read the recipe on the back of it silently for a moment. "It says baking soda," she said at last. "We were supposed to use baking soda."

We stared at each other. "Oops," I said. "Do you think it matters?"

Katie sniffed the air. "Actually," she said, "and I, unlike you, am no expert, but . . . I think they're burning."

She ran to the oven and opened it, but already it was too late. Smoke billowed out of the oven, setting off the smoke detector. *Beep! Beep!* Buster, the coward, turned tail and ran. Katie pulled the trays out of the oven. The cookies had risen to monstrous heights—due, perhaps, to the baking soda/powder mix-up—yet their bottoms were burned black.

Beep! Beep!

Katie dropped the smoking cookie trays on top of the stove and lowered herself into a chair. "I give up."

I climbed onto the countertop, trying to reach the smoke detector.

Beep! Beep!

"I suck at being a girlfriend. I will never be able to bake Martin cookies. He will never know what a nurturing figure I am."

I snorted at the word "nurturing," my fingers just brushing the smoke detector.

"Maybe I should just buy him some Chips Ahoy," Katie
said gloomily.

I finally reached the smoke detector and turned it off. The
kitchen was suddenly, blissfully quiet. "You're right," I agreed,
standing on the counter and staring down at her. "Spending
money is usually the solution."

Katie has ADD
(or a flawed moral compass)

I have ADD," Katie informed me and Hilary over a particularly revolting lunch. In an attempt at multiculturalism, the cafeteria had declared Monday "Indian Day" and was serving up a yellow-green liquid ironically referred to as curry. I couldn't help but notice that Sudipta Bhanja, at a table near us, had opted for a peanut-butter sandwich.

But I stopped being concerned with lunch when Katie made her announcement. "You have ADD?" I repeated back to her. "Oh, Katie! How did they find this out? Is it severe?"

"Isn't sixteen a little old to get diagnosed with ADD?" Hilary asked. "How did it take your doctor so long to realize this?"

"Oh," Katie said. "My doctor doesn't know yet. I just discovered it last night. I diagnosed myself."

Hilary and I narrowed our eyes at each other. "So you *don't* have ADD," Hilary concluded.

"No, I'm pretty sure I do."

"Katie, love, I don't want to make light of your disease or whatever," I said, "but on what exactly do you base this conclusion? I mean, if you had ADD, you'd be manic all the time. You're not manic."

"You're actually pretty lethargic most days," Hilary agreed.

"Until you've had your Diet Coke," I said.

"Eh, even then," Hilary said.

Katie shook her head in disgust, though I couldn't tell whether it was at our ignorance or at the cardboardlike substance (optimistically called naan by the cafeteria ladies) on her paper plate. "First of all," Katie said, "ADD is not a *disease*, Violet. It's a disorder. That's why it's called attention deficit disorder, instead of attention deficit *disease*, which makes me sound like a *leper*. Secondly, people with ADD are not necessarily manic. You're conflating it with attention deficit hyperactivity disorder, which is another disorder entirely."

"Wow," I said. "You've spent a lot of time on WebMD today, haven't you?"

"All of my free period," Katie confirmed.

"I don't get it," Hilary said. Hilary is a genius, but when

Katie and I start doing our thing, she often doesn't get it. "So do you or don't you have ADD?"

"Probably," Katie answered, at the same time I said, "Probably not."

"Well, what makes you think you do?" Hilary asked.

Katie leaned in, like she was going to tell us a secret, so Hilary and I both leaned in too. "I was babysitting for Stanley Dewey on Saturday," she began. Katie does not babysit often, but very occasionally her mother's golf buddies rope her into it. "After he went to bed, I did some precalc homework and watched some TV. Then I got hungry, so I started searching through the Deweys' kitchen cabinets to see if they had anything to eat. And guess what they had."

"Sugar cereal?" I asked.

"Better," Katie said. "A bottle of Ritalin."

"The pills you take to treat ADD?" Hilary asked.

"Exactly. Little Stanley has ADD."

"Well, he is an eight-year-old boy," I pointed out. "Like ninety percent of eight-year-old boys get diagnosed with ADD."

"Anyway," Katie said, ignoring me, "I took one of his pills."

"You did *what?*" Hilary and I gasped together.

Katie leaned back in her chair, satisfied by our reaction. "I took one of his Ritalin. Just to see what would happen."

"Let me get this straight," I said. "Unassuming parents put their helpless child in your care, and you repaid them by stealing drugs from their cabinet?" I was genuinely shocked by Katie this time.

Katie scowled at me. "Wow, thanks for showing up to the crime scene, Miss Moral Policewoman. First of all, Stanley is *not* helpless. And secondly, I didn't 'steal' his drugs. I took *one* pill. From an enormous bottle filled with pills. They'll never notice it's gone."

"It's not about if they'll notice," I countered. "It's just dangerous. What if you'd had some sort of bad reaction to the medicine while you were supposed to be watching Stanley?"

"Well, I didn't." Katie shrugged. "Martin was telling me that he used to take Ritalin a lot in high school, you know, to write papers and stuff, so I knew it'd be fine."

How did this not surprise me. "Martin's a bad influence," I shot back.

"So what happened?" interrupted Hilary, who was not particularly interested in our little morality play. "Did you become like really, really focused? Was your precalc homework so much easier?"

"You know, I thought that would happen." Katie beamed at Hilary, whose response to this story had obviously been more gratifying than my own. "I thought I would become calmer, or maybe more energized, or, I don't know, *something*. But that's the weird part: *I didn't feel anything*."

"You sure you didn't accidentally swallow a sugar pill?" I asked. She ignored me again.

"That is weird," Hilary said. "It ought to have had some effect."

Katie nodded. "But instead I just felt normal. And that's when I realized: I must have ADD. So *that's* why Ritalin makes me feel normal!"

"Oh my God, so QED," I interjected.

"So now I just need to talk to my doctor," Katie continued. "And get my own prescription to treat my ADD."

"I'm sorry, I don't buy it," I said. "You've never shown any signs of having ADD. Wouldn't school be harder for you? Focusing through a long exam or a lecture? You've never had any trouble with that."

Katie made a face at me. "You're just being contrary because you don't like that I took one of Stanley's pills."

"Well, *yeah*," I agreed. "Who would like that?"

"Violet," Katie said, somehow in that one word conveying that I was pathetically naïve, and that she was doing me a favor by explaining to me how the world works. "You have this way of seeing everything in black and white, and really it's not like that."

I raised my eyebrows at Katie, but weirdly, it seemed like she was serious. I didn't like for Katie to draw distinctions between me and her. Like *I* see the world in black and white, whereas *she* is able to comprehend the subtleties. I don't like thinking about differences between me and Katie.

Also, like—"I think *stealing drugs from children* actually is a black or white matter," I told her. "It's probably *the most* black or white matter, other than, I don't know, shooting infants with machine guns."

Katie nodded, pursing her lips together, like she was mulling it over. "So, shooting infants with machine guns . . . ," she said. "You're assuming that would be *bad*, right?"

I glared at her, and she widened her eyes in mock innocence back at me, until we both cracked and burst into laughter. Hilary just looked confused and went back to eating her curry.

Potentially hot people . . . at Westfield!

There are boys downstairs," Mischa announced to no one in particular as she breezed into the homeroom during third period.

All of us immediately looked up from our books. "Really?" we said.

"Go look," Mischa said.

Six of us had been spending our free period studying in the homeroom. Now we dropped everything and ran out to the top of the stairs, where, peering over the banister, we could just spy a group of guys in khakis and navy-blue suit jackets.

"I wonder what they're doing here," Tasha whispered.

"Don't they know this is a *girls'* school?" Pearl said.

"Trust Mischa to be the first person to know when there are boys around," I said.

"It's like she has a sixth sense," Tasha agreed.

"Guys—shut up—I think they see us!" Lily tugged at my arm, and we all dropped to the floor.

"You think the boys saw us?" I asked, curled into a ball as though trying to protect myself from enemy fire.

"Yeah—maybe. Can you tell if they're looking up here?" Lily asked.

I raised my head slightly and tried to catch a glimpse of the downstairs. "I don't know . . . maybe they didn't notice us." I craned my neck a little further. "Oh, no."

"They did see us?" Tasha flattened herself to the ground.

"Worse. Ms. Freck is coming upstairs."

We all scrambled to our feet and made a mad dash for our homeroom.

"Did you see them?" Mischa demanded as we flung ourselves back into our desks.

"They were hot," Pearl confirmed.

This may or may not have been true. All I really saw was the tops of their heads. They were definitely male, which is pretty hot in and of itself, but I was reserving judgment until I saw their actual faces.

Just then Rachel ran into the homeroom. "Did you know there are boys downstairs?"

"Yeah," we all chorused, and Mischa added, "Old news."

Rachel's entrance was followed immediately by Ms. Freck. "Hello, girls," she said. "I don't know if any of you are aware that the Two-Tones, Vermont College's all-male a cappella group, is visiting Westfield today."

We all looked at her innocently, and Pearl mumbled something like, "Really? All-male? We had no idea."

"They've agreed to sing a little performance for us during lunchtime," Ms. Freck went on. "But before then, I was wondering if any of you would be willing to give the Two-Tones a tour of the school?"

We stared at one another, wide-eyed.

"I understand that you all have a lot of work to do," she said, "but if any one of you could take half an hour out of your day, I would be very grateful."

"I'll do it!" Pearl volunteered.

Ms. Freck narrowed her eyes at Pearl. "While I appreciate your enthusiasm," she said, "I'm afraid you're not dressed quite appropriately to be representing the Westfield School."

I looked at Pearl, who, as always, was wearing a skirt that mostly covered her ass. Why not? Being able to wear whatever we want is a major benefit of not having boys in our classes.

Ms. Freck's gaze swooped around the classroom and settled on Rachel, who, in a button-down shirt and khakis, was dressed as unprovocatively as possible. "Would you mind, Rachel?" she asked.

Rachel opened her mouth. I could almost see the struggle happening inside her. "I . . . would like to," she began, but then couldn't go through with it. "I have a math test next period," she burst out. "I really need to study. I'm sorry."

Ms. Freck nodded. "Does anyone in here not have a math test?" she asked. Tasha shrugged and hung her head. We all wanted to be the one to say, "Screw math tests! My priority is showing a bunch of potentially hot college boys around school. Who wants an A in precalc when you could have a half hour with an a cappella group instead?"

But, unfortunately, we all want As in precalc.

However—"I'm in a different section," I offered. "I don't have a math test next period."

Ms. Freck looked me up and down. In corduroys and a sweatshirt, I was not looking the part of ideal school representative—plus there was the fact that the last time I gave a school tour, it was an illegal Harry Potter tour—but she checked her watch and sighed and said, "Thank you, Violet; come with me."

Dazed, I climbed to my feet and followed her out of the homeroom. Half of me was like, *I will say two words to these boys, and then I will obviously trip over a backpack and knock myself unconscious and be the laughingstock of the entire Westfield School.*

But then the other half of me countered, *Sometimes, you must take the bull by the horns! If there are boys in need of a school tour, then by God you must get your act together and go and give them that tour. You must* make it happen.

As Ms. Freck and I made our way out the door, Sydney shoved past us and squealed to the homeroom, "Hello, did anyone notice that there are boys downstairs?"

Everyone was like, "Yes."

The Vermont
Two-Tones

So here's what happened when I showed the Two-
Tones, Vermont College's all-male a cappella group,
around Westfield:

I did not trip over anything and crack open my jaw and
wind up bleeding everywhere and requiring expensive recon-
structive jaw surgery.

I did not throw up all over them.

I did not make out with any of them.

I did not actually make eye contact with any of them, which
may be why we didn't make out.

I did not show them anything they might actually have

been interested in, like the music room or . . . well, I don't know what they would have been interested in, since they are dudes, specifically *college* dudes, and I don't know what *college* dudes like. I'm just assuming that what they like is not the Lower School library, but I could be wrong there.

I did not regale them with song so beautiful that they responded, "My God! You have the voice of an angel. You must accompany us on the rest of our a cappella tour and sing solos in all of our songs because you are the next Madonna."

What I *did* do was forget the word "cafeteria." So I showed the Two-Tones to the doorway of the cafeteria and informed them that, "This is the . . . place. Where we eat lunch. You know what I'm talking about?"

I'd be inclined to deem the whole school tour an abysmal failure. But when I factor in the not-cracking-open-my-jaw bit, I guess it was really a draw.

The Boy Whisperer

The other reason I'm glad I gave the Vermont Two-Tones a tour is that I got in half an hour of practice talking to boys. Factoring in both this school tour and that evening Katie and I spent at Martin's apartment, I have probably spent more time talking to boys this month than in the past few years combined. And if I can count talking to my male cousins on Thanksgiving, too, then I am basically the *authority* on talking to boys now. Just call me the Boy Whisperer.

All this is good because I am getting into shape for the next time I interact with Scott Walsh. I have no idea when that will be. But whenever it happens, I will be ready. I will be charming and normal and Scott will realize the error of his ways and will dump Julia—but kindly, of course, always kindly—to be with his one true love: me.

Speaking of Scott's current girlfriend, I passed her in the hallway while I was leading around the Two-Tones. I almost mentioned her in my tour, like, "The Westfield School starts in sixth grade and goes through twelfth grade. Last year forty percent of the graduating class went on to attend Ivy League universities. On your left, you can see that we are passing a balletic-looking sophomore who is dressed way too stylishly for a school day. I know, she is weird and grotesque, but try not to stare!"

I didn't actually say that, of course. Julia has only the vaguest idea of who I am, anyway. All I did when I passed her was give her this look of, *Hey, you may have Scott Walsh for now, but I have a train of a dozen boys wearing matching blazers and ties. So* take that*!*

If Julia hadn't been busy looking at her cell phone, I'm sure she would have been impressed.

Maybe even worse than stealing Ritalin

Want to come over after school today?" Katie whispered to me. It was Thursday's class meeting, and we were sitting on the floor, leaning against our backpacks, and watching, appalled, as Hilary attempted to divide our class into a variety of "yearbook committees."

No one had volunteered to do layout or production, because apparently everyone had her heart set on being photo editor. Unfortunately, Hilary said we needed only two photo editors, whereas more than a dozen people could work on layout and production. So now a battle raged about how the two photo editors should be selected, whether it should be based on who *deserved* it most, or who *wanted* it most, or who would be *best* at it, and maybe all the aspiring photo editors should give speeches, so we could vote? Today's class meeting was truly the most horrifying sight I had ever witnessed, second only, perhaps, to the Internet video Katie once showed me of a mother polar bear tearing off a baby polar bear's head.

When Katie asked me to come over, it took me a moment to pull my attention away from the (now animal-themed) yearbook upheaval. Then I answered, "No, Katie. I still have the fall issue of the *Wisdom* to edit."

"You always say that," Katie whined.

"That's because I always have to do it," I replied.

"C'mon, Violet. I can't hang out with Martin this afternoon because he has to work."

Oh. So she was asking me over only because she had already asked Martin, and he had already said no. Nothing makes me feel loved like being a second choice.

Ever since Katie found Martin, I've worried constantly that I'm losing her to him. Obviously I'm smarter and funnier and prettier than Martin—not that hard to achieve—but I can't make out with Katie, and that really gives Martin a leg up on me. If Martin was at work this afternoon, it would be an excellent opportunity for some Violet-Katie quality time.

But I wasn't kidding when I said I had to work on the *Wisdom*. There was only a week left before winter vacation, and the *Wisdom* had to go to the printer before that. I mean, it *had* to. Getting the *Wisdom* to the printer before winter break is far and away my most important responsibility, as editor in chief.

Plus, exams would start right after we came back to school in January. Even though that was a few weeks away, I wanted to at least start getting my notes in order. I was going to work from now until January, and then I was going to ace my exams this semester. I wasn't taking any chances.

Katie had her phone out and was typing away on it.

"Who are you texting?" I asked.

"Who do you think?" she replied.

"What are you saying to him?"

"Nothing. Just saying hi."

A moment later her phone vibrated.

"And what's he saying?" I asked.

"He says hi."

"Scintillating conversation," I remarked.

Katie sighed. "Anyway. Tonight? You? Coming over? Watching TV, making hot chocolate, stalking Scott Walsh online?"

"I'm really busy," I said. "Aren't you really busy?"

"*I* am smart enough not to edit the *Wisdom*," Katie answered.

"Well, goody for you. But don't you have crew practice this afternoon?"

"Crew's over for the year," she said, looking down, playing with the key chain hanging from her bag.

"But you're in postseason, right? And you already skipped a practice last week to bake cookies—an event that I swear I will never speak of again. Isn't Coach Nelson getting on your case?"

"Oh, come on. If I want to skip practices, that's my decision. And anyway . . ." Katie smiled at me like an aspiring beauty queen. "The thing is, Violet, I quit crew."

"Excuse me?" I thought maybe I'd misheard her amidst the yearbook squabbling of our classmates.

"Yeah, I quit. It's been a week or two now."

Katie kept smiling, looking like she expected a prize. I stared at her, trying to figure out whether I was more upset that my best friend had lost her mind, or that she hadn't told me earlier. *It's been a week or two now?* We had talked maybe two billion times over the past week or two, and not once did she slip into conversation that, oh, hey, she wasn't a coxswain anymore!

"But you love crew," I blurted out.

Katie laughed and shook her head. "No, I don't. I'm just really good it."

"Well, whatever, same thing. Anyway, what about college, Katie? Everyone said you were going to get recruited to cox in college! Plus, it doesn't look good on an application to do an extracurricular for half of high school and then just *quit*."

Katie shrugged. "Colleges will deal. And, for the record"—she shook her head at me—"it is *not* the same thing."

Around us, our classmates were raising their hands. It seemed that we were voting on something. We're always voting on something. I raised my hand absently and hoped that I wasn't casting a vote in support of impeaching Hilary or burning down a homeless shelter or something.

"God, Vi, you look really upset," Katie laughed. "What's the big deal? I don't feel like doing crew anymore, so I'm not doing crew anymore. It's not *your* life."

But this hurt me more than anything. Because isn't Katie's life sort of my life? Isn't that what it means to be best friends?

"I can't believe people think it actually matters who gets to be photo editor," Katie muttered, already moving on from our conversation. "Like the photo editor gets *any* creative control, any choice over what goes in the yearbook. Like it's not just Ms. Freck's yearbook through and through. You know?"

And that was Katie closing the door on our conversation. She was done talking about crew. Like there was nothing more to say about it. She turned her attention back to her text conversation with Martin.

I didn't understand what was going on in her head. But to admit as much seemed to be the ultimate betrayal of our friendship. So instead I just smiled and nodded, and pulled out my precalc notes, and acted like I was really worried about the test that afternoon. Which, in fact, I was. So it wasn't even pretending.

Most likely abducted by aliens

I figured it out. Why Katie quit crew, I mean.

I worked on the *Wisdom* that night, just like I said I would, but I made barely any progress because all I could think about was Katie. She'd been acting weird lately. Stealing Ritalin from eight-year-olds, hooking up with Starbucks employees, insisting on our getting drunk . . . None of it made any sense to me, no matter how hard I thought about it. It was as if Katie had some checklist of teenage problems, culled from young adult novels and Lifetime made-for-TV movies, and she was methodically going through and hitting every one.

I stared at the computer screen, willing myself to think about the *Wisdom*'s table of contents, but all I could think about was Katie. I wanted to call her up and ask her flat out, "What the hell kind of game are you playing?" But every time I've asked her something like that—during class meeting today, for example, or outside of Martin's apartment the night I met him—she's acted like she doesn't know what I'm talking about. Like everything is fine. And maybe it is. Maybe I'm overreacting. Or maybe my best friend Katie has been abducted by aliens and this Katie is just an imposter. I wouldn't really blame them—the aliens, that is. If you wanted to abduct a perfect specimen of humanity, starting with Katie Putnam would make a lot of sense.

So I don't really know what's going on with my best friend. But I figured out the crew-quitting part of it—or, at least, I'm pretty sure I have. I realized that she probably quit crew in order to have more time with Martin.

While I hadn't thought much of him in the first place, this realization made me outright hate him. Okay, so he's not in college, so he doesn't seem to shower all that regularly, so he's aimless and boring and has no ambition and no perseverance. So, that's his business. But Katie has everything. When I think about him stealing and stealing Katie's brilliance until she's dull like him, I want to hunt down Martin in his dirty dead-end halfway home and force him to leave us alone forever.

The Candy
and Tampon Locker

Who took the last tampon?" Mischa demanded. She flung open the door to locker forty-five, aka the Candy and Tampon Locker, and gestured at it forcibly, so that the ten of us sitting in the homeroom during third period could not help but notice that it contained no tampons.

Nobody responded. I stared down at my math textbook, willing myself not to make eye contact with Mischa. Because, okay, confession: I actually *had* taken the last tampon from the Candy and Tampon Locker. I knew that was a faux pas. If you empty out the Candy and Tampon Locker, you are morally obligated to restock it. But in my defense, I was planning on running to the convenience store and buying a box of sanitary supplies during lunch. I just hadn't had time yet. I didn't need to hear Mischa's lecture. She acts like she's the goddamn empress of the Candy and Tampon Locker. She acts like she's the goddamn empress of *everything*. I bet she didn't even have her period this week. I bet she just felt like criticizing someone.

Unfortunately, since I wasn't man enough to own up to being the tampon thief, we *all* got the benefit of Mischa's lecture. "What if somebody got her period, and there were no tampons in this locker?" Mischa asked us, rhetorically. "Would you just let her *bleed all over the floor*?"

Rachel's face paled, and she looked like she was going to puke. I felt the exact same way. I'm all for the female empowerment fostered at all-girls' schools, but sometimes I really wish Westfield were coed, because I think if we had guys here, we wouldn't talk so often about menstrual blood.

Mischa's so picky, anyway. It's not like the Candy and Tampon locker was *completely* empty. There was totally a half-full bag of Rolos in there.

Wayward Girls

*T*his is probably *what hell is like.*

That's what I thought at seven o'clock on Friday evening as I sat in the Westfield computer lab, possibly the only living being left in the school, maybe even in the entire world. Who knew? I hadn't been outside in twelve hours. Maybe the outside no longer existed.

It was the last day of school before winter break, which meant the fall issue of the *Wisdom* absolutely, unquestionably, had to go out to the printer. The only problem was, it wasn't done yet. And I was trapped at school until it was.

For a while I'd had help: Self-obsessed and pretend-anorexic

Lolly, Shakespeare-loving Dolores, narcoleptic Emily, and the rest of the *Wisdom* editorial board had all stuck around after school to lend their expertise. But then they had trickled out, claiming family dinners, movie dates, and the pressing need to pack for vacations. I let them go, even though, hi, guys, we *all* have things we'd rather be doing. This wasn't my top choice for kicking off my winter break, either.

Sartre said, "Hell is other people," but Violet Tunis says hell is being stuck alone at your high school on a Friday night, with no end in sight.

So I worked away in the computer lab, singing aloud in a failed attempt to prop up my spirits. I was rocking my way through "Rudolph the Red-Nosed Reindeer" when I heard another voice harmonizing with my own.

"Jesus, Katie," I said when I spied her across the computer lab. "You scared the hell out of me. I thought I was hallucinating."

"I think I'm hallucinating from boredom." Katie flopped down in the desk chair next to mine.

"If you're that bored, you could give me a hand so I can get out of here before sunrise. Why are you still here, anyway?" I asked.

"I worked out in the gym for a while, then figured I'd clean out my locker before break. Ugh. You're here for the *Wisdom*?"

"What else? I understand now why none of the seniors wanted to be the editor this year."

Katie nodded. "They'd rather spend their Fridays getting laid than working on a literary magazine. Though I can't understand why."

"Speaking of getting laid," I said, "why aren't you out with Martin tonight?"

"Ha." Katie smirked at me. "He's working. I'm seeing him tomorrow."

Of course she was. "Do you really have time tomorrow? Don't you need to study?" I asked, sounding like her mother.

"God, I hope not. Tomorrow's the first day of vacation, in case you weren't aware. In celebration of that fact, I'd like to do something vacationy. Like make out with my boyfriend."

"Exams start in two weeks," I warned her. I hated the words as they came out of my mouth. I really did sound like someone's meddling mom. It was only a matter of time until Katie started calling me Mummy. But seriously, it annoyed me that Katie didn't feel like she had to study every minute of the next two weeks. And it annoyed me that, instead, she planned to spend that time hanging out with Martin.

"Exams start in sixteen days," Katie countered. "Which is—thank you, math class—longer than two weeks. So I'll be fine. Anyway"—she gestured to the computer—"did you write anything for this issue of the *Wisdom*?"

"Me? No."

"Why not?"

I shrugged. "Too busy editing. And I had no good ideas.

And also the literary standards of this magazine are so painfully low that people will respect me more as a writer if my work does *not* appear in it."

"We should write something for it together," Katie said.

"Yeah, sure," I agreed. "Next issue. Let's brainstorm over winter break." *If you can find any time away from your useless boyfriend,* I added silently.

"No, let's write something now." Katie leaned over me to open a blank document on my computer.

"Uh," I said, "that'd be fabulous, except for how all I want to do is send this issue off to the printer. As immediately as possible. And anything that prolongs that process is a bad idea."

Katie made a *tsk-tsk* sound. "What you need is a break."

"No, what I *need* is to be done so I can go home and study for exams."

"You're really obsessed with this exams thing, aren't you? Come on, Vi, get some perspective. They're just a bunch of stupid tests designed to make us feel bad about ourselves. Let's focus on what matters: We haven't done a project together in ages. We haven't created anything since the classist, dangerous Harry Potter tours, may they rest in peace. And the chocolate chip cookies, which we're never speaking of again. Let's write a story, just a short one, like we actually know how to have a good time together."

What I wanted to say to Katie was, "We haven't done a project together in ages because *you* have been too busy getting high with Martin and not telling me that you aced the PSATs and quitting crew." But something about the pleading look in her eyes made me realize: Katie knew what I was thinking. She didn't want us to write a story just to distract me, just to make my life harder. She wanted us to write a story to prove that, even if she was acting weird as hell lately, we were still best friends. This was an olive branch I couldn't refuse.

"Okay," I said. "We can write a story."

"Yesss." Katie pumped her fist like an award-winning athlete.

"But only a short one!"

"Obviously."

"And it has to be about something awesome."

"That goes without saying."

"Maybe it should be about witches," I suggested. "Witches are awesome."

"Too much like Harry Potter," Katie said.

"Oh, right, how could I forget that you hate Harry Potter because you think it steals too much attention from *Moby-Dick*."

"Every literary scholar would agree with me."

I sighed. "Do you want us to write a story about whales, then, since you love *Moby-Dick* so much?"

"I don't know anything about whales." Katie was being difficult.

"We could look it up," I said. "On the Internet."

"Weren't you the one who wanted to write this really fast, so you could go home? And now you're proposing that we embark on some sort of research project? Do you not know how to half-ass *anything?*"

"Fair point," I conceded, because I do not know how to half-ass anything.

"Let's just write about Westfield. We already know everything about it. We can write the whole story in like two minutes."

"Love it," I said. "Let's write the story you tell about Mr. Thompson's tattoo."

"Nah," Katie said. "Everyone's already heard that story a million times."

"Too bad," I said. "Then maybe we should write about the time that we had to take a swimming test in ninth grade, and every single girl in our class said she couldn't do it because she had her period, and Coach Nelson thought we were lying, but it turned out we really all *did* have our periods."

"Except for Rachel," Katie noted.

"Right, except for Rachel, because she hadn't started getting her period yet. So she swam two laps while the rest of us just stood there in our clothes and watched her."

Katie shrieked with laughter. "That is an amazing story," she said. "But don't you think Rachel will kill us if we print that in the *Wisdom?*"

"No one reads the *Wisdom,*" I assured Katie, "so she might never find out."

"We can change her name," Katie said. "So it won't technically be about *her.* Oh, and let's also have a bit in there about how Lily has taken the SATs every year since eighth grade, just so she'll be prepared for the real thing. And the first year she took them, she was in like the eightieth percentile—because she was only *thirteen*—so her parents sent her to a private tutor."

"Lily is so lucky," I said. "I wish my parents loved me enough to send me to a private SAT tutor."

"Oh my God, that is sick." Katie pressed her fingers to her temples. "You are sick, Violet. In our story we definitely have to mention that, instead of thinking Lily is insane, everyone in our class thinks that Lily is *lucky*."

"Because she *is*," I argued. I didn't feel like discussing SAT prep with Katie. She was never going to understand.

"I know!" Katie exclaimed. "Let's write about Pearl Jewell."

I snorted. "What *about* Pearl Jewell? I've never known Pearl to do anything story-worthy."

"Are you kidding?" Katie asked. "Everything Pearl does deserves to be commemorated for the ages! That time freshman year when she handed in her sister Opal's English essay so she wouldn't have to write her own? Only Opal's essay was about *Catcher in the Rye* and Pearl's assignment was to write about *Frankenstein*?"

I giggled, remembering. "Or the time in seventh grade when she got to take the class hamster home over break and he died because she 'didn't know you had to feed him'?"

"What about the time this past summer when the cops pulled her over for not wearing a seat belt?"

"Yes!" I was laughing so hard now that I almost couldn't get out the words to the next part of this story. "And when the policemen asked her why she wasn't wearing her seat belt, she told them that she was working on her *tan* while she drove around, and she didn't want to get any *seat belt tan lines*."

"How was she even working on her tan and driving at the same time?" Katie marveled.

"She was driving in a bikini."

"You see?" Katie crowed. "This school is like a parody of itself! Let's write a story about these girls for the *Wisdom*. It'll be a parody of a parody, and *that* is art."

I pulled the keyboard toward me and typed, *At the Westfield School for Wayward Girls, everyone was special—but some were more special than others.*

Katie laughed appreciatively. "The Westfield School for Wayward Girls," she repeated. "You, Violet, are a goddamn genius. Here, give me the keyboard; I want to write the next sentence."

As I watched Katie peck away at the keyboard, I felt good all of a sudden. Even though it was dark and cold outside and I was still at school, even though this issue of the *Wisdom* looked like it would be an epic failure, even though I was facing two depressing weeks of studying—even so, I felt good. Katie was there with me, and she had called me a genius, and for the moment that was enough.

The single most romantic night of the year

My plan was to spend New Year's Eve alone.

I didn't have to. Everyone took pity on me and invited me out with them. Even my *parents*, who were going to some party in Cambridge thrown by Dad's old graduate thesis advisor. "She has a son just your age," Dad encouraged me; though, when pressed, he admitted that his thesis advisor's son was eleven. Thanks but no, Dad.

And Katie invited me to join in on her New Year's plans, but that annoyed me almost as much as if she hadn't asked. Because it wasn't like, "Hey, Violet, what should *we* do for New Year's Eve?" No, it was, "Violet, this is what *Martin and*

I are doing for New Year's Eve. You can come, if you want."

I had barely talked to Katie since the evening when we wrote our story for the *Wisdom*. First it had been Christmas, and then she'd gone skiing in Vermont with her family, and otherwise she'd mostly been hanging out with Martin. Anyway, I had been busy too. Busy studying. Was this a boring, stressful, pathetic way to spend winter vacation? Yes, absolutely. But every time I considered giving up and, say, going out to the movies, I reminded myself of how I'd felt after getting my PSAT scores back: Hollow. Inferior. Worthless. And then I kept studying.

So when Katie called to invite me along on her New Year's Eve plans, I seriously considered it. Maybe this would be a good opportunity for us to catch up, and for me to hang out with someone other than my physics textbook.

"What exactly are you and Martin doing?" I asked.

"He and his roommates are throwing a party at their apartment."

I pictured their apartment: the water-stained wallpaper, the puke-colored couch. They invited friends into that space? If I lived there, I'd be like, "Sorry guys, someone else has to host the New Year's party. And every other party. Forever. Until I move someplace without mountains of cockroach corpses."

"Are you definitely going to Martin's?" I asked. "Because remember how much fun we had at First Night last year, and I was thinking maybe we could do that again—"

"Yes," Katie interrupted. "I'm definitely going. Violet, it's *New Year's Eve.* The single most romantic night of the year."

"What about Valentine's Day?"

"Okay, fine, New Year's Eve is the single most romantic night of the year, second only to Valentine's Day."

"And the Fourth of July."

"No. The Fourth of July is not a holiday about romance."

"My love of America is romantic."

"My *point,*" Katie went on, "is that New Year's Eve is a night to spend with your boyfriend. If you are lucky enough to have one. Which I am."

"Ouch." What, did she think I had *forgotten* that I was single? I didn't need an explicit reminder. Thanks for rubbing my face in my social failures, Katie.

"But if you come," Katie said, kinder now, "maybe you'll meet a guy! Maybe you'll start the new year off right—with a boyfriend! There will be lots of guys at Martin's party, I bet. He has so many friends. And that way you'll know boys to invite to your birthday party in January."

I thought about it. I thought about Martin's roommate Lee, who Katie said had been hitting on me when we were over at their apartment. This could be my chance. My chance to make out with Lee. My chance to make out with an under-employed, scrawny marijuana user. On a scratchy, broken, vomitous couch. My chance to start the year off right.

"No," I said at last.

"No?"

"No, I don't want to go to Martin's party."

Katie paused, apparently mulling this over. We always spent New Year's together. We always spent everything together. "Are you jealous?" she asked in a kind of small voice. "I don't mean to be rude. But are you jealous of me for having Martin, Vi? Is that why you don't want to spend New Year's with us? Because I'm sure we can find someone at the party for you. . . ."

That didn't even seem rude. It just seemed ridiculous. Out of all the reasons I might envy Katie, in a list of things she had that I constantly worked for, Martin did not even rank. I wasn't jealous of Katie for having Martin. If anything, I was jealous of Martin for having Katie.

But all I said was, "No, don't worry about it. This party just doesn't sound like my scene. You have fun. I should stay in and study, anyway."

"Study?" Katie sounded revolted. "On New Year's? Violet, I feel like I need to do some sort of intervention on you. You need to relax."

Now I definitely wasn't jealous. I was just annoyed.

"Right," I said sarcastically, "I need to relax. Because I can just hang around and go skiing and hook up with random boys and still get As on all my exams. Katie, when are you going to learn it's not that easy for us mortals? Some of us can't afford to *relax*!"

"Whatever," Katie said, sounding as fed up with me as I was with her. "Have it your way. Enjoy your holiday."

So I hung up with Katie and called Hilary, but then I remembered that Hilary and her parents were in Belize, like every winter break. And that's how I resigned myself to spending New Year's Eve alone.

After I reassured my parents one million times that I wouldn't get lonely, they left for their party. I tried to study for exams, but it turns out that studying on New Year's Eve sucks *even more* than studying on any other night of the year. As always, I kept my phone next to me, even though I knew no one was going to call, and my online chat program open, even though I knew no one was going to message me. There was no one else even online to chat with. No one except for . . . Scott Walsh?

Under any other circumstances I would never send Scott a message. Since that evening nearly two months ago when we'd had our amazing (albeit brief) IM conversation about handheld fans, I had kept his screen name on my contacts list, but just to stare at. Tonight, however, Scott and I were *literally* the only people online.

So I sent him a message. Call me crazy. I thought for a long time about what it should say. I tried many drafts. Eventually I settled on this:

ME: home on new years, huh?
[Brilliant opening, right?]

There was a long pause before Scott replied, during which I sat at my desk thinking, *Oh my God, he is never going to write back because I am a total idiot.* But then—

SCOTT: haha yah

SCOTT: u too?

ME: yeah

ME: I turned down a couple awesome parties, though

[If you can call eating canapés with an eleven-year-old boy "awesome."]

SCOTT: haha

ME: it's kind of boring here

SCOTT: yah

SCOTT: wanna do something?

ME: now?

[Oh my God oh my God oh my God.]

SCOTT: sure

SCOTT: since ur bored

ME: okay

ME: yeah

ME: sure

ME: good idea

ME: uh, like what?

SCOTT: dunno

SCOTT: lets meet at westfield

SCOTT: and figure it out

ME: ok

[OH MY GOD.]

ME: see you there

SCOTT: bundle up

SCOTT: its snowing really hard

He cares about my being warm enough! He is probably in love *with me!*

I put on a sweater and snow pants and snow boots and a parka. I looked like an obese monster, which was unattractive, but I could see out my window that Scott was right: It *was* snowing really hard, and Westfield was a solid mile's walk from my house. If I tried for a more appealing outfit, I'd have a better chance of stealing Scott's heart, but I'd also have a better chance of dying from hypothermia before he ever saw me.

I trekked through the snow for half an hour before reaching Westfield. There was no one in the entire world other than Scott Walsh who would have been worth this journey. The streets were empty, the snowfall unmarked. I couldn't see more than a few yards ahead of me, thanks to the darkness and the downpour of snowflakes. I couldn't hear my footsteps—the night's thick silence was punctured only by the sounds of New Year's parties in a few of the houses that I trudged past. Vaguely, I heard party horns and laughter before they were again muffled by the snow.

Scott was already standing outside Westfield's gates when I arrived. Unlike me, Scott did not look like an obese monster. He still looked like his normal superhumanly hot self, in a fitted charcoal-grey pea coat and matching wool cap. He even made *snow boots* look good.

"Hey," I said, sweating from exertion, except for the tip of my nose, which was so cold I couldn't even feel it. I gave him an awkward, dorky wave because I didn't know how else to greet him. Was I supposed to shake his hand? No way, that was too formal. High-five him? Only we weren't at the end of an action montage in an eighties film. Maybe one of those fist bumps guys sometimes do? Why do I never know what the right thing to do is?

"Hey!" Scott smiled at me and gave me a one-armed hug. And that one-armed hug made my entire mile-long trek through the snowbanks completely worth it. Even though we were separated by my shirt and my sweater and my coat and his coat and his sweater and whatever he had on under that, I was still convinced that I could feel his body heat as he pulled me toward him, that I could hear his heartbeat. I wished abruptly that neither of us was wearing a coat or a sweater or whatever came under that . . . and then I was glad that my face was almost entirely covered in wool, because I could feel myself turn red. I swear to God, just the thoughts I have in my mind could drive me crazy.

Scott, on the other hand, seemed to have already moved on from our brief but earth-shattering coat-to-coat contact. "I'm glad you wanted to hang out," he said with his charming grin. "New Year's Eve gets really boring alone."

"I know it," I managed.

"Can we get through here?" Scott asked, shaking the gate.

I raised my eyebrows at him, though he may not have noticed, due to the hat and scarf covering most of my face. "You want to break into my school, Scott?"

He laughed. "Yeah, gosh, being on vacation for ten days has really made me miss school. Late at night on New Year's Eve, I just want to, I don't know, break in and do some chemistry experiments. Read some books in the library."

I laughed too. I didn't know what else to do. So much for being the Boy Whisperer. If Katie had said that to me, I would have bantered back. But Scott was not Katie. And Katie was not here.

"Actually, I just wanted to wander around the fields," Scott said.

"Easy." I led him to where the fence met with a bush. "If you move this bush out of the way," I said, trying it and getting snow all over myself, "then you can make a little passage—and creep through—there!" I shoved the bush aside enough that there was room for Scott to climb through. I followed after him, and then we were both on Westfield's soccer field.

I tried to brush some of the snow off myself. "Uh, it's

easier to sneak through when there's not a blizzard going on," I muttered.

Scott chuckled. "Impressive. How'd you know about this?"

"Harry Potter tours."

"Harry Potter what?"

I shrugged and didn't elaborate.

Scott and I slowly floundered around the soccer field. There must have been nearly a foot of snow that I sank into with each step. Streetlights illuminated brief patches of the field, while the rest of it was in darkness. I felt my muscles tense, willing Scott to hold my hand. It seemed like such a little thing, for someone to hold your hand. Particularly when you were both wearing mittens and wouldn't be able to feel it anyway. He could just hold my hand to help me keep my balance in the snow. It wouldn't even have to be because he *liked* me or anything. *Come on*, I thought. *Do it!*

"So where's Julia?" I asked, in what I hoped was a casual way.

Scott sighed. "New York City. For her grandfather's funeral. I miss her. I haven't seen her in nearly two weeks."

So they were still together. Of course they were still together. Why would I have thought any differently? Because he half hugged me instead of shaking my hand?

"I had this whole perfect New Year's Eve planned out for us too," he went on. "I already knew where I was going to take her to dinner. . . ."

I was almost hyperventilating with jealousy. Scott Walsh

must be *the* perfect boyfriend. If I were Julia, I would have been like, "So sorry, family, the death of Grandpop is really sad—but I'm sure he would have wanted me to stay in Boston this holiday season, with Scott Walsh." And the ghost of my grandfather would have appeared just to confirm, "Yes, my dear granddaughter. Stay with Scott Walsh. For he is God's gift to womankind."

But I was not Julia, and, as a result, I was spending New Year's Eve with her boyfriend. Next time somebody on the *Wisdom* gets confused about what "irony" means, I'm going to point them to this example.

"It's a pretty school," Scott commented.

I looked around and tried to see what he saw. The grand brick building, the courtyard filled with snow-capped trees, the extensive fields. "Well," I said, "we don't have a theater designed by a guy who also does theaters for *Broadway*."

"Good point." Scott grinned. "I guess your school is pretty lame after all."

In the center of the field we sat down next to each other. For a crazy moment I thought he might try to kiss me, and I felt my heart suddenly pounding in my throat. I wished he would, even though it occurred to me that I didn't know how to kiss and would probably screw it up. But he didn't. He just sat in the snow, looking up at the sky.

"It's hard," he said, idly packing a snowball. Still he didn't look at me.

"Being without Julia?" I ventured, not knowing what he meant.

"Being without Julia," he repeated, nodding his head. "And being with Julia. It's just hard." He threw the snowball, fast and rough, and it disappeared into the darkness.

"Well," I said slowly, trying to figure out what he was getting at, "is it harder without Julia? Or with Julia?" *Say it's harder with her!* is what I thought. *Say it would be so much easier with me!*

My whole body ached for it. But he just said, "I'm not sure. That's what I'm still trying to figure out."

Which meant what? "Maybe, Violet"?

Maybe. I lay on my back, kicked my legs out to either side, and slid my arms up and down. I recalled the unthemed dance, when Katie and I had lain in this same field, and she had said to me "at least we have each other." Did we then? Did we now? Did I have Scott right now, as he sat beside me? Would I ever?

"Snow angels," I heard Scott say, though I was lying down and could not see him. I moved my arms and legs back and forth, back and forth, with my mouth open, hoping a snow-flake would land in it.

Scott and I lay side by side and made snow angel after snow angel until we got too cold. It was a new year by the time we returned to our separate homes. It turned out Katie was right. It kind of was the single most romantic night of the year.

If only an incorrect ellipsis were the worst thing about it

Do you see them?"

It was our first day back at school after winter break, and I had made Katie come out to the middle of the soccer field to appreciate the snow angels I had made with Scott Walsh. They were proof. Proof that night with Scott Walsh actually happened. Unfortunately, the field had completely frozen over in the past three days, so we'd had to glide our way along the ice, running the very real risk of falling on our asses, in search of snow angels.

"Yeah, sure." Katie glanced down at them, unimpressed. The ice had preserved the angels pretty well, but some snow had caved in on them, and frankly they just didn't look as magical in the daylight, with Littles scampering all around and school bags on our shoulders.

"Come on, Katie. Me and *Scott Walsh* made these."

"That is pretty great," she conceded. "That's like your dream New Year's Eve."

"Yours, too, though," I said.

She shook her head and started sliding her way back toward the school building. "Nah. I had my dream New Year's."

"I thought you just went to Martin's party?"

"I did. We drank too much and kissed at midnight and around two a.m. the cops showed up because they'd had a noise complaint and I had to hide in Martin's closet."

"And that's your dream New Year's?"

"Don't sound so proud of me," Katie said.

I heaved a sigh and almost slipped. Katie had to grab my arm to keep me upright. "Are you, like, *over* Scott Walsh?" I asked. "Because, as I recall, for the last four years of our lives, you have been every bit as obsessed with him as I am."

"Yeah, I guess I am over him," Katie said.

"How? How did you do it?" I took exaggeratedly high steps, trying to get the ice to crack under my feet. "I would love to get over Scott, since I'm getting the sense like he is *never* going to break up with Julia and therefore is *never* going to be mine."

"Well, I found Martin," Katie said, with a sort of smug

authority that made me audibly gag. She glared at me and said, "I don't know, Violet. I just realized that Scott Walsh was never going to date me, and I'd rather want someone who wants me back. Like Martin. I was sick of wanting something I couldn't have. I can't see the point anymore, of wanting what's always out of reach. You know? I've done that for years. It just makes you unhappy."

We had made it all the way across the field and back to the school building. We flung ourselves inside, desperate to escape the cold.

"Hey, look!" Katie exclaimed before I had even unzipped my coat. "*The Wisdom!*"

"Oh my God." I snatched a copy from the stack by the door. "It's here. It exists. I can't believe it." The paper stock was glossy and thick. The binding was neat and professional. It looked like a real magazine. And I had made it.

"This is awesome!" Katie congratulated me.

I flipped open to a random page, and, of course, the first thing I noticed was a typo. "It sucks!" I wailed, pointing at the error.

Katie squinted at it. "I don't see it."

"An ellipsis is supposed to have *three* dots, not *two*!"

"Violet." Katie grabbed my wrists and forced me to look at her. "It. Is. Beautiful. Trust me. Stop looking for mistakes and just appreciate it for one moment."

I breathed deeply and looked at the *Wisdom* again. Katie was right. It looked great.

"Where's our story?" Katie asked. She grabbed the *Wisdom* out of my hands and flipped through it. "Oh! Here it is." She held out the open magazine to show me.

Our piece was called "Stories from the Bestfield School"— *Bestfield*, not *Westfield*, to make it clear that this was a parody, not a factual report. And because Katie had written a motto for the school in our story: *The Bestfield School, where only your best is good enough—and even your best could use some improvement.* The byline was "Wayward Girls," because I had declared to Katie when we wrote it, "I will not have my name in any way associated with this low-quality rag."

"Your name is on the *front page*," Katie had pointed out at the time. "'Editor: Violet Tunis.'"

"Whatever. No one reads the copyright page."

Now, shoulders touching, we stood in the hall and reread our story. "It's hilarious," Katie said, leaving no room for argument. "*We* are hilarious."

I nodded my agreement. "It's too bad there aren't any college scholarships for being hilarious."

Katie groaned. "Can you imagine if there were? Everyone in our class would go around telling knock-knock jokes all the time, hoping to qualify for the scholarship. Hilary would refuse to ever hang out with us because she'd always be at home studying *Saturday Night Live*. Rachel Weiss would, overnight, become the funniest person on the planet."

"Sounds terrifying." I shuddered. "I guess I'll just stick

with trying to win one of those scholarships for lacrosse."

"You don't play lacrosse."

"Then I'm never going to get a scholarship anywhere, am I?"

Wiser and wiser

Later that day we had a special meeting of *The Wisdom* to go over the fall issue and plans for the spring. There is no rest for the weary.

My devoted editorial staff showed up looking tanner than usual. Lots of tropical vacations this Christmas, apparently. Dolores the Shakespeare fan had gotten cornrows with beads in her hair. It made the skin on her forehead look taut and white, and I could see bits of her scalp peeking through the braids. She kept tossing her hair around pointedly, sending the colorful plastic beads clattering against the back of her chair. It made me want to smack her, but as editor in chief I tried to rise above it.

"What did everyone think of the fall issue of the *Wisdom*?" I asked. The girls all nodded enthusiastically.

"I'm really proud of it," Lolly said. "I'm really proud of all of us."

"I actually like it better than either of last year's issues," Emily commented. "No offense to anyone who worked on last year's, because they were great. But I think the new layout works really well."

I nodded at everyone's comments and made a few notes. When the praise was dying down, I asked, "Did anyone see room for improvement? Anything you'd change for next time?"

There was a pause. Then Lydia said, "There's a story in here that I don't remember voting on? The one about some dumb girls at a ritzy all-girls prep school? Maybe I was absent that day?"

But everyone else in LitMag agreed that they, too, didn't recall ever having seen this story before they looked inside the finished magazine.

"How did it get *in* here?" Dolores asked, flipping her cornrows behind her shoulders with a *click-click-click*.

I began to feel uneasy. Of course we have a policy on voting on every story that goes in the *Wisdom*. It's a bullshit policy, because we have zero editorial standards and vote in all sorts of crap. But it's our policy nonetheless. Even as editor in chief, I was not allowed to undermine the *rules*. All I could do was moderate the voting, but the voting still had to happen. In my excitement over doing a project with Katie, a really good project, I had forgotten that part.

"But did we think it was funny?" I asked hopefully—only not too hopefully, so they wouldn't realize that I was the renegade who had written this story and then snuck it into their magazine.

No one admitted that it was funny, though. Lolly said, "I thought it seemed kind of mean."

"Mean?" This surprised me. "To whom?"

"To the girls in the story."

"But it was fiction."

Emily shook her head. "The main character is obviously Pearl. Okay, all the characters' names have been changed, but anyone can tell who it's about."

"And that's mean," Lolly reiterated.

"So no one liked it?" I asked, wishing my voice didn't sound as small as I felt.

"I *liked* it," Lydia said, "but it doesn't matter, because we never reached *consensus.*"

I found myself wanting to scream at them all. To stop myself, I took a deep breath, and boomed, "Okay! Enough talk about the old issue. Let's stop living in the past. It's time to start reading submissions for the spring issue. May is closer than you think, guys." I pulled the first submission from the top of the pile and cleared my throat. "This one is a poem by, of all people, Anonymous."

i cut myself
just to watch myself bleed
a reminder that i am real
red is the color of my blood
it runs like rivers down my arm
red is the color of my heart
which you break all the time
i wear red on the outside
i wear red on the inside.

I heaved an enormous sigh and tried to pass it off as a coughing fit. "Well? First impressions?"

"I like it!" Lolly declared.

Ah, yes. Here we go again.

Good-luck pajamas

I t was the evening before the first day of exams, which meant there was no time left for me to procrastinate or vacillate: I had to, right now, decide what pajamas to wear tomorrow.

The three days of exam period are the only time of year when we're allowed to wear pajamas to school, so obviously it's crucial to wear really cute ones. My problem was that I hated my pajama collection. My Disney Princess pajama bottoms seemed too juvenile. My purple silky ones had a rip in the crotch, which was fine for their usual purpose (sleeping), but less acceptable for school. My red and white plaid ones

would work perfectly, and the colors even made them season-
ally appropriate; however, I'd worn them during exams last
year and gotten a B on my history test, so they were probably
bad luck. And I couldn't afford to risk my luck this time.

Everyone in my class gets really obsessed with luck around
exams. Rachel always carries around her lucky sock puppet,
which she will pretend to talk to when she's in the middle of
a test and stuck for an answer. Pearl has worn the same lucky
tank top to every exam since freshman year. Apparently she's
too dumb to notice that it hasn't worked. Tori swears that
cracking her knuckles before she begins each question makes
the answer come to her. I don't know if the joint cracking
actually helps, but I do know that it drives me crazy whenever
I sit near her during exams.

I don't know why I jokingly called our school the Westfield
School for Wayward Girls in that story I wrote with Katie. It
should obviously be called the Westfield School for Obsessive-
Compulsive Psychopaths.

So, the evening before exams began, I stared and stared
at my pajama options, weighing the pros and cons of each
one, until eventually I collapsed on the floor of my closet
and wept into my shoes. Then I got my act together to put
on sneakers and ask Mom to drive me to the mall.

She looked perplexed by this request. "Don't your exams
start in the morning?"

I sighed. "*Yes*, Mother. That's why I need to go to

the mall *tonight* so I can buy new pajamas *before* exams."

My mother was sipping tea and reading the *New Yorker*. She gave me this particular maternal look that she has. It means, roughly, *I have absolutely no idea what's going through your head, and I suspect you of extreme mental instability, but I love you anyway.*

"Why can't you just wear your jeans?" Mom asked. "Like every other school day?"

"Because exams are not like every other school day," I said. "Plus, I would be the only girl wearing jeans tomorrow, and then I would feel so self-conscious about my outfit that I wouldn't be able to focus on the exam questions. Please, Mom. Drive me to the mall. Just do this one thing for me. Do you want me to fail? After all the money you've invested in my education, do you really want me to fail?" I felt desperate tears stinging my eyes again.

Mom just stared at me. She even took off her reading glasses to see me better. "Do you have a fever?" she asked.

I stomped my foot. "Quit worrying about my health and turn your attention to what *really* matters: the pajamas that I'm going to wear to exams!"

One thing I will say for my mother: She knows when something is not worth an argument. We hopped in the car and headed to the Burlington Mall, where she bought me two new pairs of pajama bottoms. It's hard to tell in the store, but I think I got a lucky vibe from them.

Exams: Day One

My English exam was first thing the next morning. Blah blah Innocence versus Experience, blah blah Insiders versus Outsiders, blah blah. It was a lot of writing in a little blue composition notebook, and my hand cramped up, but, other than that *physical* pain, the test itself wasn't that hard. Oh, except for the bit where I had to match lines of poetry with the poets who wrote them. Who remembers that sort of thing? Yes, okay, I read and enjoyed *Beauty is Truth, Truth Beauty,—that is all / Ye know on Earth, and all ye need to know*—but why on earth would I have cared or remembered who wrote it? *Hunger is a sin / As bad for you* *as a shark's fin*—who wrote *that* is the real question.

I sat with Katie, Hilary, Tasha, and Emily at lunch, but we barely spoke or ate, just pored over our physics notes. I asked who wrote that thing about truth and beauty. Katie said Keats, obviously. I asked how this was supposed to be so obvious, and she shrugged in that way that she does when something is obvious to *her*. Tasha said that she had answered Yeats, and she wondered if Mrs. Malone might misread her *Y* for a *K*. I said that I had answered Tennyson and I wondered if Mrs. Malone might misread my *Tennyson* for *Keats*. Then Hilary slammed her pen down and asked if we could all shut the hell up because *she*, for one, actually wanted to pass physics, even if none of the rest of us did. So then we went back to our notes.

The physics exam was tricky, not least because my hand still hurt from the morning, so I kept trying to think of shortcuts through the problems so I could use my pencil less. I pretended like I was a soldier who had been wounded in battle, yet I had to press on regardless because the fate of my country and my own honor were at stake. *Can you let down your country and your honor for a mere hand cramp?* I asked myself. *No, you cannot!*

After I finished my physics exam, I went home and fell asleep until my dad called me down to the dinner table, where I ate two slices of whole wheat bread before getting up to return to my desk. My parents tried to convince me to swallow some lasagna, but I refused.

"You need protein," my father told me.

"What if it gives me a stomachache?" I asked from the dining room doorway, glaring at the lasagna. "I cannot afford to get a stomachache this week."

My mom and dad exchanged a nervous look. "You know, sweetie," Mom said, sounding like she was launching into a speech she had practiced in front of her mirror, "your father and I will love you no matter how you do on your exams. You do know that, right? We'll go on thinking you're brilliant and wonderful even if you fail every subject—not that I expect that to happen."

"Oh, I know *you* will," I said impatiently. "I wasn't worried about *you*." *I'll* think I'm a failure, but not them. It's so easy for my parents to think I'm brilliant and wonderful, because they just don't *get* it.

Content that they had reassured me of their love, my parents let me leave the room. I went back to my bedroom and studied at my desk until ten thirty and then changed into a different pair of pajamas and went to bed. Everyone knows a full night's sleep is the most important part of exam prep.

I fell asleep almost immediately, but then I had the Harvard nightmare. Like I was in seventh grade again or something. It had been years since I last dreamed about not getting into college. I thought I'd outgrown that.

I woke up a bit past two a.m., terrified, sweating, twisted up in my sheets. I had to drink a cup of water and flip my pillow over and remind myself that it was just a dream, and that it's okay if I never get into Harvard.

Yeah, right.

Since I was awake anyway, I lay on my back, staring at the glow-in-the-dark stickers on my ceiling, massaging my still-cramped hand, and thinking about cosines.

Only three more exams to go.

Exams: Day Two

I had only one test on the second day of exams: math, in the afternoon. I got to school at eight a.m. anyway, and Katie and I sat next to each other in the homeroom, intending to spend the morning studying.

Ms. Freck found us there. "Katie and Violet. May I speak to you in my office?" That was what she said.

Katie and I exchanged a confused look but of course said, "Yes, Ms. Freck."

"Thank you. Don't worry, we'll be done in time for your exam." She smiled at us as though she was doing us a favor, then swept out of our homeroom and down the hall toward her office.

"What does Freck want to talk to us about?" I hissed at Katie.

The last time I had been in Ms. Freck's office was after the Harry Potter tours, so I knew, rationally, that when she called students in there, it was because they had done something wrong. But I just couldn't think of anything I had done that wrong recently. Okay, so *I* wasn't impressed by the B I'd gotten on my last history paper, but that wasn't the sort of thing that would get me in trouble with the Westfield administration.

So I imagined to myself that maybe Ms. Freck wanted to talk to me and Katie about how *awesome* we were. Unlikely, yes, but that didn't stop me from envisioning a scenario in which Ms. Freck said, in her refined New England accent, "Violet, Katie, never in my twenty-three years at Westfield have I seen a pair of friends as gifted as the two of you. Both of you are so bright and loyal. And actually there *is* a college scholarship for being funny, but it is only for pairs of friends, and never before has Westfield had anyone who qualified. But you do. Here is a hundred-thousand-dollar scholarship to the university of your choice."

"She probably found out about that time we got drunk," Katie predicted as we walked down the hall to Ms. Freck's office, our bags slung over our right shoulders.

"That was months ago! If she was going to hear about that, she would have heard already. No way does gossip in this school take that long to spread."

"You're right. Maybe she found out that I got drunk on

New Year's with my over-eighteen-year-old boyfriend."

"Maybe. But then why would she need to talk to me, too? *I* didn't spend New Year's getting drunk with your boyfriend."

"But you did spend New Year's breaking into Westfield campus with a boy."

Katie made a good point. We habitually broke rules that I barely recognized as existing. "I can't get in trouble for that, though," I said. "I didn't break in with any boy; I broke in with *Scott Walsh*. If she heard that, Ms. Freck would be like, 'Yeah, I would've done the same; Scott Walsh is hot.'"

Katie said, "Ha-ha," but I could tell she was too worried to really listen.

The door to Ms. Freck's office was open, and she motioned us inside. We came in and sat down in the wood Westfield School armchairs across from her. I noticed she had a copy of the *Wisdom* on her desk.

"Violet," Ms. Freck began. "You edited this issue of the *Wisdom*, correct?"

"Yeah," I said. Apparently Ms. Freck read the copyright page, even if no one else did.

"It looks excellent this year," Ms. Freck complimented me, and I swear, for one crazy second I really did believe she had called me in there to reward me for the literary magazine. Then she asked, "Do you know anything about this piece?" She opened the magazine to "Stories from the Bestfield School."

"Yes," I said. "I mean, it's in the magazine."

She nodded. "Do you know who the 'Wayward Girls' are? The supposed authors of this piece?"

"Well . . . ," I hesitated. This seemed like some sort of trick question. "The *Wisdom* receives a lot of anonymous submissions."

"I appreciate that," Ms. Freck said. "But do you know who wrote *this* anonymous submission?"

I had no idea why she was asking, and my inclination was to lie, to say I had no idea—but, really, if she already had me and Katie in her office, then she already knew we had written it. This wasn't *really* a question. "Katie and I wrote it," I answered, at the same moment that Katie said, "Violet and I wrote it." We grinned at each other nervously.

Ms. Freck nodded again, not surprised. "Why?" she asked us. "Why did you write it?"

Why did we write it? Why does anyone write anything? Because it was fun. Because it was funny. Because we had an idea and we wanted to make it happen. Because I was afraid Katie would leave me for her boyfriend if I didn't do projects with her. The normal reasons. I didn't know how to answer Ms. Freck, didn't know what answer she was looking for. I just shrugged.

"You know, it's not a very nice story," Ms. Freck told us, conversationally.

"But it's true," Katie said. "I mean, we took some liberties with detail, but it's mostly true."

"That's precisely why it's not very nice," Ms. Freck explained.

I shifted awkwardly in the *Fortiter ascende*–engraved chair. This was what the *Wisdom* board had said, too, that the story wasn't *nice*. Was that supposed to be something I cared about?

Katie narrowed her eyes. "But is it a *good* story?"

"That's irrelevant," Ms. Freck said. "What's relevant is that a number of your classmates have come to me saying they felt offended by this story."

"A *number* of our classmates?" Katie repeated.

"Yeah," I agreed. "How many people read the *Wisdom*? Do a number of my classmates read this magazine? I had no idea."

"Who exactly was in this 'number' of offended girls?" Katie asked.

Ms. Freck shook her head, same as that time when we wanted to know who, exactly, had objected to the yearbook theme of safari. She disapproved of us. "That's not the point," she said. "The point is what you have done to make them feel this way."

"We wrote a story," I supplied.

"Indeed. You wrote a story that portrayed your classmates, and the school as a whole, in a deeply unflattering light. You pooh-poohed the time-honored, esteemed traditions of Westfield, mocking it as a culture that encourages cutthroat competition at the expense of the students' happiness and friendship. You wrote a story that was mean-spirited. And why? If you had issues with a particular classmate, you could have brought those issues up with me, and we would have worked through them together. That's how the student who took issue with your story handled the situation: She came to me."

"Student?" Katie repeated. "I thought you said it was *a number* of students?"

Ms. Freck is a champion at ignoring whatever she doesn't want to hear. "I know that part of this story is about Pearl Jewell. A conscientious student brought that fact to my attention. Now, do you have a problem with Pearl, girls?" she asked us, as gentle as a snake about to strike. "Did she do something to you? Did you have an argument? If so, I'm here to mediate."

Katie and I clutched the arms of our carved wood chairs and looked at each other hopelessly. Because, of course, we had no particular problems with Pearl, and Ms. Freck knew it. "I guess," I said finally, my voice heavy, "we just thought the story was . . . funny."

There was a long pause. Then Ms. Freck said, "In that case, I worry very much about your senses of humor."

I focused on the stained-glass window behind Ms. Freck's head and tried not to cry. We weren't going to get a *merit scholarship* for being funny. We were going to get in *trouble*.

"Would you think the story was funny if you didn't think it was about our classmates?" Katie asked. Her voice came out clipped and demanding. When Katie Putnam gets angry, she gets *angry*.

"I couldn't possibly say," Ms. Freck replied coolly, "since it *is* about your classmates."

"How do you know?" Katie demanded. "We don't say 'Pearl' in here anywhere."

"A mere few minutes ago you were defending your story *because* it was true," Ms. Freck reminded us. "Now you want to defend it because it's fictional?" Neither Katie nor I said anything. Our headmistress continued. "You make a mockery of one of your classmates for no reason that I can determine. No reason other than to hurt her feelings. And, in so doing, you hurt the feelings of her friends, of the people who care about her, and of every girl who has trusted the Westfield community to be a safe space free from bullying and cliquishness."

"Oh, this is a *safe space*?" Katie asked, widening her eyes in make-believe surprise. "So *that* explains why someone drops out every year because she can't handle the pressure. That's why Violet gets depressed every time she gets a B-plus on a vocab quiz. That's why we can't be trusted to choose our own yearbook theme. Because Westfield is a *safe space*! Wow, I had totally *missed* that!"

"We didn't mean to," I choked out, my voice sounding not furious like Katie's, but like I was going to burst into tears. I cleared my throat. "We didn't mean to hurt anyone's feelings."

Trying to keep myself together, I stared really, really intently at the stained-glass window past Ms. Freck. It showed the image of a girl in a long gown wearing a crown of roses and holding a dove aloft. That stained-glass girl was some version of the Westfield ideal. But not me. I would never be the Westfield ideal, as Ms. Freck was thrilled to point out. Everything I do, I do wrong.

I'd always believed that the only thing I could always do *right* was be funny with my best friend. But now it turned out I couldn't even do that.

Ms. Freck frowned at me from across her mahogany desk. "If you really thought what you had written was clever, not cruel—if you really were proud of it—you would have used your own names in the byline, rather than using this pseudonym of 'Wayward Girls.' It's apparent that you knew you were being offensive, so you chose to hide your identities, in the hopes that you wouldn't get caught and blamed for that."

"No!" I cried, because that hadn't been it at all. Ms. Freck made it sound like Katie and I were some scheming bitches, but in fact we hadn't schemed anything. "What about that girl who wrote that anonymous poem about anorexia, two pages after our story? Or just the other day in LitMag we read an anonymous submission from a girl who cuts herself. Why are they allowed to write things anonymously, but we're not?"

"It's because we're being mean to someone else," Katie replied sharply, "and they're just being mean to themselves. Being mean to yourself is totally allowed." She jutted out her chin, a cold fury in her eyes.

"Actually, it is because they are turning to the Westfield community for support, while you are trying to undermine that very community." Ms. Freck slipped on a pair of bifocals and silently read our story for a moment, a bemused smile on her lips. "To be honest, girls, even I am disturbed by your representation of Westfield—a school that I love and believe in—as a place where undeserving students are accepted because—what are your words?—ah, yes. Because they are 'legacies' and because 'their families have a lot of money.'" She peered at us over the top of the magazine.

I felt a tear slip from my eye. It was *true*, what we'd written. Wasn't it? Did Pearl Jewell really deserve to be at Westfield more than any other girl in the Boston area? No. She went to Westfield because she was a Jewell daughter. Why did Ms. Freck insist on acting like we didn't all know this?

But she did insist on it, and she told us, "Every student at Westfield brings her own special talents and knowledge to the school. To deny that is to display an intellectual snobbery that we frown on here."

Katie giggled. I turned to her, incredulous. How was she giggling? I was nearly sobbing. "Sorry," Katie said, "we *frown* on intellectual snobbery at Westfield?"

Ms. Freck glared at Katie.

"I mean, that's cool. It's just news to me."

I wanted to slap my best friend right then. This was not the time for sarcasm. Ms. Freck had already shown herself to have zero interest in our sarcasm. No, this was the time for groveling.

"Ms. Freck." I spoke through my tears. "We're sorry. We were just blowing off a little steam before exams. We didn't think . . . I mean, we never meant to be intellectual snobs, or hide our identity, or any of that stuff you said. Katie and I both love Westfield."

Katie wrinkled her brow at me in disbelief and opened her mouth, as if to contradict me.

"I hear what you're saying, Violet," Ms. Freck said, "but you two will have to make some amends if you don't want this going on your permanent records."

"Of course," I replied, at the same moment that Katie said hotly, "Permanent record? What exactly would you put on our permanent records? That you think we're intellectual elitists? That some of our classmates get easily offended? That we're not *nice little girls*? I mean, what are the charges, here?"

Katie, shut up! I screamed internally. Did she think picking a fight with Ms. Freck was going to change our headmistress's mind? Ms. Freck had all the power! All we could do was act meek and hope for the best. And, really, what was the harm in "making some amends," if it put everything back to the way it was?

Ms. Freck pursed her lips. When she responded, her voice came out calm and collected, in stark contrast to Katie's venom. "The 'charges,' as you put it, would include that you harassed your classmates, that you attempted to conceal your identities to avoid discipline, and that you abused Violet's power as editor to further your own agenda without approval of the magazine's editorial board or faculty advisor. I assure you, none of those notes would look good on a transcript, which will be sent to colleges this fall."

Katie crossed her arms, narrowed her eyes, and said nothing.

I grabbed a tissue from the box on Ms. Freck's desk and blew my nose noisily. "You mentioned amends?" I said, trying to steer the conversation back in a safer direction. "What kind of amends?"

"I believe that we can work to keep this off your permanent record if you write a letter of apology to Pearl," Ms. Freck said.

"Done," I replied instantly. I felt bad about Pearl. I hadn't realized she would read the *Wisdom*, let alone recognize this fictionalized account of her life, let alone get worked up over it. But since all that had happened, I *did* feel bad. I mean, she really was as dumb as we had said she was . . . but if she didn't want that printed in a magazine, okay.

"You will also have to issue a public apology to the entire junior class in class meeting once exams are over," Ms. Freck continued. "You must apologize for breaching their trust and for being insensitive. For offending them and their identities as loyal members of the Westfield community."

This made me cry harder. I didn't want to stand up in front

of my homeroom and address all my classmates *ever*, let alone to apologize for being a bitch. Hilary had a hard enough time talking to all of them at once, and the worst news she ever had to break to them was that the interior of our yearbook would have to be printed in black and white, not color.

"And finally, Violet, I would ask you to resign from your position as editor in chief of the *Wisdom*. Neither your fellow editors nor your faculty advisor trust you any longer with that position."

Mr. Thompson didn't trust me? *That* was a low blow. I also, strangely, didn't want to give up the *Wisdom*. Okay, my editorial board was filled with illiterates, and okay, the best submission I could hope for was one that didn't rhyme "death" with "breath"—but still, I would miss the *Wisdom*. It was the one thing I did that made me special.

Katie also seemed to find this unfair. "Violet is a great editor in chief," she argued with Ms. Freck. "This issue of the magazine is probably the best we've ever had. And she devotes hours to the *Wisdom*. She spent all of fall semester working on it. You can't just take that away from her."

"Let it go, Katie," I muttered.

"I will not. Because this is bullsh—" Katie made eye contact with Ms. Freck and broke off speaking.

"As superb an editor as you suggest," Ms. Freck said evenly, "would not have printed this libelous story."

No longer was I even trying not to cry. Tears streamed

freely down my cheeks. So now, on top of everything else, I was a bad editor of the *Wisdom*? Goddamn it, couldn't I do *anything* right?

"And if we don't do all that?" Katie asked.

Ms. Freck said, "Katie, Violet—for your sakes, and for your futures, I highly recommend that you do." She snapped shut the *Wisdom* and said, "It's nearly noon. Why don't you go wash your face, Violet, and then you can both head to your math exam."

I stood up shakily.

"Please let me know tomorrow how you'd like to proceed." Ms. Freck turned to her computer and typed something, her Ichabod Crane fingers flickering over the keyboard. "I hope you do well on your exams," she called over her shoulder as we left the room.

Like that was even possible now. My eyes hurt from crying; my concentration was shot; I felt like a terrible person. I had spent almost my entire vacation studying for these exams, and now I was so upset that I could barely even remember what "precalculus" meant.

I felt like I had been sabotaged.

Identifying the enemy

I still want to know who the social deviant is who went crying to Ms. Freck over our story."

The two hours of our math exam had passed in a blur, and now Katie and I were sitting on the bench swing in the courtyard. Well, I was sitting. Katie was pacing and ranting.

"I don't think there was *one* social deviant who complained to Ms. Freck," I said to Katie, massaging my overworked hand. "She said 'a number of students.'"

"But then later she said 'student,' singular, remember? Maybe it was Tori. Tori hates for anyone to feel bad about herself. I could totally see her turning Pearl into one of her *causes.* Remember her crusade against the scales in the gym?"

I shrugged. "Tori's not really the type to go crying to headmistress. Why don't we just think it was Pearl? She'd have just cause."

"Because Pearl is an *idiot.* And whoever did this is too cunning to be an idiot."

I sighed. I didn't know why Katie even cared. We were screwed no matter whose fault it was. Plus we still had another day of exams. How was this my life?

"Maybe it's one of the girls who works on the *Wisdom* with you," Katie mused. "Making some kind of power play. Like that sophomore, Lolly? Does she want to overthrow you and be the new editor in chief?"

Just then I spied Mischa Amory coming out of the school. Carrying a book, she headed for a bench on the far side of the courtyard, but stopped when she saw me and Katie. Mischa strolled over to us.

"You seemed to have some trouble with that math exam," she said to me.

I would have rolled my eyes if they didn't hurt so much from crying. Why did Mischa think that *everything* that *everyone* did directly concerned her?

"You look upset, Violet," she stated next.

I glared at her. Again with the *none of your business*, Mischa.

"Well, whatever's wrong, I hope you feel better." She tossed her silk scarf over her shoulder and turned to go, then said,

"Actually, I don't. You really hurt Pearl's feelings. I hope you suffer as much as she has." And then she walked away.

Katie and I looked at each other. "*Mischa*," she said.

"Of course." I put my head in my hands. "Of course it was."

My parents totally miss the point

Y our headmistress called us today," my father told me over dinner.

"I'm not surprised." I twirled angel hair pasta around my plate but didn't feel like eating any of it. I held my breath and waited for the parental lecture. In my experience grown-ups stick together, and if Ms. Freck said I was trouble, my parents were bound to believe her. Just what I needed: Ms. Freck accusing me of undermining the Westfield community; two more exams to study for; and now my parents' disappointment with me.

"Now, I've read the work in question," my father went on,

sounding like a college professor—he can't help it; he *is* a college professor. "And, while I don't think it's the nicest story in the world, I do think your school is overreacting."

I exhaled. "Really?"

My mother nodded. "Personally, I think an apology to the girl you wrote about would do the trick. *Maybe* a detention on top of that. But when your father proposed as much to Ms. Freck, she told him that Westfield doesn't offer detention."

No, I thought. We only offer emotional torture and public humiliation.

"Have you decided what you're going to do about this?" my mother asked.

I looked at her, surprised. "I'm going to do exactly what Ms. Freck said I have to do, obviously. It's not like she gave me a choice."

"She told me she gave you the choice to let this go on your permanent record," my father said.

I thought for a moment, about the Harvard nightmare and about my PSAT scores. I thought about my two final exams the next day, and how hard I had studied for them. I thought about my college applications that would say *Literary Magazine Editor in Chief, junior fall only.* I thought about failure and mediocrity. "No," I said to my parents. "That's not really a choice."

My father said, "Your mother and I just want you to know that we'll support you no matter what you choose to do."

"Thank you," I said, my throat tight.

"But may I just ask," my mother said, "why you chose to write this story in the first place? It's a funny story, and it's very well written—the professor in me is proud of you, Violet. Another audience would have found this a hilarious parody. But you *know* how Westfield reacts to things like this. Just a few months ago, at this same dinner table, you were complaining about having to change your yearbook theme because someone got offended. Didn't you think that sort of thing might happen again?"

"They got offended because they have sticks up their asses," my father muttered, which made me smile, weakly, for the first time all day.

Of course my mother was right. If I'd been thinking, I wouldn't have done this in the first place. Or I would have written the story with Katie and told her I was going to include it in the magazine and then, at the last minute, taken it out. She would have understood.

But I hadn't been thinking, not about what Mischa or Ms. Freck or Pearl would say. I'd only been thinking about Katie. So I said to my mother now, "I don't know. Katie wanted to write it. So we did."

My mother pursed her lips and nodded sharply. Putting down her fork, she said to me, "I know Katie is your friend—"

"My best friend," I corrected her.

"—and I love her as one of my own. Who couldn't love

Katie Putnam? But she strikes me as someone who is not very happy right now. And sometimes, when people are not very happy, they don't make the best decisions. Sometimes they act in self-destructive ways. I don't want to see you getting caught up in Katie's—"

"You don't know what you're talking about," I interrupted, my voice shaking with anger. Somehow all the frustration I'd been unable to show to Ms. Freck was now directed, full force, at the very people who'd just told me they would support me no matter what I did. "This isn't Katie's fault."

"I wasn't trying to say that it was," my mother began.

"Just don't." I stood up, shoving my chair away from the table. "I've had a really crappy day, and I don't need you pretending to know what's going on in my best friend's mind. Okay? You think Katie's unhappy? You don't *know* Katie. No one else knows Katie!" I stormed out of the dining room, leaving my parents alone at the dinner table.

I marched upstairs to my room and slammed the door behind me, making as much noise as possible. Self-destructive? I'd seen it, and it wasn't Katie. Self-destructive was Genevieve's refusal to eat more than a thousand calories every day. Self-destructive was the river of blood running down an anonymous girl's arm last meeting of the *Wisdom*. Katie and I hadn't written our Wayward Girls story to destroy anything. We had written it to *create* something. My parents misunderstood that just as much as anyone else.

Getting punished for all the things I'm not

How'd your parents take the news?" Katie asked on the phone that evening.

"Meh," I replied, because I didn't want to tell her that my parents blamed her for making self-destructive decisions, and me for going along with them. I lay down on my bed, phone pressed to my ear, and stared up at the solar-system stickers on my ceiling. "What about yours?"

"Yeah, suffice it to say that Mummy is *not* thrilled." She sighed. "I showed our story to Martin, though, and at least he thought it was funny."

I wanted to make an oh-my-gosh-Martin-can-*read?* joke, but I felt like neither of us was really in the mood for my blinding humor. After all, it was our blinding humor that had gotten us here in the first place.

"What kills me most about this," Katie went on, "isn't that we're in trouble, but *why* we're in trouble. Westfield girls do worse things than this, all the time. Rachel Weiss literally made herself sick over the fact that she's only in *honors* physics instead of *AP* physics. Nadine Thomas spent hours crying when she lost the yearbook-editor election to Hilary. And that is way worse than what we've done. Yet somehow that's the *foundation* of the Westfield community. Somehow that isn't something you have to apologize for in class meeting—no, it's something you get rewarded for. What you get in *trouble* for is saying what actually goes on in this school, because no one has any perspective about it, because they are incapable of just laughing a little at themselves and saying, 'Okay, yeah, so sometimes we're ridiculous.'

"And people who break *real* rules, they just get away with it. Why doesn't Pearl get in trouble for throwing day parties in Daddy's mansion and getting dozens of sixteen-year-olds wasted until they vomit? Why doesn't Mischa get in trouble for making out with her boyfriend all over school events and then going home to have unprotected sex with him? Out of all the disreputable things Westfield girls do every day—why *us*?"

"To be fair," I said, "Mischa may have *protected* sex. Having never been in a bedroom with them while they're doing it, I can't swear one way or the other."

"It's unprotected. I once overheard her telling Pearl that the pull-out method works just great as birth control, even though it's messy."

I gagged. "Way to make this day even worse, Katie."

"I aim to please." She paused then added, "Much like Mischa's boyfriend."

"Ew ew *ew*," I squealed. "But anyway, in answer to your question"—since I had thought about this a lot since our meeting with Ms. Freck; I'd thought about this through most of the math exam, in fact—"I think the reason why we get in trouble, and they don't, has to do with money."

"Money." Katie sounded dubious.

"Yeah. Westfield wouldn't exist without tuitions and donations. That's why they let Pearl in originally, right? Ten years from now Ruby Jewell's daughter will start at Westfield, and then Opal's daughter will. . . . As long as Westfield keeps the Jewell family happy, it'll have a constant source of income.

"And as for Mischa, well, do you even *know* how much the Amory family donates to our school? Hundreds of thousands of dollars! Their names are all over the annual report that's sent to us every spring. Mischa's parents have so much money they don't know how to give it away fast enough. If you were Ms. Freck, would you really punish Mischa, and risk losing all that money? Of course not. It's fucking bribery, is what it is."

Katie didn't say anything for a moment. Finally, she replied, "I don't know that you're right, Vi. I mean, my family has money too. Just because we don't give a lot of it to the school, like the Jewells or the Amorys, doesn't mean we couldn't."

"Wow, thanks," I said. "Thank you, Katharine Cabot Putnam. I was completely unaware that your family has money."

"Shut up," Katie snapped. Obviously not in the mood for my blinding humor. "I don't need to hear you bitching about being upper middle class. All I meant was that if this were an issue of bribery, well, the Putnam family is able to bribe with the best of them."

"So do it, then," I snarled. "Go throw a few thousand bucks in Ms. Freck's face, if that's all so easy for you. That'll get you off the hook, anyway, even if it does nothing for me."

"No," Katie said. "You don't get it. One, I wouldn't do that, and neither would my parents. Two, as I said, I don't think this is about money, so I don't think money would fix it."

"So what is it about, then, oh wise one?" I asked tartly.

"Like I said: We're not in trouble for breaking any *real* rules. Real rules are things like 'Don't drink underage' and 'Don't cut class.' Even Mischa—a terrible person, by real-world standards—plays the Westfield game, so Ms. Freck can't see her for what she really is. But we're in trouble for breaking an unstated rule, which is: 'Be dutiful, be docile, be *nice*.' For all the money in Boston, we won't be forgiven for *not being nice*."

I closed my eyes briefly. Katie was right, but I was too. This was about being nice *and* being rich. It was about all sorts of things that I naturally was not. But someday I would be. Someday.

"So we apologize in class meeting on Thursday," I said to Katie, feeling defeated. "Tomorrow, we tell Ms. Freck that we're ready to say sorry for hurting people's feelings and for abusing their trust and for all that other stuff, whatever it was."

"I'm not apologizing." Katie sounded absolutely certain. This was not up for debate.

But I, as her best friend, debated her anyway. "Katie, why? Yeah, this is dumb, but it's not worth letting it go on your transcript. What if you don't get into your first-choice college because of *this*? That would be so sad. Just suck it up and say you're sorry."

"But I'm *not* sorry," Katie said. "Our story was funny. You know it was. I'm not apologizing for being clever."

"Yes, but . . ." I trailed off, not knowing how to convince Katie to save herself and her future.

"You can do whatever you want. You can apologize if you want to. Hell, you can even *feel bad about it*, if you want to. But I won't be joining you."

In that statement I felt years of my friendship with Katie suddenly crashing down around me. I realized in that moment that Katie would trade me in and sell me out for anything—for a worthless boyfriend, for stolen Ritalin, for some made-up principles. I had written this story with her to preserve us, this little team of Violet and Katie, but it turned out there *was* no us. Now that I needed her, she wouldn't be here for me.

"Are you sure?" I asked in a small voice, trying one last time to save what I had thought we were. If we could only apologize together, even that would be okay, even that would be like a project. And I loved doing projects with Katie. . . .

But—"I'm sure," Katie said. In her voice I could hear that she was annoyed by this entire thing, that she thought it was dumb that we were even discussing this, that she could not care less what happened to me as a result of this.

And, just like that, I lost it. I lost my respect for Katie. And I lost my temper.

"You know what?" I said, my voice shaking with fury, and with the enormity of what I was about to say. "My mother's right. You *are* trying to destroy yourself. And all year I've just been going along with you. You want to get drunk? Fine, let's get drunk. You want to bake cookies for your idiot boyfriend instead of doing homework? Fine, let's bake cookies. You want to run Harry Potter tours even though we're just going to get in trouble for them? Fine, sure, anything you want, Katie. Let's run Harry Potter tours.

"But this has gone on long enough. I think it's great that success comes so easily to you. I mean, wow, that must be so *awesome* for you. But I have to work really hard for it, Katie." My voice went up an octave on that last sentence, and I gritted my teeth together, trying not to cry from the sheer stress and exhaustion. "I have to work really hard.

"So if you want to undermine all your successes and make yourself as normal and flawed as anyone else—well, I think that's dumb, but I can't stop you. I've been trying to stop you for months now, and it's not fucking working. But don't you *dare* undermine my successes too. Don't you dare drag me down with you, Katie. Because my successes, as flimsy and small as they must seem to you, are all I have going for me."

Katie didn't respond for a long moment, and I thought maybe she was crying. I thought that when she spoke at last, it would be through tears, to beg my forgiveness.

Instead, when she spoke, she sounded as furious as I was. "I have spent my entire life playing by other people's rules," she spat out. "My parents' rules, and Westfield's rules, and even *your* rules, Violet. Your rules, when you're supposed to be my best friend! It's a worthless game, and I don't want to play anymore."

"I don't have any rules for you," I objected.

"Oh, please," Katie said. "You expect me to be a certain way, just like everyone else does. And if I ever don't behave exactly as you expect, then I'm—what did you say?—oh, right, I'm 'dragging you down with me.' Well, pay attention, Violet: I'm not who you think I am. And Westfield isn't what you think it is either. Deal with it."

But that wasn't news to me. If Katie had been who I thought she was, then she wouldn't be abandoning me now.

We hung up then, and I went straight to bed, even though it was barely eight o'clock. It wasn't worth staying up. If there was one thing to be said about my fight with Katie and the trouble we were in, it was that none of this made me want to prepare for my Spanish exam.

Exams:
Day Three

Before my nine a.m. exam the next day, I went into Ms. Freck's office to tell her that I would do everything she had asked—the homeroom apology, the resigning as editor in chief, anything, just please don't let this incident stand between me and college.

Ms. Freck didn't seem surprised by my decision. She just asked, "And what about Katie?"

I shrugged and said nothing. Let Katie speak for herself. Besides, I was still hoping that she might change her mind. That happens, right? Sometimes people change their minds.

But Katie has never been a mind changer. I saw her come

into the cafeteria for our Spanish exam. I was already sitting at a table, my pencils and blank blue book in front of me, ready to go. There was one seat left at my table, and Katie hesitated, looking at it—then turned on her heel and found a seat on the opposite side of the room.

Okay, so that's how it's going to be, then. Fine.

To make my life even harder, Señora Alvarez showed up eight minutes late. And it seemed like she hadn't even come to administer our exam. She was just hanging out by the hot-water machine, perusing the various tea options, before she looked up and noticed the room full of girls waiting to take their Spanish exam. So we didn't even get started until nine fifteen. Really, exactly what you would expect.

A few times during the exam, as I stared off into space, trying to remember the subjunctive form of the verb *hacer*, my gaze happened to find Katie, bent over her exam booklet, her hair swinging down to cover most of her face. I found it hard to fathom that when this exam ended we wouldn't sit down to lunch together and rehash every test question. I couldn't picture a future without Katie. I couldn't even picture the next three hours without Katie.

But I also didn't *want* to eat lunch with her. I was so fed up with her, with the way she had been treating me, with the way she had been treating herself. And when she once looked up and caught me staring at her from across the room, I immediately looked away.

After the exam ended, the Spirit Squad came parading through the cafeteria, waving pom-poms and chanting slogans like, "Only one more exam to go!" and "You are winners!" I watched them morosely, massaging my hand and not feeling at all like a winner.

As the Littles that made up the squad pranced around me energetically, I recalled how Katie and I had tried to join Spirit Squad back when we were in eighth grade. We showed up on the first day of the high schoolers' exams with our faces painted and our hair in French-braided pigtails (for some reason French braids are very popular among the Spirit Squad members). Mischa told us that she had choreographed an inspirational dance for the Spirit Squad to perform in every homeroom. Katie, who did not and does not like being told what to do, refused.

Once Katie said no, the rest of Spirit Squad suddenly realized that they could back out too, so there was a lot of grumbling from all the girls who didn't want to do Mischa's inspirational dance. Which was pretty much everyone, since her inspirational dance included a lot of ass-shaking and chest-shimmying, only none of us had asses or chests yet.

Realizing Katie's potential as a rabble-rouser among the corps, Mischa issued an ultimatum: "Spirit Squad will do the dance," she informed us. "Either you're in or you're out."

That was how Katie quit the Sprit Squad. I quit too, out of loyalty. But I remember watching the Spirit Squad perform their dance in front of the sophomore homeroom. It actually looked kind of cool. Not that I would have said that to Katie.

That was three years ago, and even then I was giving up things just because Katie wanted to give them up. That was what I thought loyalty was.

But not anymore, I realized, as the Littles attempted, with varying degrees of success, to cartwheel out of the cafeteria. And this realization, that I no longer had that old loyalty to Katie, made me feel a little bit lost, and a little bit free.

What I've lost and what I've thrown away

One good thing came of this whole scandal: I had never seen so many Westfield girls read the *Wisdom*. Every copy was snatched up, and wherever I went in the days after exams, I saw my classmates poring over Katie's and my story. Everyone had heard that we were in trouble, and everyone wanted to know what the big deal was. All of Pearl's friends were, as you'd expect, outraged. I walked into homeroom on Friday morning to hear Claire loudly declaiming, "How would they like if I wrote a story about them, huh? If Pearl's only at Westfield because of her *sisters*, then Katie's only at Westfield because of her *mother*. And

Violet, like, she's no smarter than Pearl is. I mean, she was stupid enough to publish this story."

I immediately turned around and left the room without even going to my locker.

If the *Wisdom*'s relative popularity was the best part about the trouble I was in, the worst part was everything else. And that I couldn't even talk to Katie about it, because we weren't speaking.

When I announced at the first postexam *Wisdom* meeting that I was resigning as editor in chief and that it was time to elect my successor, no one asked why. Even the freshmen knew. There are no secrets at Westfield, or, if there are, Katie's and my moral crime was not one of them.

When I told the editorial panel how sorry I was to be leaving them because I had really loved the position, they all looked unimpressed. But as the words came out of my mouth, I realized how much I meant them. I *had* loved being editor of the *Wisdom*. I already missed it.

Lolly immediately put herself up for my position, as did Dominique. No one else wanted to run for it, which was too bad. I'd been hoping Emily Ishikawa would throw her hat in the ring. But maybe she already had too much else on her plate. Like sleeping.

Lolly and Dominique each gave a speech as to why she thought she deserved to be editor in chief. "I think I give all our submissions equal attention," Lolly told everyone, her hands folded angelically on the tabletop. "I really *respect* all our authors"—here she glared at me, as though I *didn't* respect them—"and I try to *empathize* with them." Another smug glare, like she thought I didn't empathize with our writers. Actually, that was a fair criticism. I didn't.

Dominique's speech was incredibly boring and can be best summarized as: "I know how to use the computer's design program. Also, I am a year older than Lolly."

"Awesome speeches, guys," I said, in my last official lie as editor in chief. "So now it's time to vote! All in favor of Lolly being your new leader—" But it is never so easy.

"We need to vote by secret ballot!" Lolly squawked. Of course we did.

Everyone tore off scraps of paper and scribbled votes on them. I wrote *me.* Childish? Sure. So what? I wished, reflexively, that Katie were on LitMag so there would be one more vote in my favor—but, at this point, she probably would have preferred Dominique.

Mr. Thompson, galvanized into action, collected all the folded-up bits of paper and stepped out into the hall to count them. When he returned, he stood in the front of the classroom and said, "Before I tell you, uh, who your new head editor is, I want us to take a moment to thank Violet."

Everyone turned to stare at me, and I blushed.

"You've done a great job as editor, Violet," Mr. Thompson told me. "We're sorry to see you go."

"Yeah," all the girls mumbled, some sounding like they meant it more than others.

I studied Mr. Thompson. Was he really so out of it that he didn't even know why I was resigning? There are no secrets at Westfield, but maybe there are secrets from Mr. Thompson. After all, he is a guy. Maybe no one shares gossip with guys.

Mr. Thompson gave me a small wink across the room, and I realized: He *did* know. He knew exactly why I was stepping down. Yet . . . he still thought I had done a good job. Maybe Ms. Freck was lying, and he hadn't even said all the stuff about not trusting me.

I gave him a small, embarrassed smile. At least *someone* didn't think I was total screwup. Even if that one person was a vacant, pathetically tattooed math teacher.

Dominique won the vote and proceeded to boringly take over the meeting. She immediately started droning on about the placement of the *Wisdom*'s submission boxes—apparently the main thing standing between us and more submissions was that the boxes were in English classrooms, instead of in homerooms. Who knew? I desperately wanted to tell Dominique to shut up but had to keep reminding myself: This wasn't my magazine anymore. I fantasized about standing up and walking out of the room and just leaving the *Wisdom* forever. You don't want me to be in charge? Fine. Do it yourselves, bitches.

But that seemed petty. And, more to the point, if I quit LitMag entirely, what would I put on my college applications? So I stayed seated, listening to Dominique offer up incomprehensible literary criticism, and trying not to bang my head against the desk.

After the meeting Emily caught up to me in the hallway. "Hey," she said. "I'm sorry about . . . I'm sorry you're not going to be in charge of the *Wisdom* anymore."

I shrugged. "Thanks. Why didn't you want it? You would have made a better editor in chief than Dominique." Probably not a politic thing to say, not a *nice* thing to say, but it was true. Katie was right: I sucked at being nice.

"Are you kidding?" Emily grabbed my arm, forcing me to stop walking and look at her. "I think what they're doing to you is awful. I don't want to benefit from that—I don't want any part in that at all."

"Oh," I said with surprise.

Emily shoved her jet-black bangs out of her eyes and peered up at me. "Your story was funny," she said. "And you're a great editor. If I were in charge of the *Wisdom*, I wouldn't do as good a job as you."

"Oh," I said again, flattered, yet so saddened by what I had lost and what I had thrown away.

"I'm going to take a nap," Emily said abruptly, releasing my arm and heading toward our homeroom, leaving me standing, alone, in the hallway.

Four days

There was nothing to recommend second semester. Without Katie to laugh with and do projects with, I felt like everything about me had been dulled. My days were colorless and bled into one another. Without the *Wisdom* to run, I felt aimless and restless. I didn't hear a word from Scott, as though he had completely forgotten about the magical New Year's Eve we'd shared. Even the weather was crappy—cold and dry, with leftover ice tripping me up and blobs of brown slush taking over the playing fields. All I had to think about was getting back my exam results and apologizing to the entire junior class next week. Not exactly my favorite daydreams.

I ate lunch at our same old lunch table, but just with Hilary, no Katie. I don't know where Katie was eating.

Over four lunch periods, here is what Hilary and I discussed:

1. Her ex-boyfriend, Mike, and exactly
   what he had said in their most recent
   IM conversation.
2. Our physics homework.
3. The specs for the new laptop Hilary
   wanted to buy (complete with visual aids).
4. Whether there were too many drawings
   of lions in our animal-themed yearbook.

And I realized something about Hilary that I had never known before, when she was just the third wheel to me and Katie: Hilary is totally nice, highly ambitious, and recognized by everyone at Westfield as a genius—but she's *boring*. She is so, so boring.

At lunch on my fourth day without Katie, I was mushing some chilled, brownish mashed potatoes around my plate and trying not to listen to Hilary's unbelievably earnest opinions on what kind of pencil she likes to use on her math homework. But then, out of the blue, she said something that caught my attention.

"I'm sorry you and Katie are fighting," Hilary said. "It's

weird to see. I never thought you guys would be able to go this long without speaking to each other."

I grunted and focused on molding my potatoes into a mountain.

"I always used to be jealous of you, actually."

I looked up then. "Jealous of me? Hil, that's ridiculous. You're yearbook editor, you're a bona fide genius, you just got back from vacation in Belize, and you get along with everyone—even boys! You have nothing to be jealous about."

"I know," Hilary said. "You're right. But, like, I've never had a friendship like you had with Katie. And maybe I never will."

I felt an ache all through my body, and I couldn't say anything. Hilary was talking about my friendship with Katie like it was *over*. And maybe it was.

"Anyway," Hilary went on, "I'm sorry you guys are fighting. But I think it's great that you and I are getting to spend so much time together now." And then she moved on to dissecting a new pair of ankle boots that she had bought, and I tuned back out.

It's been four days since Katie and I spoke. That's the longest we have ever gone without talking, even counting the three-day falling-out at the beginning of our friendship. And that one hadn't hurt nearly so much. Because, back then, I hadn't known Katie, and I hadn't know what I was missing.

Five days

O n day five of my fight with Katie, I scheduled a
driving lesson. For the first time since seventh grade I
wanted to get my mind off Westfield and everything Westfield-
related. Plus, my seventeenth birthday, and my driving test,
were only two weeks away, and I still couldn't *drive*.

It's become clear to me that the Commonwealth of
Massachusetts doesn't want anyone to get a driver's license.
It must be some sort of pro–public transit campaign, because
if they wanted us to be able to get licenses, they wouldn't
make the process so goddamn hard.

At first I had thought the "on-road" portion of driver's ed

would be better than the classroom hours, because I would be actually *driving* as opposed to just watching shoddily produced Technicolor film shorts about marijuana. Frankly, I didn't see how the on-road hours could possibly be any worse. But they tried. Oh, did they try.

"Hang a right onto Wiltshire," Christine ordered me, chomping on her nicotine gum. I had racked up five driving hours with Christine since September, and I was sick of her Ronald McDonald hair, her wretched-smelling breath, her barked commands. I also didn't feel like I was any better at driving now than I was three months ago. It was true that driving required my full concentration, taking my mind off Katie and Westfield. Instead it focused my mind on how much I hated driver's ed. I don't know which is worse.

I started turning the wheel.

"Turn signal," she snapped.

"Oh, right. Sorry." I went to pull down the right turn signal but, in a fluster, accidentally hit the windshield-wiper lever instead.

"Why are your windshield wipers on?" Christine demanded, though with her Boston accent it sounded like "windshield wipahs." "Is it raining? No. Turn them off. And didn't I tell you to use the turn signal?"

I breathed in and out though my teeth. I turned off the windshield wipahs. I turned on the turn signal.

"You kids," Christine informed me, "you think you don't need turn signals. You think you're invincible."

First of all: False. I think I am *extremely* vincible. Second of all, even if I did, for some reason, believe that I was invincible, why would that have anything to do with whether or not I used a turn signal? Why did I ever think this driving lesson would be preferable to sitting home alone and moping?

"You missed the turn," Christine told me, as the turn signal clicked away like a time bomb. "I told you to go right onto Wiltshire."

Even though I know talking back to Christine doesn't help, I responded anyway. "That's because my turn signal wasn't on yet. And I didn't want to turn without the turn signal. You said I wasn't supposed to."

Christine ignored this, as I had known she would. What had I expected her to say? "Oh my goodness, Violet, you're *right*! I was giving you contradictory instructions! Thank you for helping me to become a better driver's ed teacher, and thus to feel more fulfilled by my career!"

What Christine actually said was, "Make this next right, then. I don't have all day."

Like she had anywhere else to be.

I took the next right but misjudged the location of the curb and accidentally drove over it. The car jolted a little, and I screamed, which was probably an overreaction. I also took my hands off the wheel, because obviously my hands *on* the wheel were only causing trouble. Christine also screamed, and then she grabbed the steering wheel and turned it so hard to the left that the car swerved into the other lane. Hers was an overreaction that put my overreaction to shame.

I screamed at her, "*Watch out for cars coming at us!*" even though we were on a quiet residential street that probably hadn't seen traffic other than driving students since 1963.

Christine, from the passenger seat, jerked the car back into the correct lane and screamed at me, "*Why are you such an idiot?*"

That did it. I freaked out. I took my feet off the pedals and buried my head in my hands, weeping. I felt Christine use her emergency brake to jerk the car to a stop.

We sat in the middle of the road for a moment. Neither of us said anything. I just bawled incoherently, snot pouring down my face.

"Stop crying," Christine said at last, sounding supremely uncomfortable.

"I am *not* an idiot," I wept.

"Actually, missy, taking your hands off the wheel when you're driving is one of the most dangerous—"

"*I am not an idiot!*" I screeched, pressing the palms of my hands into my eyes to try to stop the tears.

"Ooo-*kay*," Christine said, sounding like she had never, in fourteen years of teaching driver's ed, seen a student have this particular nervous breakdown. "Look, how 'bout we just switch seats? I'll drive. You just sit here. Don't cry. You're not an idiot, okay. Just let me drive."

"Fine," I muttered. "I'm not an idiot. Many people think I am kind of smart."

We switched seats. Christine started the ignition, and I leaned my head against the cool window.

"By the way," Christine said, as she drove us away from my inglorious accident site. "You're only gonna get credit for half an hour of driving today."

Sometimes I hate the Commonwealth of Massachusetts.

Violet Tunis's winter exam results

English: A
Math: A
Science: A
History: A
Spanish: A

Exam results redux

For my entire Westfield career, I had dreamed about getting straight As. It seemed too much to wish for, but I used to imagine what it would be like, anyway, all the time. I imagined that trumpets would blow and confetti would rain from the ceiling. My teachers would speak about me in rhapsodic tones, and my classmates would lift me up in my chair like it was a throne and carry me through the halls. For once I'd be valuable, I'd be sparkly, I'd be content.

But when I got back five exams with five As on Monday, I was none of that. I sat in class and stared at the front page of my Spanish exam and tried to will confetti to fall on me, but really I didn't feel any better than when I got back my PSAT scores. When I looked at the A on my Spanish exam, all I could think was that I had a Spanish vocab quiz next week, and I would have to get an A on that, too.

I wasn't any closer to anything.

And, normally, I'd chalk it up to my mediocrity. I'd say, "If only I'd tried a little harder, performed a little better, then now I'd be happy." But that wasn't true. I couldn't have performed any better, but I could be so much happier. The truth was, without Katie, *A* was just a letter.

I surreptitiously glanced at Katie, seated a few desks away. I wanted her to be looking at me too, but she wasn't. She was leaning back in her chair, hands clasped behind her head, with her Spanish exam lying face up on her desk for all the world to see. Like she had forgotten the rules at Westfield, that we don't do that, that we take exam results and hide them away in our school bags.

C-plus was the grade on Katie's Spanish exam. And that takes effort in Alvarez's class, since she doesn't even expect us to learn much.

I wasn't even angry at Katie any longer. I was just worried about her. It was like she had given up. I remembered how she had snapped at me that she was sick of living up to expectations, that she wasn't going to do it anymore. And I realized now just how much she meant it.

Señora Alvarez began lecturing then, and like a wind-up doll I opened my binder and started taking notes.

All year I had felt like all I noticed were the differences between me and Katie, between our lives. She knew about boys; I didn't. She excelled at school; I didn't. She was cool enough to drink or smoke or break the rules like it was no big deal; I wasn't. She was everything; I wasn't. And now, for the first time, I didn't want to just be whatever she was. But I did want to be her friend.

In class meeting the next day I would need to apologize to Pearl, and Ms. Freck, and my class. But I was also going to need an apology for Katie. And that seemed like the hardest part of all.

At least I don't drive my Lexus to school

When Westfield does emotional torture, they do not half-ass it. In Tuesday's class meeting Ms. Freck had the entire junior class sit in a circle around the homeroom so we could consider, together, the damage that Katie and I had wreaked on our community.

"As some of you may be aware," Ms. Freck began, "certain members of the class have been bullying other members of the class."

I almost gagged. *Some* of us *may* be aware? There wasn't a worm in Westfield's courtyard who wasn't aware of Katie's and my *Wisdom* story.

It felt very crowded, all of us sitting in a circle, smushed up against the walls of the homeroom. I looked around the room, trying to gauge my fifty-two classmates' reactions. In a typical class meeting, you'd have about seven girls paying attention, then maybe fourteen girls whispering to one another, and seventeen girls doing homework, and five girls sending text messages, and nine girls sleeping.

Today, everyone was paying attention. Even Katie, who was sitting in the far corner of the room, her face carefully blank.

"Let's discuss how this makes us feel," Ms. Freck went on.

Oh, dear Lord. I had not realized there was going to be a *discussion* about this. I'd hoped I could just say sorry really fast and get the hell out. But no way. Not when there was a chance for my classmates to express how offended they were about things.

Of course everyone wanted to discuss how this made her feel. The conversation opened with some general comments about economic class at Westfield, and how some girls felt that other girls were purposefully making them feel poorer by driving their expensive cars to school, and could we institute a ban on parking cars at school? But then other girls—mostly the ones with nice cars, coincidentally—said that they *had* to drive their cars to school because that was their only form of transportation. Then Lily said that cars are bad for the environment, and that we should all *walk* to school to make a statement.

Then Mischa, bless her heart of coal, brought the conversation back on track.

"Look," she said, flicking her hair behind her shoulder—my God, she'd even broken out the flatiron for the occasion of my humiliation—"I think we all know we're here not because of cars, but because of a story."

She held aloft the latest issue of the *Wisdom*, so we'd all understand what she was talking about. Nice, Mischa, bringing along relevant props. Give the girl an Oscar.

"The problem is that two of our classmates, our classmates who we *trusted*, wrote something defamatory about one of us—about *all* of us—and printed it in a public forum. Westfield is supposed to be a supportive place. We're all supposed to be nice to each other. But certain members of our class don't seem to get that."

Oh, please. *We're all supposed to be nice to each other.* Right, because Mischa was being so nice to me right now?

Mischa had her arm around Pearl, who looked put out, though I couldn't tell if Pearl's pained expression was because of the story Katie and I had written, or if it was because the chain on her Tiffany necklace was tangled.

I would never want to be Pearl Jewell. Not if it meant having Mischa Amory as my best friend. Still, I have to say this for Mischa: She knows how to watch out for her friends. Just like I had tried to watch out for Katie, before she refused my help. Just like Katie had always watched out for me, before today.

Or maybe this wasn't Mischa's loyalty to Pearl. Maybe she just wanted to be a bitch about something.

Ms. Freck turned to find me squashed between Rachel and Lily, and she said, "I think many of us share your concerns, Mischa. Thank you for bringing this issue to our attention. Westfield is much more than a school; it is a community, and we expect all of you to contribute to that community. I think the girls who wrote the story have something to say for themselves."

Right, if by *girls*, she meant *me*, since Katie was staying entirely out of this conversation, looking bored, nauseated, and not at all apologetic.

"Violet?" Ms. Freck prompted me, in her charming way of asking a question that's not really a question.

I cleared my throat—kind of—and nervously squeaked out, "We're sorry that—"

"Why don't you stand?" Ms. Freck suggested. Still not a question.

Why don't I stand? Uh, because the only thing more humiliating than apologizing to my class while sitting in a circle is apologizing to my class while everyone else sits in a circle and I stand up.

But I climbed to my feet anyway, so I was gazing down on all my classmates. Mischa looked gratified. Tasha looked entranced by the drama. Even Emily was awake, though she looked like she thought this whole deal was revolting.

I caught Katie's eye. I needed her. I needed her to say something, or do something, so I wouldn't be alone in this. But she did nothing. Or—almost nothing.

Katie gave me a very tiny smile before hardening her face back into a mask of disinterest. And that seemed, maybe, like progress.

So I apologized.

My apology

I'm sorry," I began. This seemed like a strong, if predictable way to kick off an apology. "Katie and I wrote a story about a school based on Westfield, with characters based on you. We were trying to have fun, but we weren't trying to *make* fun of anyone. And I'm sorry to the people who we hurt, to the people who we made feel worse about themselves. I truly am."

I looked at Pearl, who appeared mollified, and caught a glimpse of Mischa, who did not. Whatever, Mischa—when I said I was sorry, I did not mean I'm sorry to *you*. I went on.

"I guess I expected that everyone here should be smart and should show her intelligence in the same way. And when someone didn't fit the mold like I thought she should, I wrote a story that made fun of her for it. But what I've come to understand from this whole experience is that it's not fair for me to judge other people for failing to live up to *my* expectations. I know that everyone in this room is already under an incredible amount of pressure—from Westfield, from her parents, from herself. The last thing any of you need is for me to pressure you too, into being a certain way."

Katie was staring straight at me, her eyes shining, and I caught her gaze. *See, Katie? I get it now. I get it.*

"What I think is that sometimes we are blind to the best parts of ourselves. And we want to change ourselves to be more like someone else, or someone else's idea of what we should be. Because we can't see what's valuable about the way we are. It's like looking in a mirror and seeing a distorted, much uglier version of yourself."

I was talking straight to Katie now, and I'm sure she knew it, but I was also talking to myself. Meanwhile, a lot of other girls had guilty expressions too, including Genevieve, who awkwardly set aside her Diet Coke. Ms. Freck just looked confused and annoyed: This was not the contrite apology she had expected. I realized it was probably time to wrap this up myself before Freck wrapped it up for me.

"Basically, what I'm saying is that I'm sorry for the feelings I hurt. That was never my intention.

"But even though I'm sorry about the content of my story, I'm not sorry for writing a story with my best friend. Because *that's* what's best about me."

Katie's apology

After I finished speechifying, I sat down. Rachel and Lily scooched away to make room for me, both looking at me with awe in their eyes. I couldn't tell if this was awe like, "My God, you are a truth teller! You are a sage!" or if it was awe like, "Ms. Freck and Mischa are still going to kill you, and we are awed that you actually managed to make things *worse* by apologizing."

"Thank you, Violet," Ms. Freck said, looking less than thrilled by my apology, but she didn't press the issue, I guess since I did say the word "sorry" a number of times. "Katie," she went on, and fifty-two heads turned toward my best friend. "Do you have anything to add?"

And I thought that was decent of Freck, to give Katie one last chance to make amends, to wipe her slate clean. At this point, all she really would have to do was agree, say, "Yeah, ditto to whatever Violet said." And she'd be off the hook.

Katie stood up and said, "I apologize for the way I treated Violet. I'm sorry, Vi, and I hope you forgive me."

She sat back down.

"That's all?" Ms. Freck asked.

"That's all," Katie said. And that was all.

To strive
for something else

During lunchtime I skipped the cafeteria scene that I knew would be filled with chatter about our apologies, and I went outside to sit on the bench swing in the courtyard. It was freezing outside, the sort of cold that bit at me even through my parka and scarf and hat, but I'd rather suffer the cold than the gossip. Katie found me there.

"I liked what you said this morning," she said, slipping onto the seat beside me.

I looked down at my mittened hands. "I liked what you said too."

Katie snorted. "You mean, 'I'm sorry, Violet'?"

"Yeah. I liked that part."

"I *am* sorry."

"Thank you," I said, looking up from my hands to stare her in the eye. "I really am sorry too. I guess you were right about what you said on the phone last week. I do expect you to be a certain way. I expect you to be, I don't know, how you always have been. I guess I can see why that upset you. But, honestly, Katie"—and this was the hard part to ask—"what changed? Why *aren't* you how you've always been? Is it Martin? Did you quit crew and stuff to have more time to spend with him?"

Katie looked genuinely baffled. "That's not why I quit crew," she said. "Did you really think that? I mean, I like him all right, but no."

"So what happened?"

Katie's brow furrowed, or at least as much as I could see of her brow under her hat.

"I don't know how to explain this to you, Violet, but I'm going to try. I have parents with all the money I could want. I'm able to ace tests without really working. I'm naturally skinny and pretty. I was born lucky."

"Uh, if you're trying to make me feel sympathy for you," I said, "you're doing a really shitty job of it."

"I was born lucky," Katie repeated, "but it's all luck. I don't deserve any of it. I don't deserve money or intelligence or beauty or anything. I don't deserve to be at

Westfield any more than Pearl does. And I'm just trying to get what I deserve."

I didn't understand what Katie was saying. Or, if I understood it, I didn't like it. Kicking at the icy remains of New Year's Eve's snowstorm, I told her, "*I* think you deserve all that. I think you deserve the best."

Katie chuckled sadly. "I know you do. That's one of the things I love about you. But I've tried and I've tried, and I can't make myself agree with you. *You* deserve this." Katie flung her arm out, encompassing the crystalline-white courtyard, the state-of-the-art gym, the acres of playing fields. "You're willing to work for it; you care about it. Westfield makes sense for you. But it doesn't make sense for me. I feel like I've been trying to make you see this for ages now, and you just haven't heard me, or haven't wanted to hear me. Years of being extraordinary has never made me happy. It's just made me anxious and guilty and less happy every day. And that's why . . . well, I don't know how to tell you this, but . . . I'm leaving Westfield."

We sat in silence for a moment, watching our breath form clouds in the air, as I tried to figure out what she was talking about. For a moment I thought she was saying she was leaving Westfield, like, for the afternoon. When I finally got what she really meant, I still didn't understand.

"But where are you going?" I asked.

"Public school. I'm starting at Brookline High on Monday."

"*Monday?* That's so soon!" I felt short of breath all of a sudden, and dizzy.

"I've been planning this for a while. It's really not as sudden as it seems. Just this whole deal with the *Wisdom* has, I don't know, sped things up. But it was going to happen sooner or later. Even my parents have agreed that it's not working out for me here, not anymore."

Katie had been planning to leave Westfield for "a while," and she hadn't mentioned it to me? This was a huge life decision. I would never keep a secret like this from her. This was way more than "Oh, hey, I aced the PSATs" or "By the way, I quit crew." This was, "Guess what, Violet? I'm not going to see you every day anymore. We're suddenly going to lead totally separate lives. Just thought I'd mention that. Okay, later!"

"See, I knew you would be mad at me," Katie went on, resting her head in her hands. "That's why I put off telling you. It's hard to tell you things you don't want to hear, Violet. I didn't want to disappoint you. I mean, I *really* . . . I tried so hard not to disappoint you."

I looked up from my mittens and frowned. "I'm not *mad* at you. And it's not even about my being disappointed with you. I just . . . don't understand. Westfield's not perfect, but it's one of the best high schools in the country. Can't you just take that, and ignore the rest of it? Okay, it has some problems, like how today's class meeting was the most hellish forty-five minutes of my life, but it's not a *bad* place."

"You're right," Katie conceded. "But it's bad for *me*." She elbowed the school motto on the back of the bench swing. "I don't want to 'strive for success' anymore."

So Katie was quitting. Just like that. Just because she could.

"Then what do you want to strive for?" I asked her. "If not success? You have to want something."

She threw her head back, pondering it for a moment. "Happiness," she said at last.

"They're the same thing, Katie," I told her. "They can be the same thing, if you would just let your successes make you happy."

"Right, that should really be Westfield's motto right there. 'Success can make you happy.' But it doesn't, really. You can never succeed *enough*, and then you're always wanting more. Sometimes you just have to accept second best."

Was Katie lecturing me? Was Katie *blind* to the life that I led? "Hello," I said, "I *do* accept second best. All the time. If I'm *lucky* I am second best, if not third or fourth or fiftieth best. You don't even . . . I mean, you have no idea what that's like. You have never known what that's like."

Katie shook her head. "But when I say *accept it*, I mean, you can't think that's failure. You have to embrace your second or third or fiftieth best."

"Oh." I frowned.

"Right. That's the secret part that Westfield never tells you," Katie said. "And I'm not sure, because I've never been there, but I *think*, when you can do that—I think that's happiness."

I thought about what I'd said at the end of my apology in class meeting. What really made me happy was doing projects with my best friend. I knew the Wayward Girls story was mean, but—I'd been so happy writing it with Katie. Even though it totally blew up in our faces.

Actually, I guess *all* my projects with Katie blew up in our faces. The Harry Potter tours, the pool-shark plan, baking cookies, even getting drunk . . . all epic failures. But they'd made me happy.

And maybe that was what Katie meant.

Life without Katie

K atie didn't bother to tell any of our other classmates that she was going to public school. She just didn't show up on Monday morning, and then a few days passed and everyone figured out that she was gone. A lot of girls seemed to think that Katie had left because of our Wayward Girls story. Like maybe she had gotten expelled for being *too mean*. I let them think this, because it was easier than explaining the truth. For fifty-two supposedly brilliant girls, it's funny how much we miss or misunderstand.

Suddenly Katie and I didn't see each other every minute of the day. We didn't even talk every evening. We're friends, still—we're *best* friends still—but as soon as she was gone, I felt a distance between us. Maybe we just needed more time to pass, to completely get over our disagreements. Or maybe that distance would always be there.

I talked to Katie on the phone after she'd been gone for a few days. "It's weird," she said when I asked what her new school was like. "Like, we're not allowed into the school building until the first bell rings."

"Why not?" I asked.

"I don't know! And also you have to get a pass to go to the bathroom during class. And there's only one pass."

"I remember that from elementary school," I said. "But we're like *adults* now. Why do adults have to take turns using the bathroom?"

"I have no clue. Oh, and during lunch you have to be in the cafeteria. You can't eat in the halls or outside or anything. They're obsessed here with knowing exactly where you are, like at all times."

"Sounds even more controlling than Ms. Freck," I said, hoping maybe Katie would say, "Yes, and therefore I have decided to return to Westfield."

But actually what she said was, "No way. Here you're allowed to *think* whatever you want. And you can be as nice or as mean as you want to be. There are hundreds of students just in the junior class, so no one even notices!"

She sounded excited, but I said, "It just sounds lonely."

"It is, kind of. But I'm getting used to it. I'm making friends."

"Anyone you can bring to my birthday party next weekend?" I asked. "Since half our class still thinks I'm a bully and wouldn't come to my party if I paid them, I might need to fill in with some strangers."

"Hmm," Katie said. "Well, I met this girl Janie in my U.S. history class. . . . She seems fun, and like she has the same sort of sense of humor as us."

I didn't say anything.

Katie laughed at me. "Don't worry, Violet. I'll always like you best."

Embracing failure

"All right," said the cop who was about to administer my driving test. "Violet Too-nees."

"Tunis," I squeaked. I was sitting in the driver's seat of the driving-test car. The policeman sat in the passenger seat, scribbling on his clipboard. I couldn't figure out what he was writing, since I hadn't even started the car yet.

"It's Violet Tunis," my dad piped up from the backseat, even though I had just clarified that.

"Rhymes with 'vunis,'" my mother chirped, also from the backseat, even though "vunis" is not a word.

"Born January thirtieth, huh?" the cop asked, still scribbling. What was he writing? A grocery list?

"She's seventeen years old today!" my mom confirmed. I could have lived without any parents in the backseat. Or, if they were going to be there, it would have been nice if they were wearing muzzles. Unfortunately, they both insisted on witnessing this momentous event in my life, and they refused to wear muzzles. I don't know why.

"Happy birthday," the cop said, sounding impossibly bored. It was eleven a.m. on Saturday, and he had probably already given the driving test eight hundred times today. "Put the car into drive," he told me.

I wiped my clammy hands on the steering wheel, then pulled at the gear shift. Nothing happened. Oh my God. Was this car broken? Had they give me a broken car for the driving test? Was this some kind of cruel prank?

"Turn the car *on*," the cop advised me. "Then put it into drive."

Oh. Okay. I turned the key and shifted into drive.

"Drive forward, please," the cop instructed me.

"Yay!" my parents cheered from the backseat. "Yay, Violet!"

"Be quiet!" I shouted. The cop gave me a dubious sidelong glance. "I meant my parents," I explained. "Not you. You can talk as much as you want."

"I know I can," he said. "Drive forward."

I drove forward until I was at the end of the parking lot.

"Right-hand turn," the cop said.

I put on my blinker, spent about three minutes leaning forward, looking for nonexistent oncoming traffic, then turned right on to the road.

"Careful of that car!" my mother screamed from the backseat.

I slammed on the brake, causing the four of us to jerk against our seat belts. "What car?" I screamed.

"That one!" My mother pointed at a parked car that I would not have hit if I'd been driving blind and drunk.

I started moving forward again. "Mother," I said threateningly. "I swear to God . . ."

"Can everyone in the car shut up?" the cop said. "Except me. I will talk. Left-hand turn at this stop sign."

I spent another three minutes watching for oncoming traffic before making my left-hand turn. My mother made whimpering noises and clutched my father's hand, but both kept their mouths shut because the policeman had said to. We respect the law in my family.

Then he told me to make a three-point turn in a little side street. I drove forward—easy does it—turned the wheel—so far so good—put the car into reverse—drove backward—and the back wheels of the car went up onto the curb.

I hit the brakes, but it was too late. Everyone in the car had felt me go up onto the curb. I was twisted around in my seat, looking for obstacles out the rear window, and now all I could see were my parents' horrified faces.

The cop was writing furiously, and I wanted to yell at him,

"What the hell are you writing? *Can't make a three-point turn.* It's one sentence, max! You're not fucking *Thoreau.*"

But I didn't say that. I didn't say anything, just turned back around in my seat, and ever-so-slowly drove forward, the car bumping off the curb as I completed my three-point turn.

"Drive straight to go back to the lot," the cop instructed me.

"Um," I said. "It was an accident—" But "accident" is not actually a good word to use when you're trying to convince someone to give you a driver's license.

I drove us back to the RMV parking lot in silence. I did a flawless job pulling into a parking space there, but did I get any credit for that? No.

"Sorry," the cop said as he opened the passenger-side door, not sounding really emotionally invested in his apology. "Lots of people fail their driving test the first time around."

I shrugged ungraciously and wrinkled my forehead to hold back tears.

"Who was your driving instructor?" he asked me.

"Christine."

The policeman nodded. "She needs to work harder. I've seen a lot of her students come through here not properly prepared."

I knew I should be cheering that Christine was finally, finally getting blamed for totally sucking at her job. But, since I totally sucked at driving, it wasn't much of a consolation.

The policeman left us alone. "I'm sorry, Violet," my mother

334

said, petting my hair. "We'll practice so much over the next couple months, and when you come back to try again, you'll be perfect."

I shrugged her off and climbed out of the car. I just wanted to talk to Katie.

"Happy birthday!" she screeched into the phone. "Happy license day!"

"I failed," I told her.

Katie was silent, then heaved a long, put-upon sigh. "Violet. For the love of God. When I told you to learn to embrace second best, I didn't mean you should *fail your driving test.*"

"What about 'success doesn't make you happy,' blah blah?" I asked.

"Uh, I think passing your driving test is one the few successes that *would* make you happy," Katie replied. "It's bizarre, really: You are so smart, and yet you have zero real-life skills."

"You forgot that I can bake," I said.

"No, I didn't."

I snickered then, and Katie did too. "All right," she relented. "I didn't want you to get your license anyway, because I don't want you to have it before me. I'll admit it: I did voodoo spells to ensure that you would fail your driving test today."

"You did not," I said.

"You're right, I didn't. But it seems I didn't have to."

I was outright smiling now. A few minutes ago I had wanted to cry on a policeman's shoulder, and now Katie had made me smile. "Look," I said, "my parents are waiting for me, and we have to go so I can get ready for my birthday party tonight. Can you come over to my house in an hour?"

"I don't know . . . ," Katie answered. "I might not have a way to get there, since you can't pick me up. . . ."

"Oh, shut up," I laughed at her.

Seventeen years and counting

I can't believe I'm throwing a coed birthday party," I whispered to Katie. "My last coed party was when I was eight years old."

My party was on the second story of a Mexican restaurant. My parents had rented out the space just for me and my guests. There were waiters mixing virgin daiquiris and serving chicken shish kebabs. I wore dark skinny jeans, a babydoll-cut shirt, and bright purple heels that I couldn't really walk in. I felt mature. I felt *seventeen*.

The way I made my party coed was: I texted Scott Walsh. It took me all afternoon to work up the courage. "He will think I'm a loser!" I kept saying to Katie.

"Right, because only *losers* invite people to their awesome birthday parties," Katie replied. "Come on. If he doesn't want to come, he just won't come."

Eventually, and very carefully, I texted him, Having a birthday party 2nite. Want 2 come? Bring friends—we need more boys!

"See, that's good," I explained to Katie, "because then he'll know I invited him simply to even out my girl-boy ratio, and not because I actually have any interest whatsoever in *him*, as an individual."

And it must have worked, because Scott texted back wanting to know where the party was, and promising to bring many friends. Being seventeen was going to be awesome. I could already tell.

Of course, a lot of girls from my class were not at my party, because they still thought of me as that snob who tried to ruin Pearl's life and undermine the core values of the Westfield School. But I didn't want them there anyway.

I left Katie getting another drink to totter over to where Scott and one of his friends were playing darts. Not because I am in love with him or anything. Just because a good hostess says hello to all her guests, you know, to be polite. "Violet!" Scott said when he saw me. "Great party."

"Thanks!" I was wearing like seventy layers of makeup. Maybe he couldn't see me blushing.

"Love that they have darts here. Do you think they have a pool table too?"

I shrugged. "Katie and I are pool sharks, you know," I said.

"Really?" Scott sounded intrigued.

"Uh, no."

Scott gave me a funny look and changed the subject. "This is my friend Alex."

"Happy birthday." Scott's dart-playing partner shook my hand and smiled. I looked him up and down quickly. He was cute. I mean, not as cute as *Scott Walsh*—but cute. Surprisingly deep-blue eyes. Great lips. Great all-around smile, in fact.

"Alex goes to Harper Woodbane with me," Scott explained.

"Do you do plays and stuff too, like Scott?" I asked, already knowing that he did not. Not like I've been to every single play Scott has ever been in and therefore know all the other Harper Woodbane guys who act too.

"Nah," Alex said. "I get stage fright. I do lacrosse. And I edit our newspaper. Things where I don't need to speak in front of people."

"Oh, cool!" I said. "I edit our literary magazine. Or, well, I used to."

"Oh!" I saw Scott and Alex both raise their eyebrows. "So *you're* the one . . ."

I got a sinking feeling in my stomach. "I'm the one, what?"

Scott said, "I hadn't realized it was *you* who was all caught up in that Westfield literary-magazine scandal."

So it was a *scandal* now. A scandal that had traveled as far as our brother school. Great. "Yeah," I sighed. "That was me." So now Scott and his cute friend could hate me too, just like Mischa and Claire and my own headmistress.

But then they did something that surprised me: They laughed. Alex clapped me on the shoulder and said, "Sometimes girls are really oversensitive, aren't they?"

"Yeah," Scott said. "If something like that had happened at Harper, everyone would have been like, 'Boo-hoo, so someone was mean to you. Get over it.'"

I grinned as I tried to picture how Ms. Freck would have reacted if I'd said that to Pearl or to Mischa. I legitimately think that boys must be a different species from girls.

"I'm going to grab another drink," Alex said. He handed me his darts and left me alone with Scott.

"Want to play?" Scott asked, taking aim at the dartboard.

"Well, I'm more of a pool shark than I am a darts shark. But yeah, okay."

We threw a few darts. Most of mine didn't even land on the board. I don't know what my sport of choice is, but at least now I can say it's definitely not darts.

"So, how's Julia?" I asked casually. I stood next to Scott, trying to look sultry and skinny and other things that might cause him to leave his girlfriend for me.

"Actually," Scott said, taking careful aim at the dartboard, "we broke up."

Oh my God.

Scott Walsh was *single* now. That meant he could date *anyone*. He could date *me*. And it wouldn't be like last time he was single and chose not to date me either. He didn't really know me then. But now we had spent New Year's Eve together, he had come to my birthday party . . . We knew each other now.

"I'm sorry you two broke up," I said as sincerely as I knew how, since I think that's what you're supposed to say when people break up. I don't think you're supposed to say, "*Now you can kiss me!*"

"Thanks," Scott replied, "but it was for the best. I wanted to tell you something, actually, and now seems as good a time as ever."

Was he going to ask me out? Now? Already? Being seventeen was for real *the best thing ever.*

"So," Scott Walsh said to me, lowering his darts and looking me in the eye, "I'm gay."

"Gay?"

"Yeah."

"Gay."

"I guess I've always kind of known," he said, like I'd asked him a question, "but I've only recently really come to terms with it. I just realized that it wasn't fair to Julia, and it wasn't fair to me, to stay in this relationship. I cared about her a lot—I still do—but despite that, I'm just never going to be attracted to girls."

"Never going to be attracted to girls," I repeated.

"Right. I felt like I was acting all the time, you know? And the conversation you and I had on New Year's helped me figure out that I need to be true to myself. So I've been coming out to my friends and family and stuff—a lot of Harper Woodbane knows now, and everyone seems cool with it. And you and I have gotten kind of close over the past few months, so, I don't know, I wanted to tell you, too."

I stared at Scott, momentarily frozen into silence. Eventually I realized I had to say *something* or he would believe that I was some kind of raging homophobe. "Good for you," I squeaked, which may or may not be what you're supposed to say when the love of your life comes out of the closet. "So are you . . . dating anyone new? Any . . . boys?"

Scott shook his head. "Not yet. You've probably noticed: Harper Woodbane doesn't have that many great options."

"Ha-ha," I said, while thinking *Harper Woodbane has* you! You *are a great option!*

"I mean, Alex is cute," Scott said, pointing at his friend at the bar. "But straight as they come."

I glanced over at the bar too, and saw Alex trying to drink his virgin piña colada without accidentally snagging his eye on its little decorative umbrella.

"Hey, Violet?" Scott said, looking at me closely, vulnerably. "Thanks for being so supportive. You know, I never know how people are going to react when I tell them, and, well . . . it's just good to see that my friends will be my friends no matter what." And he pulled me in for a hug. I inched my arms around his neck and pressed my face into the soft fabric of his T-shirt, breathing in his fresh, clean, Scott Walsh scent. I felt like my heart was breaking.

He let me go and I let him go and I mumbled something else like, "Congratulations," or, "Good job on being gay," and then I ran as fast as my high heels would take me over to Katie.

"Wow," she said. She was sitting on a table, sipping a daiquiri from a straw and kicking her legs back and forth. "Nice Scott Walsh hug over there. Want to tell me about it?"

"He hugged me," I said, collapsing next to her on the table, "because he is gay."

Katie let the straw drop from her lips. Her eyes widened. "He's *what?*"

"Yes," I said. "You heard me correctly. I am such an *enormous loser* that the boy I have loved for four years—the *only* boy I have *ever* loved—is a homosexual."

Katie laughed. She laughed and laughed; she laughed until she was doubled over crying.

"You're welcome," I said. "I'm so glad my life can provide you with such amusement."

When she could speak again, Katie crowed, "At least we know now why he was never interested in us!" This just made her crack up again.

When she had finally calmed down, she said, in a more serious tone, "In other dating news: I broke up with Martin last night."

"Um," I said. "I'm sorry?"

"Come on," she scoffed. "You're thrilled. That's why I didn't tell you earlier: I wanted to give you my breakup as a birthday present." While I resented not being told the moment that this had happened, I was glad that Katie was now telling me about her major life changes within twenty-four hours of the time that they happened, as opposed to waiting weeks to drop the bombshell. She was improving.

I mulled it over. This news didn't make me as ecstatic as I had expected. Even without Martin, Katie still wasn't a coxswain, she still wasn't at Westfield with me, she still wasn't the Katie I remembered from seventh grade. I supposed now that none of those changes had ever been Martin's fault. So I said, "If Martin made you happy, then I guess I really am sorry."

Katie shrugged. "He kind of made me happy. I don't know, I just realized that I wanted something . . . better." She twisted her ponytail around her finger and looked at me. "I was thinking a lot about what you said about how I deserve better. I don't really think I deserve anything that good at all . . . but it means something to me that *you* think I do."

"I think you deserve everything," I told her softly.

"Thank you," she said seriously. Then she grinned. "Plus, hello, there are so many hot guys at public school. I can't be tied down until I've explored my options!"

I groaned. "Why didn't you bring any of these hotties to my party, Katie? We could use them here."

"I've only been at Brookline High for two weeks," she replied. "Give me another week or so." She paused. "Wow, I can't believe you're already seventeen and you still haven't kissed anyone."

"Thanks, Katie. Rub it in."

"You know you have ridiculously high standards, right? Did you even listen to what I said to you about accepting second best?"

"Yes, dear. I'm working on it. I might even make out with that cute friend of Scott's."

"Really?"

"I don't know. Maybe." I caught Alex's eye across the room and waved at him. He waved back, then blushed and looked at his shoes.

"You should totally make out with him. And then we can double date."

"Who's *we*? Me and Alex and you and . . . ?"

"Me and the boyfriend I'm going to find soon! Have a little faith. I go to a coed school now. Boys are everywhere. They swarm the halls. They *sit next to me in class*. I can't help but find someone."

"Can we have a joint wedding, too?"

"Obviously! On a cruise ship."

"But what if one of our fiancés gets seasick?" I worried.

"Then we'll dump him at the altar and find a new one. Come on, Violet. Show a little *vision* here."

I missed Katie so much right then, even as she sat next to me. I missed how our friendship used to be, back when we agreed on everything and shared everything, or at least I thought we did. Back when Katie was perfect and Westfield was perfect, or at least I thought they were.

Suddenly I recalled my goals for the school year, so innocently written back in September. I was halfway through junior year now, and it was too late for me to get a perfect score on my PSATs or save the *Wisdom* from itself. I had failed my driving test, and Scott Walsh had just made clear that he was never going to fall in love with me. Maybe, if I worked really hard this semester, I could maintain an A or A-minus average for the year. So maybe I could achieve one of my goals.

Or maybe, I thought, that wasn't really the point.

"Katie?" I ventured. "Even though you don't go to Westfield anymore, can we still do projects together?"

"Of course! Only no more cookie baking. Not even for our husbands-to-be."

"God forbid," I agreed.

"So did you have a particular project in mind?"

I looked out over my party, at my friends, with Hilary creaming Mike at darts, and Alex having a Tabasco sauce–chugging contest with Scott, and Emily trying to French-braid Tasha's hair. "Anything," I said to Katie. "Anything with you."

Acknowledgments

Publishing a novel has been my guiding dream since I was old enough to read, so for it to actually come true has been an extraordinary experience. Of course, a dream does not come true in a vacuum, and there would be no *Mostly Good Girls* without the contributions of the following people.

First and foremost, a thank-you to my editor, Anica Rissi, who loved this story for what it was, and who understood how to mold it into the best possible version of itself. Anica makes killer cookies and mix CDs, she often knows what my book is trying to say better than I do, and, bonus, she's tall. Anica, thank you for believing in me.

Boundless gratitude to Stephen Barbara, who sold the hell out of this book. Stephen, every day you go above and beyond an agent's call of duty. I don't know how you find the time to show me so much individualized care and attention—but I'm very glad that you do!

A huge thanks to Kendra Levin for her emotional support, brilliant editorial guidance, and friendship. I don't know what this book would be without Kendra's feedback, but "not very good" comes to mind.

To Lauren Oliver—thank you for so generously sharing with me your time, your storytelling wisdom, and your agent.

To Clare Hawthorne, Leslie Prives, and Molly Thomas for telling me what was and was not funny.

To Katie Hanson for helping me come up with synonyms and for never complaining when I don't wash my dishes because I am "writing," even when she can see that I'm really just looking at Facebook.

To Emily Heddleson for sharing her high school memories, and for standing by my side throughout this entire process.

To Kathryn Hurley for being Violet and Katie's first fan.

To Leslie Dewan, Clare Hawthorne, Emily Haydock, Reed Keefe, Allie Smith, and the rest of the mostly good girls I met in high school. Thank you for inspiring this story.

To my high school, which provided me with a top-notch education, inspiring teachers, and some of the best friends I've ever had. Although I couldn't help incorporating your fire drill practices in here, I promise that you are *much* more functional than Westfield.

Finally, of course, to my parents. Thank you for providing me with the support, education, and confidence to become a writer—and to do anything else. I love you!

And for now, I think that's mostly good enough.